VATICAN FILES
AN ALICIA YODER NOVEL

M.A. ROTHMAN

Copyright © 2024 Michael A. Rothman

Cover Art by M.S. Corley

This is a work of fiction. Names, characters, businesses, places, events, locales, and incidents are either the products of the author's imagination or used in a fictitious manner. Any resemblance to actual persons, living or dead, or actual events, is purely coincidental.

All rights reserved.

Paperback ISBN-13: 978-1-960244-41-3
Hardcover ISBN: 978-1-960244-42-0

CONTENTS

Chapter 1	1
Chapter 2	19
Chapter 3	40
Chapter 4	63
Chapter 5	80
Chapter 6	98
Chapter 7	119
Chapter 8	143
Chapter 9	158
Chapter 10	178
Chapter 11	189
Chapter 12	199
Chapter 13	222
Chapter 14	234
Chapter 15	245
Chapter 16	265
Chapter 17	277
Chapter 18	285
Chapter 19	296
Epilogue	300
Author's Note	307
Preview of Perimeter	313
Addendum	357
About the Author	366

"What is past is prologue."

—*William Shakespeare, The Tempest*

CHAPTER ONE

Father Alessandro Montelaro sat hunched over the ancient manuscript, the soft glow of the desk lamp cast eerie shadows across the vaulted ceilings of the Vatican's secret archives. His eyes strained to decipher the faded Latin text, his gloved finger tracing the delicate curves of the script. The silence that enveloped the underground chamber was broken only by the occasional rustle of parchment and the muted ticking of a distant clock.

In the depth of the night, when the world above ground was lost in slumber, a door at the far end of the archives creaked open. The priest's head snapped up, his heart quickening with a mixture of curiosity and trepidation. The dim light flickered as a couple of Swiss guards wheeled a series of crates into the room. Their expressions showed a combination of exhaustion and surprise at seeing him at such a late hour.

"Father Montelaro," one of the guards said, his voice hushed but urgent, "these boxes contain items from a site revealed by a nearby landslide."

"Landslide?" The priest frowned. "Is this from the tremor I felt earlier today?"

The taller of the two guards nodded. "Yes, Father. The earthquake unveiled a previously unknown cavern on one of the hills about four kilometers away. It turns out that items had been hidden away in this place and the prefect was afraid that looters might disturb the site."

Intrigued, Father Montelaro rose from his chair, his curiosity piqued. He followed the guards, his footsteps echoing in the vast chamber. The two large men carefully placed the crates on the metal shelves reserved for holding items that needed to be catalogued, and left the underground archives as quickly as they appeared.

Retrieving a nearby crowbar, he pried open the first crate and Father Montelaro's eyes widened in astonishment. The air was thick with dust and the scent of age wafted up from the wooden box.

Inside were relics from a time long past, items adorned with the unmistakable chi-rho symbol, the intertwined letters '☧' representing Christ.

His white-gloved fingers brushed over a seemingly ancient chalice; its surface adorned with intricate engravings. There were brittle scrolls and carved wooden boxes, all of them adorned with iconography from a time long past, and as he carefully retrieved items from within the crate, the priest spotted hints of hand-written text in both Latin and Aramaic.

His heart raced with excitement and reverence. The items before him were evidently from the early days of the Church, a tangible connection to the roots of his faith. The mild earthquake, it seemed, had unveiled a trove of history, hidden for centuries beneath the earth.

Father Montelaro carefully lifted an ornate box from the crate, its lid adorned with the chi-rho symbol inlaid with precious gems. He opened it with trembling hands, revealing a collection of delicate jewelry—rings, pendants, and bracelets, each bearing the same ancient symbol. The flickering lamplight danced on the polished surfaces, casting a warm, golden glow.

It was easy to understand why such things might have been concealed in those early years. If indeed it turned out these items were from the first century, it stood to reason why such identifying markers would have been kept hidden. In the first hundred years of the faith, it was a secret sign for Christians to identify themselves to each other.

It was at that moment, Father Montelaro felt a profound sense of awe and responsibility. He had been entrusted with preserving these artifacts, tangible links to the dawn of Christianity. The discovery filled him with a renewed passion for his work, a deep appreciation for the intricate tapestry of history that he was now a part of.

As he emptied the last item from the first crate, he noticed that one of the scrolls he'd placed on his table had opened up on its own volition.

The priest stared at the ancient object and muttered a prayer under his breath, making the sign of the cross.

Scrolls as old as these items rarely opened themselves willingly to scrutiny. After centuries or even millennia, such things became impossibly brittle and only through the miracle of modern technology could the contents of the scroll be extracted, without ever having to unroll the item.

Father Montelaro was seventy-five, and even though he understood the concepts behind what the technology did, how the CT scanning device or advanced computer software worked were well beyond his comprehension.

The priest put on a surgeon's mask, fearing that even the slightest breath might damage the ancient object. He stared at the flowing, handwritten message from another time.

It was perfectly preserved, causing the priest's heart to race as he shook his head in disbelief at the improbable level of preservation.

As his eyes darted across the page, he quickly recognized this as an eloquently-written testimonial by a man named Gaius.

An ancient Roman name, yet the language descriptions read almost as if written by a person from modern times.

In the dim flicker of candlelight, I find myself huddled with fellow believers, our faces illuminated by the soft glow, and our hearts alight with an unwavering faith. Among us sits Mark, the very disciple whose words had earlier painted the story of Christ's life.

The priest gasped and his eyes widened at the impossibility of such a find. He was immediately torn between running out of the chamber to alert the prefect and continuing. It was past midnight, and the scroll pulled at his attention.

. . .

His eyes, usually bright with enthusiasm, now held a somber depth as he unrolled a scroll before us. The parchment crackled softly, echoing the anticipation in our hearts. We were about to witness a profound secret, a revelation intended only for the most steadfast among us. I am Gaius, and this moment will be etched into my soul for eternity.

As Mark began to read, the words that flowed from his lips were not the familiar verses we had known. They were different, profound, and laced with mysteries that seemed to unlock hidden chambers of understanding. The Gospel we knew, the one that had been cautiously circulated among us, suddenly felt like the outer courtyard of a grand temple, and what Mark shared was the sacred sanctum, the holiest of holies.

In this new Gospel, Jesus' teachings were not mere stories but profound discourses, weaving together threads of wisdom that resonated with the very core of our beings. The words were bolder, daring to challenge the status quo with a fearless spirit. They carried the weight of revelation, hinting at the divinity of Christ in ways we had scarcely dared to ponder.

As I listened, my heart swelled with a mixture of awe and trepidation. These words were revolutionary, capable of transforming the souls of those ready to receive them. Yet, they were also dangerous, like a blazing torch in the heart of a dry forest, waiting to ignite a conflagration.

As the echoes of Mark's voice faded into the silence of the chamber, he fixed his gaze upon me, his eyes reflecting a blend of wisdom and urgency. In that profound moment, he entrusted me with a sacred task, a responsibility that weighed heavy upon my soul.

"Gaius," he said, his voice steady, "these words are not for the present, but for a future yet unseen, a time when our faith will flourish without the shackles of fear. You, my dear friend, are the keeper of this hidden Gospel. It is your charge to safeguard these revelations until the world is ready to receive them with open hearts."

His words hung in the air like a solemn oath, binding me to a destiny I could not yet comprehend. I nodded, my heart pulsating with reverence for the trust he placed in me.

"Find a place, a sanctuary far from prying eyes and seeking hands," Mark continued, his tone measured and deliberate. "A place where the wisdom of these teachings can rest undisturbed, shielded from the storms of persecution. Bury this scroll deep within the earth, beneath the roots of an ancient tree or within the heart of a hidden cave. Let the earth itself become its guardian."

I nodded again, my hands tingling with the gravity of the task. Mark's gaze bore into mine, his faith in me unyielding.

"When the time is right," he said, his voice carrying a note of hope, "when our faith stands tall, unbroken by the chains of oppression, and when the hearts of humanity are ready to embrace the full brilliance of Christ's teachings, then, and only then, shall this hidden Gospel see the light once more."

With trembling hands, I accepted the scroll from him, feeling the roughness of its ancient parchment against my fingertips. As I clutched it to my chest, a profound sense of purpose settled within me.

I would honor Mark's trust, protect these sacred words, and await the day when they would illuminate the world, guiding humanity toward a future of enlightenment and spiritual awakening.

Mark laid a gentle hand on my shoulder, his touch imbued with a silent blessing. "May your faith remain steadfast, Gaius." His voice carrying the weight of centuries yet to come. "And may you find the strength to guard this treasure until the appointed time."

With a final, lingering glance, he turned away, leaving me alone with the scroll that held the secrets of a future yet unwritten. I tucked the precious document into the folds of my robe, my heart resolute, and set forth to find the perfect sanctuary for this hidden Gospel, a beacon of hope awaiting the dawn of a new era in our faith.

Father Montelaro looked at the array of tightly-bound, brittle scrolls on the table and wondered aloud, "Could a new gospel of Mark be lying right in front of me?"

Noticing a scrap of vellum partially hidden underneath the bottom end of the scroll, he grabbed a pair of tweezers with trembling hands and retrieved the fragile item.

The archivist's eyes widened with astonishment as he noticed Latin script etched in a handwriting starkly different from Gaius's elegant script. The message was concise but laden with urgency: *"The Romans have vowed to eliminate us. The Gospel has been moved to a place of safety."*

The priest's heart raced with the weight of the revelation, realizing that even in antiquity, there were guardians, unknown and unsung, who valiantly safeguarded the sacred words, ensuring that the light of truth would endure against the tides of persecution.

With tears welling up in his eyes, the priest stared at the hastily scrawled message.

Pulling in a deep breath, the septuagenarian slowly let out his breath and gazed at the ancient scrap of animal hide. Still holding the item with his tweezers, he looked on the flipside of the brittle object and noticed more hastily scrawled Latin.

"In the land where the river's gift meets the sun's eternal gaze, beneath the guardian palm's shade, the hidden words shall find sanctuary."

Father Montelaro stared at the message and wondered what it could mean.

"Yo, Rosie! Where's my Puttanesca?" A well-dressed man with a thick New York accent bellowed from his table on the far side of Gerard's, a hole-in-the-wall eatery in New York City's Little Italy.

The man behind the bar counter yelled back, "Rosie's getting it, keep your shirt on. The kitchen's backed up a bit."

This was her father's favorite eatery in what he liked to call the old neighborhood, a somewhat rundown part of

Little Italy. The unassuming place brought with it a raucous atmosphere, and it gave Alicia a sense of comfort. Her father had brought her to this place countless times over the years, and despite the familiar surroundings, her stomach churned as anxiety weighed heavily on her.

The last couple weeks had been an emotional rollercoaster. Not only was she was having second thoughts about working for the Outfit, a clandestine government agency nobody was supposed to know about, Alicia had confronted her father over what she believed was his relationship with *La Cosa Nostra*—the Italian Mafia.

Even though he never admitted to it—frankly she didn't expect him to—he wouldn't outright deny some of the things that she'd confronted him with. He didn't have to admit it for her to *know* that he was a member of the mob, and in turn, all the people she'd grown up with as uncles or cousins were obviously members of the Bianchi crime syndicate.

Life had become very complicated.

Alicia had started off as a kid who'd been trafficked out of Asia by some very bad people, and she'd lucked into being adopted by her father. All of that was locked away in her past and despite the rocky start, she felt like she'd had a somewhat normal childhood. But as she sipped at her coke, it was starting to sink in that her definition of normal was way off kilter.

Here she was at a place that held the reputation of being a mob hangout, yet it was probably the one place she felt the most at ease. She knew almost all of the people in this place on a first name basis, they were associates of her father, and only now did she realize that these guys were all probably part of the same mob family.

As Alicia stared at the bead of sweat dripping down the side of her Coke bottle, Tony Montelaro slid his considerable bulk into her booth. "I know your father's out of town and you're crashing at his pad, but why are you ducking his calls?"

"Hey, Tony, good to see you too." Alicia sat back in her bench seat. "He put you up to talking with me?"

"Maybe." Tony shrugged.

Alicia couldn't help but smile at the man's look of discomfort. Tony was pushing three hundred pounds, much of that muscle, and was dressed in a fitted suit. She knew that he was probably one of her father's Mafia soldiers or whatever they called them, and he might have been involved in some terrible things, but she still saw him as a kind of jovial uncle.

"I told him I was fine," she said. "He knows I'll call when I'm ready. I'm just dealing with some things."

"I understand." Tony leaned forward and spoke in a conspiratorial tone. "Hey, I've been hearing things... You thinking about quitting that job you just got?"

"Not you too, Tony. Look, I just need some time to sort this all out. I've taken a month off. I'm going to use it to get my head right and make a few decisions, okay?"

"No, that's not going to work," Tony said. "A month, you

said?"

"Yeah. Why?" When he didn't answer right away, Alicia sighed, leaned forward, and pushed the Coke bottle to the side. "What's with the hesitance from everyone today? *Spit it out.*"

Tony's expression darkened and he spoke barely above a whisper. "It's a family thing. Kind of delicate."

"What kind of family thing?" Alicia raised an eyebrow.

"A 'missing person' kind of thing. I've got family back in Italy. A priest assigned to the Vatican. He's gone, and no one knows what the hell is going on." Tony paused, then nodded to himself as if he'd made some sort of decision. "Look, I heard some of what you've said before… you want to help people. Really help actual people without an agenda. Right? So help *me*."

"You want *my* help?"

"No," Tony said. "I *need* your help."

A strange feeling of release grew in Alicia's chest. It was almost as if God himself had come down from heaven and put an angel in front of her to guide her next steps. She gazed at Tony's sincere expression… and it felt right.

She never could have imagined that her angel would come in the form of a three-hundred-pound mafioso named Tony.

"Okay, Tony. Tell me everything."

"To make a long story short, we haven't heard from my uncle in over a month and nobody at the Vatican seems to know what's going on." Tony dug a sheaf of folded papers from within his suit jacket and placed them on the table along with a photo of an older man wearing a Catholic priest's collar. "It's all in there. Uncle Alessandro is an archivist for the Vatican."

"Archivist?" Alicia began scanning the papers, all of which looked like they'd been hand-written and then faxed. "Is that some kind of record-keeper?"

"It is, sort of." Tony sighed and ran his fingers through his salt-and-pepper hair. "I should probably give you a bit of background. My uncle is a family legend. I remember as a kid hearing stories about Uncle Alessandro traveling everywhere, tracing the steps of the medieval knights in search of lost Church artifacts. He was my family's version of Indiana Jones, and he'd send weekly updates to my father back then, and since my father's passing, I now get the family updates. Or at least I did." Tony leaned forward with a somber expression. "He's never missed a weekly update to us. *Never.* And we haven't heard anything since his last telegram over a month ago. He's now in his seventies and those days of traveling everywhere are over."

"This looks like it's all written in Italian." Alicia frowned as she began flipping through the stack of hand-written pages. "I can make out some of this, but I'm not exactly fluent." She slid the pages back over to Tony and asked, "Can you give me the gist of what I'm looking at?"

"Sure." He scanned through a few of the pages and said, "Most of this is pretty normal day-in-the-life stuff about what he's doing at the *Archivio Apostolico Vaticano*. The place he's working in used to be called the Vatican's Secret Archive—basically from what I understand it's where they store a lot of really old documents. Uncle Alessandro is one of the people charged with record keeping and translating lots of that old stuff from Latin, Greek, and Aramaic into Italian." He flipped to the last page in the stack, picked it up and pointed at the neat handwriting. "This is the last telegram I received, and it's really out of character with what he normally sends. Notice that he wrote it in English. He never does that."

Antonio,

Four years and three months since you've visited, I hope you, Sophia, and the kids are doing well.

Recalling our last visit, I would very much like it if you came soon.

Let's plan this, I will do everything I can to make your visit entertaining and educational.

Our time together is limited on this Earth, and it's always cherished.

Maybe we can also catch up on recent events here. We had a little bit of excitement this week with a small earthquake.

Brilliant as you are, I'm sure you know that we occasionally get rumbles from the ground to remind us that God is watching what we do.

Artifacts from the past were uncovered recently due to the most recent of rumbling.

Recall how long of a history our Church has, I can't begin to tell you how amazing it is to be in the presence of things that were created during the time of our Lord and Savior.

Despite my desire to, I can't really speak on what it is that I've been charged with overseeing most recently.

I had to inform the prefect of the archive about some of what I've encountered. Based on his reaction, it might cause a bit of additional frown lines on the princes of the Church. I would very much like to see you and the family soon. Maybe then I can share more of what I'm working on.

Sending my love as always,
AM ♊︎♊︎♊︎

"Princes of the Church?" Alicia asked. "What does that mean?"

"The cardinals are typically thought of as the princes of the Church." Tony pointed at the bottom of the printout. "Do you see those symbols after his initials?"

Alicia nodded. "Does it mean something to you?"

Tony shook his head. "I was hoping maybe you can help. This Friday it'll be five weeks since I last heard from my Uncle and I've called everywhere I know to call at the Vatican—nobody will give me a straight answer of where he is, and

I've even called the police in Rome and they've said it's a Vatican issue unless I have solid evidence of something that needs their attention." He pulled out another envelope and slid it across the table. "That's for you and your expenses."

Alicia picked up the heavy envelope and peered inside. Her eyes widened, she shook her head and slid the envelope back toward Tony. "I can't take that. First of all, how in the world do you think I can figure out where your uncle is when—"

"You're your father's daughter by training if not by blood." Tony said as he reached across the table and placed the envelope back in Alicia's hand. "There's something about that last message of his that screams to me that something's wrong. I can't trust my emotions on this, I'm just too close—and I'm not exactly known for my level-headedness when it comes to family things, I need someone I can trust to think straight about this stuff. Can you help me with this?"

Alicia nearly jumped out of her skin as her phone vibrated in her pocket. She grabbed it and the moment she put the receiver to her ear, she heard her father's voice.

"Alicia, I just got off the phone with Mason, what's this I hear about you taking time off from the Outfit?"

"One second, Dad." Letting out an audible groan, she got up, glanced in Tony's direction and said "I'll be right back" as she walked toward Gerard's entrance. Over the phone line Alicia heard the sound of music and someone in the background yelling in Russian. As she walked out onto the street in Little Italy, she turned her attention back to the phone and said, "Dad, just trust me on this, I need some time to get my head straight on this whole Outfit thing, and I really need to talk to you about something else."

"Alicia, I just want what's best for you and I know how hard you've been working toward being a fulltime agent. What's up, I don't have much time before I have to get off the line."

"Dad, Tony Montelaro just dropped a missing person's case in my lap and wants me to help him find his uncle. I'm not sure—"

"You want me to talk to him? I can pull him back and tell him not to bother—"

"No, I'm actually kind of interested in helping, but I don't even know how to go about it."

"What do you mean you don't know how to go about it? A missing person's case is as good as whatever information you have. If Tony's got a missing uncle, I'm sure he gave you something to start with. Just think of it as a case dropped into your lap from the Outfit, what would you do if they asked you the same thing?"

"I'd go to the analysis team and have them help me take apart the letters Tony gave me and maybe see if there's any other comms or SIGINT stuff that Brice can find."

Her father chuckled from what likely was the other side of the world and said, *"SIGINT? Comms? You're starting to talk like a spook... okay, in all seriousness you want to do this?"*

"I'd like to help Tony if I can, though he offered me a bunch of money to do that, and I don't feel right taking it."

"Alicia, don't be ridiculous. Take the money, you'll have bills to pay. I remember Tony once speaking about his uncle being a priest up at the Vatican, so you probably are going to have some decent expenses for an international search. If you're even thinking about freelancing, which I'm not against, I want you to remember that you're not a charity. This is business, even if it's someone like Tony as a client."

Alicia wasn't sure how she felt about the idea of Tony being a so-called customer. "I get that, but I don't know that I'm worth it. I don't have a research team or—"

"Baby girl, this is where some of my people can help you get started. You know Denny, right?"

"Of course, I'm actually standing just outside of Gerard's right now. Why?"

"Well, I'll go ahead and text Denny. I want you to treat this as you would anything that's classified. Nobody is to know, but get whatever information you need to start the case from Tony and then talk to Denny. He'll help you piece things together."

"Denny will?" Alicia frowned as she glanced at the entrance to Gerard's. "The same Denny who is serving drinks at Gerard's, that Denny?"

Her father chuckled. "Yes, Denny Carter, that dark-skinned fellow you've known for years as a bartender and owner of Gerard's. Trust me... talk to him when you're ready. I'll open that door for you. Hey, listen, I have to get going, my target is in sight. Let me know what happens and best of luck."

The phone line went dead and Alicia stared at the entrance to Gerard's, not sure how the bartender would help with any of this.

CHAPTER TWO

Alicia's stomach lurched as she watched Tony walk out of Gerard's. "I can't believe I agreed to this," she muttered to herself. Tucked inside her jacket she had Tony's payment and in her hand was all of Uncle Alessandro's recent communications.

With an eerie feeling of déjà vu, Alicia felt exactly like some of the nightmares she'd had back in college. It was that same panicky feeling she'd had when going to take a test and realizing that she'd studied for the wrong subject. It had never actually happened to her in real life, but those nightmares still clung to her, giving her a level of anxiety that she'd never been able to fully get rid of.

Drumming her fingers on the table, she took a deep breath and let it out slowly. "Okay girl, you can do this."

Getting up from her chair, she looked across the eatery and spotted Denny chatting with someone at the bar.

She walked over to the bar and he must have seen her approaching because he ripped his attention away from the local, who'd been nursing a beer, and set his gaze upon her.

"What can I do you for?" Denny asked.

"Talk to Denny and he'll help you piece things together."

Her father's words replayed in her mind.

Alicia leaned across the bar and whispered, "I need a bit of help, and Dad said you might—"

"Hold that thought," Denny said and looked over his shoulder at the woman coming through the swinging doors that separated the kitchen area from the front of the eatery. "Rosie, I need you to man things for a bit?"

The Puerto Rican woman gave Denny a harrumph that the bar owner chuckled at. She then shifted her gaze to Alicia and stared with a mildly surprised expression. She muttered something and turned to the older gentleman nursing his beer.

Denny lifted up a section of the bar's counter and motioned for Alicia to follow.

He led Alicia through a beaded curtain and into a back room.

Despite Alicia having been at Gerard's for years, she'd never been back behind the beaded barrier, which seemed like a throwback to the seventy's disco era.

They were in a small windowless room lit by a weak fluorescent bulb overhead. There was nothing notable about the room except that the far wall was covered with a tiled mural of a beach scene, the individual tiles were no bigger than one-inch square.

Denny turned to her and put a finger to his lips, the universal sign for quiet.

Alicia nodded her understanding.

He turned to the mural and said, "Fortune's fool."

Alicia heard a click somewhere in the room.

Denny pressed on a combination of tiles, and with a beep, the outline of a door appeared. He pushed the door open, and the two of them stepped through the hidden entrance, which sealed itself seconds after Alicia walked into the darkened room beyond.

Lights flickered on to reveal a large supply room filled with rows of shelving holding a variety of electronic equipment. "Woah, I had no idea this was back here."

Denny laughed as he picked up what looked like a police baton. "Not everything is always as it seems. I'd have thought you'd know that by now. Bear with me." He pointed at Alicia with the baton. "Raise your arms, and let's just make sure we're alone."

Denny moved the black wand slowly along Alicia's body. As it passed over her front right pocket, it let out a loud squeal. He made several passes with the wand, covering both sides of her body as well as the front, and the back.

"Empty your right pocket."

Alicia dug her phone out of her pants pocket and put it on a nearby shelf.

Denny waved the wand back over Alicia. It remained silent. Denny picked up her phone and held down the power button, physically turning it all the way off. He waved the wand over it again and nodded at the silence. He turned to Alicia and smiled. "Okay, now that we know nobody's listening, your father said you might need some help. What is it I can do for you?"

Alicia's heart was racing as she stared at her surroundings. "How is it that I... that you... holy cow, Denny. This place looks like it comes right out of a mad scientist's lab." She pointed at one of the shelves, "You've got oscilloscopes, laptops, phones... are you some kind of mad scientist/engineer/computer guy?"

Denny walked deeper into the maze of floor-to-ceiling shelves, leading her to a corner desk with a computer, a large monitor, and a nearby rack of electronics with all variety of LEDs that randomly blinked on and off. "Your father likes to compare me to Q from the James Bond movies, but let's just say I'm pretty good at electronics and anything having to do with extracting information. How can I help?"

Alicia handed Denny the sheaf of papers that Tony had given her and said, "Here's everything I know about this case that just landed in my lap."

Alicia stared up at the computer monitor hanging from the ceiling as Denny scanned through some database coming out of the Vatican.

"As with most missing person's cases, we look for any signals intelligence we can get. But given that our missing person is not exactly what I'd call part of the digital age, there's not much to be had. However, I am seeing some references to a Father Alessandro Montelaro." Denny tapped aggressively on the keyboard and the image on the monitor refreshed with several fragments of text.

Fr. Montelaro: translation of Vat.lat.14117

Fr. Montelaro: translation of Reg.gr.38

Fr. Montelaro: erratum to the Italian translation of Codex Vaticanus Graecus.

Fr. Alessandro Montelaro: private meeting with prefect

"Is that all in chronological order?" Alicia asked.

"It is. The last one has a last-updated directory entry of about five weeks ago."

Alicia pursed her lips as she continued staring at the screen. "That matches up with the time that the last letter was sent."

Denny nodded. "Vatican City is a bit frustrating due to the lack of cameras." The keyboard clicked loudly as he typed. "Most people don't realize it but cities nowadays have cameras everywhere. That usually lets me trace people pretty easily if I have a starting location and time. With the Vatican being what it is, I guess they're behind the times. I'm not getting much else electronically." He placed the letters Alicia had given him from the missing priest into something that looked like a fax machine and pressed a large green button on the device. "Let's see what we can learn from the letters."

The first printout got sucked into the top of the machine, a light flared from within the box-like unit, and the letter spooled out from the bottom of the device onto the table.

The process continued as Denny focused on the computer, pulling up what ended up being a scanned image of the first letter.

"Let's get this processed..." With a few clicks of the mouse the screen split into two regions, with the left-hand side showing the original letter and the right showing a blank white screen.

Elements of the handwritten letter automatically zoomed large, the program highlighted the text and on the right side of the screen the text was transcribed in both Italian and an English translation.

Alicia stared wide-eyed as the next pages were processed automatically. "That's pretty cool. Is this some kind of off-the-shelf software?"

"Parts of it are, but I had to write some scripts and injection code to get things to work together and make it seem seamless. The real magic is the advent of some of the OpenAI plugins that help process text and images. What I'm now doing wasn't something you could automate just five years ago."

The screen continued flickering with new images and data for a full minute until finally a collage of each scanned image appeared, one of them highlighted in red.

"Look what we have here." Denny clicked on the red image and the monitor pulled up a copy of the most recent letter from Uncle Alessandro. He pointed up at the left side of the screen. "Look at the highlighted text—our septuagenarian is into basic encryption it seems. The first letter in each sentence seems to be significant."

Alicia stared intently at the highlighted text. "F-R-L-O-M-B-A-R-D-I, what does—oh crap. That spells out Father Lombardi. Is that what I'm seeing?"

Denny pointed at the report on the right side of the monitor and nodded. "The AI flagged that text as being significant."

*** Acrostic letter placement detected ***
Eighty-eight percent chance of purposeful encoding.

Alicia asked, "Is there a Father Lombardi at—"

"I'm already on it," Denny interjected as a new window popped up on the monitor.

Several screens flew by, all in Italian, and most of them with the Vatican logo.

"Got it," Denny announced as he pulled up what looked like an employment record. "Our Father Lombardi is eighty-three. Has been at the Vatican for eighteen years, before that spent time in Argentina, Japan, and he's originally from Northern Italy."

"Any phone number or anything like that? Email maybe?"

He shook his head. "Don't see anything."

Alicia leaned back in her chair. "This all seems really thin. It's as if this missing priest literally vanished and nobody has anything to say. Is there anything outside of the Vatican on Father Montelaro?"

"No, I already looked to see if there was anything out of Rome. Nothing comes up." He turned in his chair and faced Alicia. "I've never had to track anyone at the Vatican, but your father's been to some places that also don't have much in the way of remote surveillance equipment, and in the end the only way to track some folks down is actually being there."

"Well, there is this Father Lombardi, assuming he's still alive and kicking, and it isn't a weird coincidence that his name sort of popped up in Montelaro's letter." Alicia pointed at the screen. "What about those symbols at the end the priest's signature? Can you tell what those are?"

Using the mouse, Denny highlighted one of the characters and within seconds a summary popped up on the screen.

. . .

The Chi Rho symbol, combining the Greek letters Chi and Rho (XP) from "Christos," represents an early Christogram. Initially used by Roman Emperor Constantine I in military standards, known as the Labarum, it evolved from earlier symbols like the Staurogram and the IX monogram. Before Christianity, it denoted significance in marking valuable passages or abbreviating "good." While originally Greek, it's commonly seen as an abbreviation in Latin texts, representing "to Christ" or "Christian."

Alicia scanned the text and nodded. "Doesn't seem very conspiratorial to have a priest use that symbol. If it's supposed to mean something, I have no idea what it's telling me."

Denny tapped away at the keyboard and after a moment shook his head. "Nope, I've got nothing else. Its use goes back to forever ago, but it's not exactly something that's commonly used today." He turned back to Alicia. "You have anything else that I can help narrow things down?"

"No, you've got everything I have." She pulled out her phone. "I guess I need to book a flight and brush up on my Italian."

"Oh." Denny's eyes widened. "When are you leaving?"

Alicia shrugged. "I guess the sooner the better. Depends on when I can get a flight, but I'm guessing in the next couple days. Why?"

"One second, wait right here." Denny got up and disappeared into the maze of floor-to-ceiling shelving and within a minute returned lugging what looked like a very heavy device with a view finder attached to it. He carefully placed it on the nearest table, plugged it in, and motioned for her to approach. "Do me a favor and look into this viewfinder."

"What is it?" Alicia asked as she walked over to the device and peered into the box-shaped item.

"Trust me, it won't hurt a bit. It's an auto-keratometer. Just stare straight ahead at the green light. The machine will do the rest."

Alicia held her forehead against the viewfinder and stared at the green LED as the machine hummed and occasionally made a clicking noise. "What's it doing?"

"It's measuring the curvature of your eye. I'll have something for you to take on your trip if you give me half a day to get it ready."

The machine gave out a long beep.

"Okay that's good enough. It got what I need."

Alicia looked up and Denny handed her the copies of the priest's letters. A wave of awkward uncertainty washed over her as she looked at the bar owner and asked, "How much do I owe you for the help?"

Denny grinned and shook his head. "Your father and I have an arrangement. If this becomes a habit for you, then maybe we can make our own arrangement regarding my fees. For now, let's just think of this as a free sample of what I do."

"If you say so." Alicia laughed as she pointed at her

surroundings. "All these years and I thought you were a good bartender, but *this,* this is all new to me."

Denny led her back to where they'd entered this hidden area and said, "I'd have thought you're used to people not always being who they seem to be."

Alicia snorted and shook her head. "I guess I'm a bit naïve at times. Thanks a lot for the help, Denny. I really appreciate it."

Denny stopped in front of the door and pointed to the phone that was in her hand. "Oh, before I forget, I added my business number to your contacts. Text me if you need anything while you're out there." As Denny opened the door leading to the eatery he whispered, "Come by tomorrow afternoon. I'll have something for you."

Sitting at the dining room table in her father's apartment, Alicia twirled her fork to collect some of the spaghetti she'd made for dinner as her father tried to advise her from wherever he was.

"Alicia, don't take this the wrong way, but you're female. I know you can take care of yourself, but being a woman alone in this world opens you up as a target. Any street thug is looking for an easy mark, and a petite woman by herself is just begging for unwanted attention."

"I get that, Dad." She swallowed her bite of pasta and took

a swig from the bottle of Pellegrino she'd found in the fridge. "I asked Tony if he'd accompany me, especially since he speaks the language, but he's got something else cooking. I'll figure something out." Bagel, her precocious black cat yowled from the nearby dining room chair as he listened to the conversation. "And besides, I've got Bagel to watch over me."

"*Baby girl, I don't like it. Give me a little bit before you book the flight. I'll make some calls to folks I know in Italy and see what I can do about getting someone we can trust to at least act as an escort.*"

"Dad, you don't really—"

"*Nonsense, don't worry about it. I'll take care of it.*"

Alicia rolled her eyes and knew it wouldn't do any good to try to argue with her father about having a chaperone. Even though he meant well, and was probably doing what any dad would do in this situation, this was one of the reasons why she sometimes didn't want to talk with him. "Fine, I'll hold off booking the flight until tomorrow."

"*Okay, it's midnight in Rome right now, so I might not get anyone until the middle of the night your time. I'll try not to wake you, but expect a call from me in the morning.*"

"Dad, where are you right now?"

"*Let's just say it's 2:00 AM here. I'll call you when I have some information. I love you.*"

"I love—" the phone line went dead and Alicia shook her head. It was six o'clock local time, which put her father's time squarely in the same time zone as Moscow. Not a big surprise. And given that her father also worked for the Outfit as a sort of freelance agent, he could be there for mob-related or national security reasons. She wasn't the only one whose life was complicated.

Bagel reached across the gap between his chair and hers and gave her leg a series of well-coordinated taps, a system they'd developed to communicate based on Morse Code. *"Hungry."*

She turned to her golden-eyed companion and held up a forkful of spaghetti. "You want some?"

Ignoring her question, the cat hopped off the dining room chair, jogged over to the kitchen cabinet that held the cans of tuna she'd bought him, and yowled loudly.

"Okay, okay... I'll feed you. But if we're going to Italy together, you might want to get used to some other types of food."

Alicia put down her cell phone and looked over at Bagel who was lounging on the top of a leather sofa. "That was the vet. You've got an appointment first thing in the morning to get an EU Health Certificate for travel."

The cat seemed unfazed by the news but suddenly hopped off the sofa and approached the front door to the apartment, letting out a long, multisyllabic yowl.

"What?" Alicia asked just as there was a knock at the door.

Nobody ever knocked on her father's door.

Alicia looked through the peep hole and immediately opened the door. "Uncle Vinnie, this is a surprise. Dad's not home."

Vincenzo Bianchi was the head of the Bianchi crime family. Though this was something that wasn't talked about in her presence, she now knew, and had suspected it for a long time.

"You think I don't know that?" The man gave her a warm smile, they kissed each other's cheeks, and he let himself in the apartment.

For anyone else, the act of walking into someone's apartment without asking would seem presumptuous, but this guy owned the entire building, so it was something that Alicia didn't even give much thought to.

Bagel followed Vinnie as he made his way to the leather recliner, and just as the mob boss settled onto the plush seat, the cat hopped up onto his lap.

Alicia smiled as the mob boss stared down at the black ball of fur that had claimed his lap as his own. "His name is Bagel, and he's not really good at acknowledging people's personal space."

"I can see that." The mobster held an amused expression as he pet the cat's head. He motioned to the nearby sofa and said, "Please, I just wanted to have a quick chat."

Alicia felt a mix of anxiety and curiosity as she sat across from the man who'd ostensibly been her father's boss for as long as she'd been his daughter. The man had always seemed friendly and pretty laid back, but she was always aware that the people around him worked for him. And in a mob family, the guy at the top typically earned that position through ruthless exercise of whatever the mob life required.

Vinnie looked directly at her and gave her a warm smile. "You know, your father is very proud of you. You and your sisters have grown up to be beautiful women. And Alicia... you working for the feds was always something that had its plusses and minuses."

A chill raced up and down her spine. Vinnie knew that she was working for the government, and it was something that she'd never mentioned out loud, certainly not to him. Dad obviously told him, but what exactly had her father told him? Could he have told the mob boss about the Outfit?

"I know you're taking some time from that work—"

"How does everyone seem to know that?" Alicia asked.

"Some of us know things." Vinnie waved the question away. "One of the reasons I'm successful is that I know what's happening to those in my circle. Since your father isn't here at the moment, I feel responsible for you. You going off on this trip to Italy—" he held up his hand to stop the question that was about to spill out "—yes, I know all about it. I know you're quite capable of taking care of yourself, but you're a girl—sorry, a woman—and the streets of Italy aren't a place for a lone woman to be. Even though I don't greatly worry for your safety, that's your father's job, I don't like the idea of the distractions you might encounter. I know in this day and age it may seem old fashioned, but I'm responsible for you while your father is... indisposed."

"But Uncle Vinnie, you're really not," Alicia managed to interject even though she didn't like the idea of talking back to her father's boss. "I'm an adult and—"

"Listen, I know that. But you're going to place I know very well and one you aren't familiar with. Take my advice. Even though you might think of yourself as a lion, you don't serve up an intimidating figure, it's not fair, but I'm telling you the way it is. You need some muscle, even if it's for appearances. I won't take 'no' for an answer on this. Give me a second." Vinnie dug his phone out from inside his suit jacket and put it to his ear.

Alicia stared at the man as he talked to someone in Italian. Her mind was racing as she realized that she wasn't really being given an option. The man had come to tell her how it was going to be, very much like her father would have done when she was younger. But she was twenty-three, and she choked down the urge to protest, took a deep breath, and let it out slowly.

Uncle Vinnie's message was largely the same as what her father had already said earlier.

It probably wasn't fair, but nonetheless, both her father and the mob boss were probably not wrong. All she knew about Italy was the men were supposedly more "macho" and outgoing, and her experience with Italians had mostly been her father's acquaintances—which almost certainly wasn't a good representation, since they all knew her father and would all be on their best behavior.

Vinnie put the phone away and stood, Bagel leaped off his lap and clambered up onto the sofa. "Okay, it's settled."

There was a knock at the door and Vinnie walked over, opened it and Tony stood at the doorway, wide-eyed with a nervous expression.

The mob boss motioned for Alicia and gave her a kiss on both cheeks. "Tony will accompany you. The flights have been arranged for tomorrow at three-thirty in the afternoon." He walked over to the mob enforcer and hitched his thumb in Alicia's direction. "She's your responsibility, *capiche*?"

Tony nodded.

"Good." He patted Tony on the cheek, turned once again to Alicia and tilted his head toward the other mobster. "He's good, you just need to keep him in line."

Vinnie walked out the door and Tony gave Alicia a weak smile. "I guess I've had a change in plans."

Alicia laughed and felt a warm sense that everything would be okay. "I'm glad to hear it. I guess we both need to pack."

Tony nodded and said, "I'll arrange for us to get a ride together to the airport tomorrow. Be ready by noon so we don't have to rush."

"Noon?" Alicia grimaced. "Tomorrow morning is going to be really busy; I've got a vet appointment and..."

Tony cleared his throat loudly, slowly shook his head and frowned.

"Okay, okay... I get it. The airplane won't wait." Alicia's mind raced with everything she had to do. She glanced over her shoulder at Bagel, who was giving her a disapproving stare from the back of the sofa. She sighed and focused again on Tony. "I guess I'll see you tomorrow, at noon."

Alicia heard Italian being spoken from the MP3 file Denny was playing, but the ear bud he'd custom-fitted for her ear canal was simultaneously whispering to her the English translation.

"Is it working?" Denny asked.

She nodded. "That's amazing."

"Try this." He handed her a small plastic item.

Alicia stared at what looked like a plastic contact lens container. She shook it lightly, and heard water sloshing inside. Contact solution? "Why the heck do you think I need this?" Alicia didn't wear glasses—in fact her vision was nowadays better than it had ever been before.

Denny smiled. "Humor me. Open it and put that contact in your right eye. If you've never done it before, I can do it for you."

Alicia felt a tingle of excited anticipation... almost like unwrapping a present. She unscrewed the cap and examined the contact submerged in contact solution. "Why does this thing look like it has little silver stripes running through it?"

"Those are fiber-optic channels. Actually, it's a bit more than that, they're bundled arrays of carbon nanotubes, let's just keep things simple. Trust me, you won't even see them when you put it on."

Alicia looked at her hands. "Shouldn't I wash my hands or something?"

"Really?" Denny gave her an amused look and pulled out a large retail bottle of Bausch and Lomb contact solution. "Show me your right hand."

Alicia extended her hand, and Denny squeezed the solution on her hand and all over the floor.

She rubbed her fingers together, not sure that they were any cleaner now than before. "What's this thing do?"

"Stop being a baby, I'm not going to steer you wrong. Just put it in your right eye. That's the one I measured it for."

With a sigh, Alicia scooped the contact onto the top of her index finger. The idea of putting something directly on her eye seemed wholly unnatural. Yet here she was doing exactly that, and she was curious about what the contact lens was going to do.

"Just press it on gently and it should just suction cup right onto your eye. It'll automatically orient itself once you blink a few times."

Alicia did as she was told, and the world turned blurry as she blinked the excess contact solution away. But as she was about to rub her eye, Denny stopped her.

"No—don't rub your eyes. Here." He handed Alicia some tissues. "Just dab the wet away."

Alicia dabbed away the wetness, then looked around. "Okay, now what? I don't see anything different. Am I supposed to?"

"That lens is linked to the app I installed onto your phone. The lens has AR capability and—"

"AR?"

"Augmented Reality," Denny replied. "Let me show you." He grabbed a sheet of paper from the computer desk and handed it to her.

Alicia recognized it as a copy of one of Father Montelaro's handwritten notes.

Almost instantly, the letters on the paper glowed and English text overlaid on top of the Italian writing.

"Holy crap! It auto-translates," Alicia exclaimed as she quickly scanned the letter, which she'd normally not be able to read.

"Yup, and using some built-in AI features in the app, it can even do a pretty good job on translating handwritten text. It's really no different than the earpiece. It's known technology, but I've miniaturized things and for maximum capability, I've linked it to your phone via Bluetooth so that you can both hear and see translations from dozens of languages. Just be warned that it might not always work right if you don't have a data connection with your cell phone."

Alicia panned her gaze across Denny's hidden sanctuary

behind Gerard's and smiled as she looked back down at the paper. No wonder her father thought the world of Denny, this guy was amazing.

Impulsively she gave Denny a hug and said, "Thank you so much for this. I'm sure it's going to be a lifesaver when I'm in Italy."

Denny shook his head. "Let's just hope it doesn't need to be a lifesaver." He glanced at the wall clock and pointed at the far end of the room, toward the exit. "You have a flight to catch."

Alicia's eyes widened as she looked at the time. "Oh crap." She rushed toward the exit as she called up an Uber on her phone and yelled over her shoulder, "Let me know what I owe you."

"Have a safe trip," was Denny's only response as Alicia rushed to catch her ride.

CHAPTER
THREE

"*Ladies and gentlemen, welcome onboard Flight 609 with service from New York to Rome. We are currently third in line for take-off and are expected to be in the air in approximately seven minutes time. We ask that you please fasten your seatbelts and secure all baggage...*"

Alicia fastened her seatbelt as the jet slowly taxied closer to the runway. She peered over the half-height barrier between the business class seats in the center aisle. "Tony, I don't even want to think about how much you paid for these seats. We could have gone in the back—"

"Are you kidding me?" Tony held an amused expression as he shifted his bulk to face her. "The Don—I mean Mr. Bianchi made these flight arrangements. Remember, I didn't think I was going anywhere until I got sucked in at the last minute. I don't make the kind of bread it takes to fly fancy like this, especially at the last minute."

She grinned at her beefy companion and wondered how he'd fit in a coach seat. Alicia leaned closer and spoke in a conspiratorial tone. "You know, I know about Uncle Vinnie. The whole Don thing and stuff…"

Tony tilted his head and said, "I don't know what you're talking about, and it's best to leave it at that, if you know what I mean."

"Dad would never say anything to me either, and I get it. I'm not an idiot. I might have deluded myself for years, but I now understand what's up and I just wanted you to know."

"Little lady, you don't have *any* clue what you know or don't know." Tony smiled and gave her the slightest of nods. "Nonetheless, heard and understood."

Alicia leaned forward in her seat and grabbed a folder from the backpack stowed at the foot of her business class pod. She pulled out some notes that she'd taken from her session with Denny and said, "Let's go over some of the plans for when we land. I was thinking that the first thing we should do is—"

"Alicia, I don't mean to interrupt your train of thought or nothing, but this is going to be an eight-hour flight and it'll be morning when we land in Italy."

Alicia felt the plane turn onto the runway and it then slowed to a stop.

As the jet engines began giving out a high-pitched whine,

Tony raised his voice and said, "You're old enough to drink, so when the nice stewardess comes by, let's grab some cocktails, put them down quickly, and get ourselves some sleep. I've done this trip a few times and if you follow my recipe, we'll be there without too much jet lag or anything. We'll have plenty of time to go over stuff after we get some shuteye."

"Actually, you're right." Alicia stowed her folder back into her backpack, took a deep breath and let it out slowly.

"I can tell you're all wound up and excited." Tony's voice was a bit muffled by the barrier between them. "Just relax. We're just taking a little trip."

Alicia's mind raced, the weight of responsibility for finding Tony's missing uncle rested heavily on her shoulders.

Suddenly Alicia felt herself getting pushed back against her seat as the jet accelerated down the runway.

Trying to control her breathing, Alicia tightened her grip on the armrests and wondered how Bagel was doing down in whatever hold they'd stowed him.

Alicia opened the latch on the cat carrier, and Bagel, displaying a touch of irritation from his confinement, maneuvered into the papoose-like sling she had purchased just before leaving the US. The thought of having to carry him everywhere in Italy wasn't appealing to either of them, and the anxiety of letting him roam freely, risking loss, theft, or accidents, was equally unsettling. They reached a compromise with the baby sling, initially designed for snugly holding infants against the chest. However, her feline companion wasn't a fan of such close contact. With the straps loosened, Bagel settled into the sling, transforming it into something akin to an oblong purse. He squirmed a bit, found his comfortable spot, poked his head out, and curiously observed their new surroundings.

Passaggeri in arrivo, benvenuti all'Aeroporto Internazionale Leonardo da Vinci–Fiumicino...

The announcement, which she didn't understand, broadcast through the baggage claim area and Bagel tapped on her chest. *"Hungry."*

Alicia nodded. "You'll have to wait a little bit. Let's get past customs and out of the airport."

She turned her phone back on and heard a chime in her ear from Denny's device syncing back with her phone.

Arriving passengers, welcome to Leonardo da Vinci–Fiumicino International Airport. To ensure efficient processing, please have your travel documents ready for the customs officials.

. . .

Her ear bud automatically translated the Italian.

Tony emerged from the bustling crowd, his grip firm on their suitcase as he stepped away from the chaos of the baggage turnstile. His eyes locked onto them, a mischievous grin spread across his face as he moved closer, his focus fixed on the furry bundle nestled on Alicia's chest. "How's Mr. Bagel?"

Bagel, peered up at the mobster and gave him a prolonged, multi-syllabic yowl that uncannily resembled a well-articulated sentence in cat.

Acknowledging the cat's "response," the mafioso nodded, gesturing toward the customs processing area. "We'll get you something to eat when we get out of here."

Alicia slung her backpack over her right shoulder, snatched up the now-vacant cat carrier, and trailed behind Tony as he skillfully carved a path toward customs.

The woman at the customs booth waved her forward. "*Documento di viaggio, per favore.*"

"*Travel documents, please,*" her earbud automatically translated the question.

Alicia handed over her passport as well as Bagel's travel documents.

"Ah, an American. Welcome." The middle-aged woman spoke with a heavy Italian accent and Denny's translation device kicked in, speaking in her ear with a bland, yet more understandable form of English. The customs agent flipped open the passport and placed it under a scanner. A green LED flashed and she asked, "Purpose of your visit to Italy?"

"I'm here as a tourist. Going to see the Vatican."

"Ah, it is a beautiful place." The woman nodded and opened Bagel's documents. A smile bloomed on her face as she flipped open the EU document that had been filled out in the veterinarian's office—effectively a kitty passport.

Bagel popped his head up from within the sling and peered over at the customs agent.

"*Madonna mia, che visino di gatto più—*" the translation from the ear bud for some reason lagged a second or two and then rapidly translated. "Oh my God, that is the most beautiful cat face I've ever seen! Those golden eyes are just precious." The agent leaned closer, a big smile plastered on her face. "Are you enjoying your trip?"

Bagel meowed in response.

The agent let out a warm laugh as she put a stamp into Alicia's passport and handed back their paperwork.

The purring cat reached toward the woman with his paw and the agent waved in response.

Alicia walked past the customs booth and spotted Tony waiting for them.

"Any problems getting Mr. Bagel through?" Tony asked.

"No." She scratched at the top of the cat's head and followed Tony as he led them to the pickup area. "This little guy is a ham. I think he made that lady's day by flirting with her."

Bagel looked up at her and tapped out a rapid sequence, "Hungry."

"Okay, okay... we'll get you some food."

As Alicia exited the main terminal, she was hit with a gust of warm air. The scent of diesel was almost overwhelming.

A man in a suit jogged toward them, waving a sign with "Antonio Montelaro" printed on it.

He focused on Tony as he called to him in Italian. "Sir, Mr. Montelaro." The man was panting, and beads of sweat dripped down the side of his face. "I've got your car. I'm Marco, the driver."

Tony frowned and responded in Italian. "I didn't ask for a car."

The man looked taken aback. He pulled out a printed sheet, glanced at it, then showed it to Tony. "Sir, it was prearranged by your travel agent. This is the order. You are Antonio Montelaro, are you not?" The driver shifted his gaze in Alicia's direction and said, "And I assume you are the 'plus one' on the order."

Alicia walked up to Tony as he examined the printout. She felt a slight sense of vertigo as Denny's contact lens flashed translations of the Italian text printed on the travel business's stationery. It included a scanned copy of Tony's passport—with his picture—and his arrival itinerary, including the flight and even his seat number.

"My travel agent." Tony chuckled as he turned to Alicia and whispered to her in English, "It seems like another one of the boss's people made arrangements I didn't know about."

Alicia's brow furrowed as her mind raced with all sorts of realistic and outlandish reasons why she shouldn't trust this stranger driving them anywhere. *This isn't a cloak and dagger mission. We're just tourists visiting Rome.* At least that's what she tried to convince herself of. Some of the Outfit's training had become engrained in her psyche and she'd grown paranoid. Maybe there wasn't a boogieman behind every tree?

Tony shifted his attention back to the driver. "I see my travel agent forgot to tell us about the car."

The man held out his hand. "Sir, I can take your luggage. The car is parked in the express parking lot nearby, if you'll follow me."

Tony tightened his grip on their suitcase and shook his head. "Don't worry about the bags. Let's get out of the heat. I assume your car has good air conditioning?"

"Yes, sir."

A minute later, Alicia was settling into the back of a brand new Mercedes S-Class sedan. The scent of the plush leather seats enveloped her as the driver started the car and turned on some soft classical music. Tony sat in the front seat, his body angled slightly toward the driver, who looked particularly nervous.

Tony held a relaxed expression, but as the two men

chatted in Italian, Alicia noticed the mafioso paying close attention to the road ahead as well as the driver.

Alicia couldn't get rid of the feeling that this driver wasn't being totally on the up-and-up.

"*Keep right to continue toward Via Alessandro Guidoni.*"

The car's navigation system spoke up in Italian, and Alicia leaned her head back on the plush seat. As the two men spoke in Italian and her ear bud translated, Alicia focused on the words being spoken both in the car and in her ear. Thanks to Denny's device, she had something to focus on. Not knowing the the language being spoken all around her was a very awkward thing for her.

She had no idea how much Denny would charge her for these gadgets she was using, but whatever his price, it would be worth it.

"*At the roundabout, take the 1st exit onto the Via Mario de Bernardi ramp to Roma.*"

"How far is it until we get to the hotel?" Alicia asked.

The driver glanced back at her with a puzzled expression and Tony quickly translated.

"*Ah, sì sì. Stiamo andando alla Via dei Cavalleggeri, l'appartamento che hai prenotato è a circa 26 chilometri di distanza. Sei così*—so close to the Vatican City wall that you can wave to the Pope from the apartment."

Alicia glanced at her phone, whose signal was barely registering at one bar. No wonder the translation fell out in the middle.

Tony looked back at her and said, "He says it's about

sixteen miles away and in spitting distance of the Vatican. It's past early morning rush hour so the traffic shouldn't be too terrible. I'd say we should get there in a little over half an hour."

"Do you know anything about this place we're going?"

"Nope." He shook his head. "Remember, I'm a late add to this little adventure. I know absolutely nothing other than how to speak the language and what my uncle looks like. You're in charge for the most part. I'm just the meat wall to prevent any of the guys from getting fresh with you."

Alicia gave Tony an evil grin. "What if I want them to get fresh?"

He shook his head. "Not on my watch, young lady. Not only would my boss kill me, your father would probably scrape up what's left of me and drop my remains in a volcano or something."

Bagel shifted in the sling that was now laying in her lap. He stretched both of his arms up into the air. She kissed one of the pads on his feet and felt a purr as the cat shifted once more and lay like a lump in his private cocoon.

Alicia closed her eyes as Tony and the driver began chatting again. She listened to the dual conversations in the car and in her head and slowly tried to learn more than the handful of words she knew in Italian.

She focused so intently on the words that she must have fallen asleep, because the next thing she knew was her startling awake as the car slowed to a stop.

"Welcome to the House of Cavalleggeri," the driver announced.

Alicia was glad the apartment wasn't very fancy. Thankfully, it was clean. It had two en-suite bedrooms, a very tiny kitchen, and a small living area. All totaled, it was probably five or six-hundred square feet. By American standards it was small, but evidently quite spacious for Italy. In the pit of her stomach, she worried about expenses. Her father's warning about *"you'll have bills to pay"* repeated in her mind. Was she going to be responsible for the plane ticket? She had no idea how much Denny's services would cost. She'd asked the driver about the price for the apartment, but evidently one of Uncle Vinnie's people had already paid for it. That was yet another expense that she couldn't quantify, and could only assume that at some point she'd have to pay for it.

She had no idea about budgeting for this kind of "mission" and this whole thing got complex very quickly. Alicia couldn't stand excuses from other people, much less herself. She hated not having all the information she needed, and from here on out, things would have to change. Either way, starting off with an unknown quantity of debt gave her a stomach ache.

Wrenching her thoughts away from things that she

couldn't do anything about at the moment, she looked out of her bedroom window and smiled.

It was just like the driver had said. Alicia saw a building with an impressive domed roof within a stone's throw of her tiny bedroom. It closely matched the images she'd seen of St. Peter's Basilica. It was probably impossible to have a place closer to Vatican City than where they were staying.

Alicia closed the window and made her way to the kitchen, where the scent of fish filled the air. There, she discovered Bagel enthusiastically devouring the remnants of the freshly-cut sardines placed in a bowl she'd found in one of the kitchen cabinets. "You sure seem to be enjoying your meal," she remarked.

Tony walked into the kitchen, buttoning up a fresh shirt. "I don't see why he wouldn't like it; those fish were probably swimming in the ocean just this morning."

Alicia bit into on one of the apples they'd gotten at the market and the juice practically exploded into her mouth. "Wow, is all the food like this in Italy?"

"What do you mean?" Tony asked.

"So fresh and tasty." Alicia wiped her chin and took another bite. "This is the best damned apple I've ever had."

The large man shrugged. "If there's one thing Italians are known for, it's our love of good food. Are we ready to go?"

"Sure." Alicia took another large bite of the apple, and laid the other half on the kitchen counter for later. "Bagel, are you almost done."

The cat made loud eating noises as he tilted his head to the side and chewed heartily on the last of the sardines.

"Tony, what do you know about getting tickets into the Vatican? I was reading something about needing tickets to get into the Vatican and it's faster to get them online."

As Alicia crouched on the floor and let Bagel climb into his pouch, the cat yowled at her with his fishy breath.

With his palm up, Tony pinched his fingers together and gestured up and down in a classic Italian way that Alicia had witnessed countless times. "Why the heck would we need tickets to check out my uncle's workplace? We're not some tourists trying to get into a museum or something. Just come with me; I remember enough to get us to where my uncle worked. After that, we'll figure it out."

Alicia followed the large man out the door, and within moments they were walking along the Via della Conciliazone.

All along the street were souvenir shops with vendors hocking wares having to do with Catholicism, the Vatican itself, and an innumerable number of trinkets that spanned the gamut of tourist-oriented items.

Tony pointed ahead, "See the big domed building?"

"Yup, isn't that St. Peter's?"

"Yup. It's actually pretty amazing this stuff is all still standing."

"Do you know when it was built?" Alicia asked as she dodged a group of kids running along the expansive sidewalk.

"Nah, but I'm sure it's way older than any building we have back home."

"Antonio?"

Tony stopped midstride as a dark-clothed, collar-wearing priest called out again.

"Antonio Montelaro? Is that really you?" The man spoke in heavily-accented English.

Alicia looked back and forth between the middle-aged priest approaching at a fast pace and Tony's confused expression.

"*Madonna mia!*" Tony's eyes widened, he took a few steps toward the priest and with outstretched arms the two men embraced. Kissing each other on both cheeks. "What is this?" He pointed at the priest's white collar. "Leonardo, how is it I didn't know you're a priest now?"

The Father laughed and draped his arm over Tony's shoulder. "It's been what, thirty years since I last saw you? You're an American now. I'm no longer the troublemaker my mother worried over. Things change." He nodded in Alicia's direction. "Who are you with? This couldn't be your daughter... or—"

"No, it's nothing like that." Tony laughed; a genuine expression of amusement plastered on his face. He waved Alicia over. "This is Alicia, the daughter of a close friend. I'm her escort."

Alicia asked, "Are the two of you related?"

"Second cousins." They both responded at the same time.

Tony patted the priest on his chest. "Leonardo... or I suppose he's probably now called Father Marino, his mother and my mother are first cousins."

"It's a pleasure to meet you, young miss." The priest gave her a warm smile. "What brings you to the Vatican?"

Tony's happy expression faltered as he focused on his cousin and switched into Italian. "Have you heard from Uncle Alessandro recently?"

"No, I live up near Bologna where I have a modest parish and attend the people there. But Momma had gotten sick and she'd asked for me to come. It turns out that she's getting a little..." he tapped the side of his head and shrugged. "Anyway, she thinks that her apartment needs to be cleansed of evil spirits and per her instructions, I must get holy water from here. As far as Momma's concerned, my blessings aren't strong enough for her spirits."

"Is she okay?" Tony asked.

Father Marino waved dismissively. "She's fine. Since Poppa passed, she's lonely and a little bit crazy. I'll have to talk to some of the neighbors and see about getting her more socialization. Anyway, as for Uncle Alessandro, I was planning on paying him a visit before I left. Is that why you're here?"

"No, not really." Tony shook his head. "Alicia's never been in Italy before and since we were nearby, she wanted to take a look at the Vatican."

The priest turned to her and spoke in English, "I'm sorry, I should have been speaking in English. It's a habit—"

"No, don't worry." Alicia grinned. "I understood what you two were saying about your mother and the evil spirits. I just don't really speak Italian."

Tony looked at her with a surprised expression and it suddenly dawned on her that she hadn't told him about any of the gadgets she was using to help bridge the language gap. She gave him a wink and wondered why Tony wasn't telling his cousin the truth about why they were here—Uncle Alessandro.

"Excellent." The priest switched back to Italian. "I'm sure you'll be speaking just fine soon enough." He gave her a warm smile and motioned for them to follow him. "Let's go. I don't have time right now to give you much of a tour, but I can at least walk with you up to Saint Peter's."

Alicia followed as the cousins talked animatedly about family members she'd never heard of.

It took only minutes before the buildings loomed large and the priest turned to Alicia and pointed at St. Peter's. "Up ahead is St. Peter's Basilica. It's truly a spiritual and architectural marvel. It was conceived by Pope Julius II in the early 1500s, but its construction spanned over a century and involved famous architects that I'm sure you've heard of like Bramante and Michelangelo. The basilica was erected on the burial place of Saint Peter, one of Jesus Christ's apostles.

"Michelangelo's dome, a Renaissance masterpiece, crowns the basilica, while Gian Lorenzo Bernini's grand colonnade embraces St. Peter's Square. The basilica's interior, adorned with intricate mosaics and sculptures, houses iconic works like Michelangelo's Pieta. Throughout history, St. Peter's Basilica has been witness to significant events, from papal ceremonies to historic proclamations.

"As I'm sure you know, this place is a sacred pilgrimage site for millions of Catholics. It symbolizes the Church's continuity and spiritual significance. St. Peter's remains a testament to the enduring power of faith, the artistic brilliance of the Renaissance, and the unbroken connection of the Catholic Church to its apostolic origins."

"*Wow, quello è stato... molto buono.*" Alicia struggled to recall the right words in Italian and immediately switched back to English. "Wow, that was really good." She focused on the priest. "You should be a professional tourist guide. Your enthusiasm is infectious."

The priest laughed and shook his head. "I appreciate that, but we each have our own calling." A nearby clock chimed and he glanced at the tourist stand with several Catholic-themed wall clocks. "Speaking of a calling, I need to get the holy water I promised my mother. It was nice meeting you, Alicia. I hope this visit gives you a strong spiritual awakening." He gave her a nod, kissed Tony on both cheeks and was off toward the basilica.

"He seems like such a nice man," Alicia remarked.

Tony chuckled and motioned for her to follow him as he turned right at the first cross street onto Via di Porta Angelicato. "You didn't know him as a kid."

Alicia glanced in the direction the priest had gone. "Are you implying he wasn't as nice back then?"

"My parents certainly held that opinion. They hated the idea that he and I had grown close. Had I not left for America, who knows how things might have evolved."

"Maybe another Father Montelaro?" Alicia smiled as she imagined Tony in a priest's vestments.

He shrugged as they turned left on another street corner.

Alicia was always conscious of who Tony was and what he was likely capable of. He was a working member of the Mafia. He'd probably killed people, and he'd developed a mindset that allowed him to live with what he'd done and might likely do again. These things were never talked about. She wasn't on the inside circle of that sort of trust, and frankly wanted no part of it. It was a hard thing to reconcile, the man almost certainly being a killer, yet a trusted companion... but with Tony it just seemed natural. After all, her father was also a part of that same world, and she didn't like to think about what he'd likely done as well.

It's not like Alicia had much choice in who her family was, and that was okay. She cast a sidelong glance at Tony, a smile breaking across her face as she teased, "Are you saying Father Marino was a bad influence on *you*?"

"He wasn't Father Marino back then." Tony pointed at the gates they were walking past. "This is Chiesa di Sant'Anna dei Palafrenieri. It's one of the churches built in the 1500s. Uncle Alessandro and I would sometimes go in there for Sunday Mass. We're almost at the Apostolic Archive where he worked."

"Do you think the people there will talk with us about your uncle?"

Tony cracked his knuckles, sporting a determined expression. "Oh, someone will talk, I'm sure of it."

Alicia spoke in a barely audible whisper, "Tony, you know you can't force people to talk if they're not willing."

Tony harrumphed. "I think you underestimate my determination when it comes to family."

Bagel poked his head out from within his sling, took in his surrounding and let out a huge yawn.

Alicia gently touched the back of Tony's arm. "Tony, if you don't mind, let me handle things if you feel like you aren't making any progress with the folks here, okay? I already have a lead or two we can try if this doesn't pan out."

Tony's facial expression darkened, and he remained silent for a full thirty seconds as they approached a familiar building. Alicia recognized it from her internet research—the Vatican Apostolic Archive. The burly mobster slowed his pace to a halt, focusing his gaze on her. "As long as we're getting closer to an answer about where my uncle is, I'll do what I can to control myself."

She grinned at him. "You hired me to do a job; it's about time I start." She pointed at the building. "Let's go and see what we can learn."

Seated in an office lined with books, Alicia's eyes widened as tension gripped the room. A standoff had unfolded between the prefect, overseeing the archive, and Tony, who appeared ready to launch from his chair, the frustration evident in his inability to extract anything useful from the clergyman.

"What do you mean you can't disclose my uncle's whereabouts?" Tony's voice grew louder.

Alicia discreetly squeezed the back of Tony's sturdy arm, wary of a potential physical confrontation, while the prefect maintained a solemn gaze on both of them. The last thing anyone needed was a trip to an Italian jail.

"*Signore*, I have nothing to share with you," the middle-aged priest spoke in a calm, soothing tone, though it only appeared to further agitate Tony.

Alicia put her hand firmly on Tony's shoulder, leaned forward in her chair and said, "Father Russo, I have records of you and Father Montelaro meeting privately just before he went missing. You must know something."

The prefect leaned forward and put his elbows on his desk. "Young lady, it's true that Alessandro and I met privately. In my role as prefect of the archive, it is something I do with all of our archivists and researchers." The man's voice, which had only a slight Italian accent, maintained the same even tone. "I have no information on Alessandro Montelaro's whereabouts."

Alicia frowned. "I'll be direct. It seems to be that you're being evasive. You have to have more information than simply 'I don't know.' You're familiar with his routines, his comings and goings. What efforts has the Church made to locate him? Have you checked his apartment? What other actions have you taken? What aren't you telling us?"

For a fleeting moment, a hint of something in the man's expression signaled to Alicia that she'd struck a nerve. This man was holding *something* back.

Nonplussed, the priest maintained his calm tone as he addressed her. "Miss... I'm sorry I didn't get your last name."

"My name is Alicia. That's good enough." Alicia kept a neutral expression even though she was starting to feel the same frustration Tony exuded.

"Fair enough, Alicia. Are you familiar with a man named Armand Jean du Plessis?"

"No." Alicia's interest was piqued. "Who was he?"

"He was a Cardinal of this church in the seventeenth century. You may have heard of him as Cardinal Richelieu. There is a quote attributed to him that I've long ago taken a lesson from and it goes like this: 'If you give me six lines written by the hand of the most honest of men, I will find something in them which will hang him.' This is why I rather not speculate on things I don't know about. If I knew something useful, I would tell you. I believe we have the same desire, and that is to see Alessandro back with us."

"Fine." Alicia had heard the quote before, and felt a rising sense of annoyance with this man, who now seemed more like a politician than a clergyman to her. "What you don't seem to realize is that you might hold some information that you believe is unimportant, but may in fact lead to us finding him. You've worked with him or at least known him for years and you have to have some guesses as to where he might be. Who might know where he is? Who are his associates outside of work? There has to be something, because what you've told us amounts to absolutely nothing."

The prefect shook his head. "I'm sorry. Father Montelaro was a scholarly man who mostly kept to himself. He was either working here at the archive or, as best as I know, in his apartment. And yes, of course we sent someone to check on him. We even asked the landlord to open the apartment and do what I think you call in America a wellness check. I was told the apartment was empty.

"I even looked into his Vatican records and know that in his younger days he would often seek knowledge to further his studies in remote parts of the world, but always with the blessing of the Church. It is possible that he's left to seek knowledge yet again, but at his advanced age, he might not have gotten the blessing of the Church to do such a thing. I know of no formal requests on his behalf for such a trip, so it's pure speculation on my part. I truly have nothing useful to share with you. I'm at a loss as to his whereabouts."

"Any colleagues? Friends?" Alicia asked.

"I'm sorry, I don't have any names to give that could help you."

There was a knock on the office door and one of the Swiss guards opened it, poked his head in and said, "Father Russo, your afternoon appointment is waiting for you in the archive."

Alicia got up and motioned for Tony to do the same.

"I apologize that I couldn't be more helpful with this." The prefect stood, shifted his gaze to Tony and said, "Your uncle is in my prayers."

Before Tony could respond, Alicia grabbed the large man by the arm and practically dragged him from the prefect's office.

As they stepped outside of the building, Tony growled. "That man knows more than he's letting on."

Alicia nodded. "You might be right, and even though he was practically useless, I know where to go next."

Tony paused at the street corner and looked at her with a serious expression. "Where is that?"

"We're going to pay a visit to a Father Giuseppe Lombardi." Alicia replayed in her mind the information she'd acquired from Denny's research.

"And why in the world are we visiting him?"

"Actually, it was your uncle who told us to visit him," Alicia said with a lopsided smile.

"He what?" Tony furrowed his brow.

Alicia motioned for him to follow her. "Come on, I'll explain on the way."

CHAPTER
FOUR

Alicia scanned *Via della Stazione Vaticana*, searching for any address number to orient herself. They strolled along a narrow two-lane road, with apartment buildings towering on the right. A single-file row of cars was parked against the buildings on the right, while on the left, a twenty-foot-tall wall, sloping slightly inward at the top, delineated the outer edge of the Vatican.

"So you're expecting me to believe that my seventy-something year old uncle put a coded message in his last communication to me?" Tony frowned as they walked along the narrow street.

Alicia nodded. "It was actually there plain as day once you're looking for it. Just take the first letter from each sentence he wrote to you and it spelled out F-R-L-O-M-B-A-R-D-I. Father Lombardi."

"Never heard my uncle speak of anyone by that name. I don't know Alicia, this seems pretty shaky."

Alicia halted as she spotted the number three above the lintel of an entrance to the next apartment building. It was directly across the street from a small guarded entrance to the Vatican—one that tourists likely wouldn't have used. She motioned to the apartment building entrance and said, "Well, there's only one way to find out. Father Lombardi's apartment is in that building, second floor, apartment eleven."

"What do we know about this Lombardi guy?" Tony asked as he opened the door to the apartment building.

In her mind's eye, Alicia saw the Vatican's personnel records that Denny had pulled up and said, "He's eighty-three. He's been at the Vatican for eighteen years. Before his stint here, he'd spent time in Argentina, Japan and he's originally from Northern Italy."

"The Lombardy region is in the north, so that's no surprise." Tony panned his gaze across the old and somewhat dingy foyer and veered to the right where there was a sign indicating stairs.

Alicia took the stairs two at a time and when Tony caught up, she spoke with a hushed tone and pointed at their target. "Let me handle this, okay?"

Tony nodded and they walked along the poorly-lit hallway until she found number eleven.

The scarred wooden door showed its age as did the rest of the building. She stepped closer, listening and hearing nothing behind the door. Unlike the other apartments they'd passed, there was no obvious sound of a TV or radio playing. Alicia rapped her knuckles firmly on the door and listened.

No noises in response.

She waited a few moments and then knocked harder. Only then did she detect the sound of shuffling feet and someone muttering something unintelligible behind the door.

There was the sound of someone fumbling with a lock, and Alicia watched as the doorknob rattled a few seconds before the door finally opened, the unoiled hinges emitting an unpleasant squeal.

In the doorway stood a stooped elderly man, leaning heavily against the doorframe. He gazed at Alicia with a puzzled expression, clad only in a coarse brown robe. His disheveled hair suggested that he'd just gotten out of bed. "Yes?"

"Padre Lombardi?" Alicia asked in Italian.

"Yes?"

"*Posso parlare?*" Alicia struggled coming up with the right words. Tony interjected, "*Possiamo parlare?*" which her earbuds picked up as what she'd intended to say: "Can we speak?"

The man stepped back into his apartment, leaving the door open.

Alicia turned to Tony and whispered, "Can you translate for me?"

He nodded as they both walked into a tiny apartment.

There were only two spindly chairs and one was occupied by the frail clergyman who began sipping at a steaming cup of something that smelled heavily of herbs.

With a rheumy gaze, the man looked at Alicia and motioned to the unused chair. He asked in heavily-accented English, "British?"

Alicia sat and shook her head. "No, I'm American. Can we speak in English?"

The man held a confused expression and just as Tony was about to translate, the old man said in English, "I think so." He seemed to snap out of whatever stupor he'd lapsed into and nodded. "Yes, I think I can speak English." He looked up at Tony, switched to Italian, and said, "I'm sorry that I don't have a chair for you, my son."

Tony smiled and with a warm tone that Alicia wasn't used to hearing from the large man he said, "It's okay Father. I'm more comfortable standing."

"Father," Alicia leaned forward and Bagel yowled as she accidentally pressed him against the table. The cat squirmed, popped out of the sling and onto the floor.

The clergyman's eyes widened and said something indecipherable as he made the sign of the cross. "Where did he come from?"

Bagel walked away from the table and began sniffing at his new surroundings, indifferent to the people in it.

Alicia reached across the table and patted the man's hand. "I'm sorry, he was asleep in his carrier. He's harmless."

The priest's eyes followed the cat as Bagel explored the

empty kitchenette, and sniffed at the air coming in from the window that was cracked open an inch.

"Father," Alicia continued, "do you know a fellow priest by the name of Alessandro Montelaro?"

The clergyman shifted his gaze back toward Alicia and his bushy eyebrows furrowed and after seconds-long pause, he nodded. "I remember my younger days when I too would adventure."

Alicia pressed her lips together, unsure if the elderly priest misheard her or was otherwise confused.

The priest sat up straight, his eyes took on a faraway look and he began speaking in Spanish. Thankfully Denny's earbuds handled things automatically.

"I remember in Argentina, I was in San Carlos de Bariloche at the foot of the Andes Mountains. It was many years ago, but I'd embarked on a journey that would change my life forever," Father Lombardi began, his voice stronger and sounding like a younger man. "In those days, my spirit burned bright with the passion of youth, and my calling led me to places where few dared to tread."

He recounted the tale of stumbling upon an ancient, hidden chapel nestled in the remote mountains. Father Lombardi's eyes sparkled with the remnants of youthful wonder as he described the breathtaking beauty of the forgotten sanctuary, its walls adorned with murals that seemed to whisper stories of centuries past.

"As I stepped into that sacred space, a profound sense of awe enveloped me. It was as if time itself had stopped, and I had been granted a glimpse into the divine mysteries woven into the fabric of that remote corner of the world. That had started me on my path."

The priest slumped in his chair, whatever had lit his internal fire had been snuffed. He looked up at Alicia and nodded. Switching back to English he said, "Yes, I know Alessandro. He's a good man. A thoughtful one as well."

Alicia glanced at Tony who gave her an approving nod.

"Father Lombardi, when was the last time you saw Father Montelaro?"

The old man frowned as she stared at his arthritic hands. "Oh, I don't know... it has to be years... I think."

Alicia winced.

Bagel yowled as he walked back from wherever he'd explored, carrying a scrap of paper.

"Bagel!" Alicia bent over and took the paper out of the cat's mouth and scooped him into her lap. "Are you done exploring?"

The cat turned away from her and reached for the scrap of paper she'd taken from him.

"What are you doing?" She grabbed the paper, it was some receipt from a courier.

"Ah, yes... I remember now." Father Lombardi pointed a thick finger at the paper. "Alessandro sent me something via a courier. I don't get many things hand-delivered anymore. It was very thoughtful of him."

Alicia studied the receipt. The date on it would make it roughly around the time of Father Montelaro's disappearance. There was no obvious return address. Her heart thudded heavily in her chest. With a wide-eyed expression, she asked, "What did he send you?"

"I suspect it was a birthday gift. At my age, I have very little need for such things, but I appreciated the gesture."

Bagel complained as Alicia leaned toward the elderly man and asked, "You suspect? What was in the package?"

The old man shrugged. "I don't know, I never opened it. I ended up giving it to one of the boys I know who lives nearby."

Alicia's felt a wave of nausea come over her. *He gave it away?*

"Anyway, it felt like the weight of a book, and my eyes are not so good anymore. Reading gives me a headache, even with spectacles." He pointed at the far wall with bookshelves stacked with all variety of tomes. "I have more books than I know what to do with anyway."

Trying to keep her voice calm, Alicia asked, "Can you tell me who you gave it to?"

"It was the Bandini boy," Father Lombardi said with an air of certainty. "He's a good one. May the book serve him well."

"You don't by chance know what apartment he lives in?"

The man shook his head. "No, but he's usually playing out front with the other boys. By the car lot outside the Vatican entrance. They're good boys."

Tony cleared his throat and asked, "Did you by chance hear at all from my uncle?"

"Your uncle?" The priest seemed confused.

"I'm sorry, I forgot to explain. Father Montelaro is my uncle. Are you sure you haven't otherwise heard from him?"

The old man pursed his lips and remained silent for a moment. "You know, I do remember young Alessandro calling me. Yes, it was before I received my birthday gift." He held his index finger up to emphasize his point. "I know this because I would have thanked him, but I didn't thank him, because I hadn't..." The man paused mid-sentence. "...because I hadn't received it yet. Yes, I'm pretty sure of that."

"What did he call about?" Alicia asked.

The man gave her a weak smile and patted her hand. "You know these young fellows. Always on an adventure. He was asking about my trips to Egypt, but I don't remember why. I know we talked of palm trees for some reason. It seems odd now that I think on it, but that led to other fascinating discussions of some of my past adventurers when I was much younger." The man's eyelids began drooping. "I'm sorry, but I'm in need of a nap."

Alicia tucked Bagel into his sling without too much squirming from him and stood. She held out her hand, helped the old priest to his feet, and kissed his hand. "Thank you for being such a gracious host. I hope it might be okay if we visit again some time?"

"Of course, of course." The priest patted her on the shoulder and nodded. "It's good to talk. It keeps the mind awake."

Alicia waited at the door as Tony thanked the priest and made sure he was okay.

They both walked out of the apartment and Tony said, "Well, that was actually more productive than I expected."

"Uh huh." Alicia began texting Denny. It would be early morning in the US, and hopefully he was around.

She needed to know what that package might have contained.

*

"I'm seeing only one Bandini listed in a quarter-mile radius, and it's in the same building as Lombardi. You should find the Bandini family in apartment five, first floor."

It had taken Denny only a few minutes to respond to her text, and as they walked down the hall, looking for the apartment, Tony asked, "How do you know this is the place?"

Alicia held up her phone. "With a smartphone and the internet, the world's information is at our fingertips."

Tony harrumphed. "You're sounding a lot like your father."

"I'll take that as a compliment."

"We'll see." Tony pointed at the door on the right. "This is the one."

Alicia glanced at Tony. "Same as before. Help me with the translation."

Before Alicia even had a chance to knock on the door, a

kid bolted out of the apartment and raced down the hallway toward the building's entrance.

A thirty-something-year-old woman yelled a stream of curses in Italian and muttered to herself, "Damn boy never closes the—" she halted as she saw Alicia and Tony standing in front of her door. With a baby on one hip, her cheeks flushed red as she ran her hand through her mop of dark-hued curls. "I'm sorry if my boy ran into you, he's a bit... spirited. Can I help you?"

Alicia nodded. "We're here because of Father Lombardi from the second floor." Tony translated as she spoke, "He mentioned giving the Bandini boy a package. The Reverend Father I think was a bit confused." She hitched her thumb in Tony's direction, "The package was from his uncle. We wanted to check if your boy still has it, and we're willing to compensate for the trouble."

The mother shifted her toddler from one hip to the other and said, "The only Bandini boy in this apartment is the one who just ran out the door to go play. One second, let me see if he's out on the street." The woman motioned for them to come in.

Alicia entered the small, cluttered apartment. The floor resembled an obstacle course of toys and assorted trinkets meant to amuse the children. With what looked like a one-year-old on the mother's hip, Alicia couldn't help but empathize with the evident exhaustion the woman must be experiencing. It was clear she had her hands full.

The mother walked across the apartment to the open

window, peered outside and yelled, "Luigi, come up here. I have a surprise for you!"

"What surprise?"

The boy's response barely registered with Alicia before the mother began yelling threats at her pre-teen.

"There will be no surprise if you don't get up here, and I mean, *now*!"

It took less than a minute for the sweaty boy to appear inside the apartment, panting, and holding his hand out. "Mama, what's the surprise?"

"I'll give it to you later tonight after you answer this man's questions."

Tony crouched low and said in a firm voice, "Do you remember Father Lombardi giving you a package a few weeks ago?"

The boy nodded and gave Tony a sour expression. "It's in my room. You can have it." He wrinkled his nose. "It's just a book."

Alicia and Tony glanced at each other.

The boy looked up at his mother. "Is that it? Can I go back out and play?"

His mother nodded and the boy bolted out of the apartment as if the Devil was chasing him.

Alicia turned to the woman and asked, "Do you mind if we go look for it?"

Tony translated and handed the mother a twenty-euro note.

Alicia made a mental note of the expense.

The mother smiled at the sight of the money, pocketed it, and pointed at the door on the far end of the main room. "His bedroom is right there."

The mother led them to her son's bedroom, opened it, and she let out a gasp. With her face turning beet red, she stormed over to the open window facing the street and began yelling at her son about cleaning his room.

Alicia walked into the bedroom and was unfazed. She'd seen much worse in some of her friend's dorm rooms in college.

Tony sifted through the boy's bed, even at one point lifting the mattress and finding all sorts of discarded candy wrappers hidden under the bed.

Alicia carefully moved the piles of clothes scattered on the floor and after a few moments, she found under one of the piles a discarded shipping box with an old leatherbound book sticking halfway out of it. She peered at it and saw the gilded lettering in latin: *"Tractatus de bibliothecis mundi, praesentibus et praeteritis."*

Her contact overlaid the letters with the English equivalent and she read it aloud, "Treatise on the libraries of the world, present and past."

"That's got to be Uncle Alessandro's," Tony said as he moved the bed back into its original position.

The boy, whose room they were in, walked in carrying a gloomy expression. "Hey! You moved all my stuff!"

The mother smacked the back of the boy's head and she

looked at Tony with embarrassment clearly etched on her face. "Have you found what you need?"

"Yes, thank you." Tony pulled out another twenty-euro note, handed it to the mother, and said in a hushed tone, "You're doing great. I was just like him as a child. We all eventually grow up."

The mother flashed a tired smile at Tony, shifted her gaze back to her son and Alicia sensed the storm that was coming for young Luigi.

Alicia motioned to Tony and they both left as the frustrated mother grabbed one of the piles of clothes and began giving her son orders for him to follow. With the book in her hands, she tapped on its cover and said, "Let's go back to our place and figure out if this thing is some sort of clue, or it's a dead end."

For a handful of hours Alicia had been sitting at the small kitchen table poring over the book Father Alessandro had sent to the other priest. It was an old text, printed in the early 1800s, and was probably valuable. And even after hours of scanning through the chapters, she hadn't yet gained any revelations.

It was near dinner time and Bagel was the only one of them who'd eaten. She glanced at the cat as he chomped on a fresh serving of sardines.

Tony sat at the small kitchen table, reached down and gave Bagel a scratch between the ears. "It's funny how the cat managed to rummage through that old man's apartment and of all the things he decided to play with, it was a receipt from the courier my uncle had used. If it weren't for Mr. Bagel, that old priest might not have even remembered getting the delivery."

Alicia looked down at Bagel and couldn't help but smile. In many ways she owed that cat her life. Bagel's origin story was still a bit of a mystery to her. Even though she'd found him in the woods as a kitten, there was something preternatural about him. She'd dreamed some rather strange things about the cat, and in some sense, those dreams were more real than not. He was definitely smarter than the average cat, but what were the chances of him just managing to find something in that apartment that would lead to what they needed? At some point, she wouldn't be surprised if Bagel one day just started talking to her with a British accent, informing her that she was a pretty ignorant two-legged creature.

As Alicia's skimmed the yellowed pages of the book filled with Latin, Tony remarked, "I'm surprised you learned Latin. I didn't think they taught that anymore in school. Anyway, are you getting anything out of the book? Why would my uncle send it to Lombardi?"

Alicia's contact worked overtime as it overlaid the foreign text with its English equivalent and she still hadn't told Tony about her little gadgets. This was something she'd gotten from Denny, and because it would be impossible for her to explain about where she'd gotten such a gadget without compromising Denny's confidence or her father's, it seemed better to keep some things to herself.

"I'm not yet sure why this was sent. This is an almost two-hundred-year old book, and it's talking about libraries old and new. I'm pretty sure some of the new ones from the perspective of the book might not even be around anymore. Anyway, it has a pretty strong emphasis on the ancient past, but there might be something in here. Even skimming the text, I'm barely a third of the way through this thing and I'm starving."

Tony stood. "I'll go get us something and bring it back."

Alicia rubbed her eyes and shifted her gaze back to the tome. With her thumb on the current page, she began riffling through the remaining pages, realizing just how much she had yet to go over. Suddenly, she froze mid-page flip as a scrap of something fluttered down to the kitchen table. "Woah, what's this?"

Tony walked back into the kitchen. "You find something?"

With trembling hands, Alicia carefully picked up the scrap, which was covered with handwritten text, and said, "This isn't from this book."

"What do you mean?" Tony asked.

"It's a different color, texture, heck I don't think it's made of paper. It's thicker. Probably vellum. Some kind of animal skin."

"What's that doing in the book?" Tony crouched low and stared at what was in her hands. "Can you read that writing? It looks like Latin."

"It is." Alicia gasped. "My God, if this is real, it could be over a thousand years old. It says, *'The Romans have vowed to eliminate us. The Gospel has been moved to a place of safety.'*" She turned over the stiff scrap of animal hide. "There's more. *'In the land where the river's gift meets the sun's eternal gaze, beneath the guardian palm's shade, the hidden words shall find sanctuary.'*"

"What does that mean?"

Alicia shook her head. "I have no idea, but you know who might?"

"Lombardi?"

She nodded. "You remember what he said? Lombardi mentioned talking to your uncle about his trips to Egypt and about palm trees." Alicia held up the ancient fragment. "I don't know about you, but this thing talks about a river, which could very well be the Nile, and explicitly mentions a palm. A coincidence?"

Tony shook his head. "Do you think my uncle went to Egypt? At his age?"

"I don't know. It's getting late, but I think a visit to Father Lombardi in the morning is more than warranted." She lay the scrap down on the table and tapped her finger next to it. "Just like that receipt Bagel found, maybe this thing will jog something out of his head that might help."

Tony patted Alicia on the shoulder. "I may not say this

often, but I think you're doing a great job. I would never have gotten this far."

Alicia shook her head. "We haven't really gotten anywhere yet. Congratulate me when we find your uncle. Until then, there's work to do."

"Fine." Tony walked out of the kitchen and said over his shoulder, "I'll go get us something to eat. Rest your eyes for a bit."

Alicia heard the sound of Tony leaving through the front door as she stared at the scrap of animal skin. She flipped it over and stared at the message.

"The Romans have vowed to eliminate us. The Gospel has been moved to a place of safety."

What in the world could that mean?

CHAPTER
FIVE

Walking down the hallway toward Father Lombardi's apartment, Alicia passed a group of clergymen, two of whom were dabbing at their eyes with linen handkerchiefs.

She paused at the entrance to the priest's apartment, its door stood ajar as other members of the Church consoled a middle-aged woman who was sitting on the same chair Alicia had sat on yesterday.

As a priest approached them from within the apartment, Tony asked, "Is Father Lombardi…"

With a grim expression the priest nodded. "Our Reverend Father was called home in his sleep. Son, are you related to Father Lombardi?"

Tony's expression darkened and he shook his head.

Alicia's mind reeled as she stared through the doorway.

She wasn't sure how to react to what the priest had just said. They'd just yesterday talked with the man... how could it be?

The priest spoke in a hushed tone. "I don't want to offend, but can we please give our Reverend Father's daughter some space? She just now learned of her father's passing."

Alicia stared at the apartment and a chill ran up and down her spine.

It was Tony who had to tap her on the shoulder and whisper, "Let's go. There's nothing we can do here."

They walked down the hallway in silence, and it was only when they exited the apartment building that she blurted out, "Something's not right about his death. Do they do autopsies in Italy for unexplained deaths?"

"Unexplained deaths?" Tony looked at her as if she were crazy. "Alicia, the man was quite old. You saw him, he wasn't exactly all there."

The hairs on the back of her neck stood on end and she shook her head. "Did you notice the scratches on the doorframe, near the strike plate?"

"What are you talking about?"

Alicia closed her eyes and studied the image of Father Lombardi's door. It was an image so clear that it might as well have been a photograph. "Tony, I'm not crazy. I remember looking at the door jamb yesterday as that priest was fumbling to open the door. There were no scratches on the doorframe where the strike plate would be. But today I saw some deep gouges on the doorframe. As if someone broke in." Her eyes widened. "Do you think someone might have seen us talking to Father Lombardi and paid him a visit afterwards?"

"No." Tony shook his head and held a worried expression. "I think you're jumping to conclusions. It could just as easily have been someone having to jimmy the door to do a wellness check and found out that he'd passed. In fact, I'd wager that might be what happened. How else would half the Church be here and his daughter notified as well?"

Alicia paused as she processed what her large companion had said. What he'd said made sense, and her jumping to conclusions was making her sound like a crazy person. She felt her cheeks getting red. "Maybe you're right."

The mafioso chuckled and patted her on the shoulder. "You're almost as paranoid as your father, and that's saying something."

She nodded, retrieved Uncle Alessandro's book from her backpack, opened it and began flipping through the pages.

"What are you looking for?" Tony asked.

"I was riffling through the latter half of the book when that scrap fell out of it. I think I remember roughly what page I was on, or at least I remember seeing a couple of the words at the top of the page."

Alicia's fingers were a blur as she flipped through the book's pages, looking for the sentence fragment that stood out in her mind and within seconds she stopped.

This was the page.

The sound of her heart thudding echoed in her ears as she stared at the page and knew this was something important.

On that page someone had underlined in blue ballpoint ink a phrase.

Custodes Veritatis.

She repeated the words out loud.

"What does that mean?" Tony asked.

"It means Guardians of Truth."

"Is that supposed to be significant in some way?"

With her heart racing, Alicia pulled in a deep breath and let it out slowly. She showed Tony the underlined phrase and then, written with the same blue ink in the book's margin was a word. "This is your uncle's handwriting. I recognize it."

"*Venezia?* That's Venice in Italian." Tony frowned. "It sure seems like my uncle was leaving this behind like a breadcrumb for us to follow."

Alicia nodded. "It's a sheer miracle that we found it, if that's what it is."

"No, it's no miracle." Tony gave Alicia a one-armed hug. "You managed to find a hint he sent me that I would never have recognized. That led us to Father Lombardi, and in turn led us to this. I don't know how you or your father do this stuff, but somehow you're solving a puzzle that I don't think very many people could solve. I sure as hell couldn't do it, not on my own."

In her mind's eye Alicia saw the map of Italy. Venice was

nowhere close to Rome. At least a few hundred miles away. "I guess my vote would be to go to Venice."

Tony nodded. "The fastest way to get there will be by train. I'd say it shouldn't take more than a handful of hours."

"Okay. Let's pack things up and I'll book us some tickets."

"I support this plan." Tony smiled and they began walking back to their apartment.

"Good." Alicia's mind was racing as she sorted through the facts they'd uncovered so far.

The butterflies in her stomach were definitely doing a dance as she worried about maybe forgetting something. Was there anything they'd overlooked in Rome or Vatican City?

She couldn't think of anything.

The one thing that lay at the forefront of her mind was the thing she hoped was easy to resolve.

Who are the Guardians of Truth, and why did Tony's uncle underline a reference to them?

Alicia frowned as the taxi slowed to a stop just outside of the train station. Noticing the large backup of cars preventing any forward progress, she leaned forward, paid the taxi and looked over at Tony. "Let's go." With the empty cat carrier in one hand, and Bagel snuggled up against her in his sling, she stepped out of the taxi and felt the first dots of rain coming from the overcast sky. She took in the sight of the *Roma Termini*, which to her resembled an airport terminal, minus the sight or sound of any planes. There were also no obvious trains in sight, which would be no different than New York's Grand Central where a lot of the railways approaching the terminal were underground.

Bagel yowled and patted at her from his sling. "Wet."

"I know, we're almost there." Alicia covered the cat the best she could with her arm as Tony grabbed their suitcase from the trunk and then they both jogged toward the terminal and the protection of the large overhanging roof.

Following Tony, he led them through the atrium and as always, the crowd seemed to part for the beefy man as he made a beeline for one of the red self-service ticket stands.

Alicia pushed her way in front of Tony and popped her credit card into the slot. "I'd rather be the one making the expenses so I can keep track of things."

"Sure thing," Tony responded as he watched Alicia navigate the touch screen.

She successfully managed to get to the page where she was booking tickets for two from Rome to Venice. "Looks like the non-stop train will get us there in four hours."

"Told you it would be around that."

The ticket choices staring back at her were Standard, Premium, Business, Business Quiet, and Executive class tickets. The prices ranged from around one-hundred euros to around two-hundred-and-fifty euros a person.

Her finger was hovering over the Standard choice when Tony loudly cleared his throat and said, "No chance my ass is going to fit in one of those seats."

"Premium?" Alicia glanced back at him, thinking that an extra twenty euros a piece wasn't too much.

He shook his head and pulled out some cash. "Listen, the premium seats aren't any bigger, and business is going to suck. Let me go ahead and pay for the tickets—"

"No," Alicia barked. "I'll go ahead and—"

"Listen, you wouldn't be spending the extra—"

"Tony, I've got this." Alicia raised her voice, getting annoyed that he wanted to pay as if she were a kid. "No more discussion."

"I don't think so, young lady." Tony's brow furrowed. "Listen to me, let's compromise. I'll pay the difference between the cheap sets and what I want. You wouldn't normally be paying extra if it weren't for me." He handed her three one-hundred-euro notes.

Alicia hesitated, not sure what the right thing to do was in this situation. Was she being treated like a kid who didn't know any better for letting Tony pay or was she being ridiculous for not taking the money? With a loud harrumph, she took his cash and bought the two executive class tickets. "Fine, I won't argue this time. I've never been on these trains and the last thing we need is you getting some blood clot from lack of circulation or something."

Tony nodded his approval as the machine spit out the freshly-purchased tickets. He grabbed them and motioned for her to follow. "And besides, the menu in the executive car is much better than the others."

"That's exactly what my father would say," Alicia said as they walked through the concourse. As they hurried to their destination, she noticed a wide variety of stores like Nike, Benetton, and Swatch. If they weren't in a rush to catch the train, which was leaving in twenty minutes, she wouldn't have minded window shopping a bit.

"Your father knows better than to waste calories on crappy food."

Alicia rolled her eyes at the back of Tony's head as they neared their train's platform. It was almost like traveling with her father.

Taking the nearest escalator up to platform fifteen, Alicia blinked at the brightness of the daylight as they emerged on a surprisingly clean and not overly crowded train platform.

"Over there." Tony pointed ahead and to the right at the train that was actively boarding.

Following his lead, Alicia walked past almost all of the cars until Tony paused at the first car, it had "Executive" stenciled on it.

Tony held out his hand, "Give me Bagel's carrier, I'll stow it for us."

Alicia handed him the carrier and they both stepped into the car. The first thing that hit her was the scent of pine wafting out of the first conference room she'd ever seen on a train. A cleaning crew was actively cleaning the conference-room table as Tony stowed their stuff and led them to their seats.

There were only eight seats in the entire car. The interior had the feeling of what she imagined a private would jet be like.

Even though her naturally frugal nature protested at the idea of spending so much extra on this kind of luxury, Alicia had to admit that this wasn't all that bad. She'd probably never allow herself such a luxury, but the trip to Venice was probably not going to suck.

Tony pointed at a set of luxurious leather seats that were facing each other and asked, "You prefer facing forward or backward?"

"Either works for me. I'm probably going to have my nose in my phone most of the time trying to track some things down." Tony took his seat and just as Alicia settled in hers, a man sitting a row behind Tony stood with a wide grin.

"Antonio!"

Tony looked up at the man standing next to his seat and his eyes widened. "*Signore* Bianchi?" He stood and the two greeted each other with the customary kiss on both cheeks.

The man pinched his fingers together and gestured up and down just like Alicia would have seen it in the Godfather. "What are you doing here and you don't reach out?"

Tony smiled and motioned for Alicia. "I'm sorry, it was all last minute. The Don made the arrangements before I knew what was happening." He motioned for Alicia. "This is Alicia Yoder, Levi Yoder's daughter. You remember him, right? He's a friend of ours."

Alicia smiled and was surprised to learn that some of the quirks of the Mafia language she'd learned about in English actually translated to Italian as well. "A friend of ours," between two members of the Mafia meant the so-called friend was also a member, which yet again confirmed to her that Dad was who she'd concluded he was.

The man, who was roughly the same age as Tony, nodded at Alicia, "*Buongiorno*. Your father is a rather interesting man. Is he in Italy as well?"

"No, he's..." Alicia struggled to find the right word in Italian, "on business other places."

"Ah." The man smiled. "That is a shame."

Tony put his beefy hand on the man's shoulder and looked over at Alicia. "This is the Don's cousin. He lives in Rome."

"Non, that is a not true." The man spoke in broken English and then switched back to Italian. "I moved back to Sicily last year." The man snapped his fingers at one of the crew members and pointed at the three of them. "Three *Prosecco*." The fellow-mobster patted Tony on the chest. "Let's you and I talk a bit."

The crew member vanished, presumably to fulfill the request.

Alicia gave Tony a quick nod and sat back down as the

two men conspired over whatever two mafiosos might conspire over.

She pulled out her phone just as the crew member appeared with her a glass of sparkling white wine.

Taking a sip of the cold and sweet drink, she allowed herself a moment to sink back into the plush cushions of her seat.

This was pleasant, but as she thought about their destination, Alicia suspected that this might be the peak comfort level of this particular mission.

Glancing at her phone, she noticed that the train had WIFI and smiled.

It was hopefully a good sign that she'd have a solid connection to the internet for the next four hours.

Without it, doing research on these so-called Guardians of the Truth would be very difficult.

Alicia winced as it suddenly dawned on her that it was probably very early in the morning on the East Coast. "Sorry Denny, I hope it isn't too early to call." She spoke softly into her phone as Bagel lay spread-eagle on her lap, without a care in the world.

"It's 5:00 am, but that's okay. It wouldn't be the first time a Yoder has interrupted my beauty sleep. And besides, I'm just now getting home from closing the bar. What's up?"

"Denny, my father told me that you're a wizard at getting info nobody else can, and I was hoping you might be able to help. I'm sort of stuck and wanted to see if you can help me get unstuck. I don't exactly know where to start."

"The beginning is usually a good place." Denny sounded distracted as she heard through the connection the sound of keys jingling in the background.

"Well, let's just say I'm on a train heading to Venice on what I hope isn't a wild goose chase. I'm looking for more information on what seems to be a group of people called the *Custodes Veritatis*, which roughly translated is the Guardians of Truth.

"The only reference I've found is in a two-hundred-year-old book about libraries." Alicia didn't need to get the book out of her backpack, she closed her eyes and saw in her mind's eye a crystal-clear image of the page she was referring to. "All the book said was exactly this, 'Rumors abound that in Venice, there's a group of scholars whose purpose is to safeguard ancient knowledge. If one can find a member of the Guardians of Truth, who knows what wealth of information they might have hidden away. Imagine the tomes they might have in their possession that are otherwise lost to those who seek scholarship from such works.'"

She heard the clicking sound of Denny typing. *"You said Custodes Veritatis?"*

"Yes."

"Hold on, I'm sending out a query to the UDC."

"UDC? What exactly is that?"

"It's a set of computers I have access to."

"Go on." Alicia made a rolling motion with her hand even though Denny couldn't possibly see it. "Unlike my father, I have some clue about computers. I'd like to understand what you're doing. Can you give me a bit more than that?"

Denny chuckled and a stream of keyboard clicking noises followed before he responded. *"The UDC is a big building filled with some of the most powerful information crunchers we possess."*

"We being the US?"

"Sure." Denny said it in a somewhat vague and airy manner that told Alicia he wasn't exactly telling her everything. *"The Utah Data Center is actually managed by the NSA. It's officially known as the Intelligence Community Comprehensive National Cybersecurity Initiative Data Center, but nobody sane calls it that. Just about all comms coming and going from the continental US gets filtered and routed through servers that are located in that building."*

Alicia furrowed her brow and leaned slightly to her right. Tony was still huddled up with Uncle Vinnie's cousin, likely chatting about something Mafia-related. "Denny, correct me if I'm wrong... the UDC resources aren't generally available to the public, yet you somehow have access."

"You might say that."

"I did say that." Alicia shook her head and shrugged. That meant either Denny was up to no good and had penetrated US security, or he was a member of the Intelligence Community and she didn't know it. Either way, it was probably just as well that she didn't know. "Fine, I know nothing..." she muttered more to herself than to Denny.

"You don't make a very good Schultz imitation."

"What do you mean?" Alicia asked.

"Hogan's Heroes? Sergeant Schultz... either of those ring a bell?"

She shook her head. "Nope. If that's some movie or something, I haven't seen it."

"Never mind; I forgot I was talking to a fetus," Denny chuckled to himself and there was an electronic ping in the background. *"Looks like I got a bit of something on your Guardians of Truth. Want to hear it?"*

Alicia stared open-mouthed at the phone, not sure whether to laugh or be insulted. She'd never been called a fetus before... "Sure, the *fetus* is ready to hear about whatever your sneaky computer partner came up with."

"You know I'm teasing you, right?"

"Yeah, I get it, I'm younger than my father. Big surprise. Anyway, what did you dig up?"

"It turns out that the Library of Congress archives has electronic copies of just about everything ever written here and abroad. It looks like this set of data comes from scanned pages of a book from Thomas Jefferson's own collection. Interestingly enough, there doesn't seem to be any known copies of this particular book elsewhere... so we have nothing to corroborate what it's saying. It could be real, or it could be the ravings of a long-dead madman, or something in between. I'll e-mail you the scanned images, but if you want, I can read it to you now."

"Go ahead."

"Okay, just so you know, the images I'm sending you are handwritten in Latin and since I don't exactly know more than handful of words in the language, I'm reading what the AI translated:

"In antiquity, amidst the sinuous waterways and intricate thoroughfares of Venice during the Renaissance, a covert fellowship by the name of the Guardians of Truth emerged. Conceived by erudite scholars, adept craftsmen, and prescient intellectuals, these Guardians sought to preserve knowledge and shield truth from manipulation and subjugation.

"The inception of this clandestine organization traces back to the seventh century when enlightened minds, inspired by the intellectual currents of their time, laid the foundations of the Guardians of Truth. Within the heart of the Serenissima Republic, these Guardians covertly established a hidden refuge, exploiting the labyrinthine water passages and concealed alcoves of the city to veil their endeavors. Amid opulent palaces and time-honored libraries, they meticulously assembled a repository of wisdom, accumulating rare manuscripts, artifacts, and revolutionary ideas. Venice, steeped in cultural opulence and historical commercial eminence, provided an impeccable backdrop for the clandestine machinations of this esoteric society.

"As murmurs of their presence meandered through the resonant alleyways and secluded chambers, the Guardians of Truth metamorphosed into a fable. Whispers alluded to their possession of age-old scrolls housing profound elucidations of existence, *cryptic codes unveiling concealed chambers of enlightenment, and artifacts permeated with mystical attributes.*

"Over the annals of time, the Guardians of Truth adroitly preserved their confidentiality, bequeathing their vocation from one progeny to the next. Their covert operations transpired in the shadowy realms, intervening when the equilibrium of knowledge faced peril from malfeasance and despotism, with their clandestine activities mostly concealed within the recesses of Venice.

"In contemporary epochs, the speculation regarding whether the Guardians of Truth exist occasionally resurfaces. It usually occurs as modern-day protagonists stumble upon clues that illuminate their possible existence.

"I personally believe that this mysterious brotherhood exists to this day, but I have yet to solidly grasp evidence of anything but the most ephemeral details. The one thing that seems a certainty is that they have an unwavering pursuit of enlightenment and it's centered amid the eternal allure of Venice."

"That's it... that's the end of the passage."

"Wow, that's some kind of weird yet fascinating testament." Alicia pressed her lips together. "How the hell am I supposed to find these people who evidently elude everyone's attention?"

"I admit that this sounds like a tough nut to crack. I might be able to at least give you a person to start with."

"Oh?" Alicia sat up straight, which forced Bagel to shift positions, look up at her as if she'd done something offensive, and then curled himself up into a ball and began sucking on the tip of his tail.

"Yup, I'll send it in the e-mail with the images I got from the UDC. Viktor Sokolov is a rare book vendor who has gotten into some trouble in the past for smuggling rare books or buying stolen property. However, he fancies himself as a purveyor of the unique and extremely rare. If anyone I know has information about these Guardian folks, it might be him. And he's based out of Venice."

"Thank you so much! That's awesome—"

"Don't thank me yet, he might have information... then again he might not. It's a total shot in the dark on my end."

"Either way, this is way more than I had to start with, I can't really thank you enough."

"We'll figure out a way. Your father and I have an agreement, and if this is something you're doing longer term, we'll come up with our own agreement.

"Also, and I want you to pay careful attention to me on this, Alicia. If you have a serious need, don't hesitate to call this number. You'd be surprised at the extent of what someone can do with a keyboard and mouse if the need arises.

"Anyway, unless there's something else, I'll go ahead and send you the stuff we talked about and then get a few other things finished up and get to bed."

"No, that's it. Thanks again, Denny, you're a lifesaver."

"For everyone's sake, let's hope it doesn't have to come to that."

The phone line cleared and in less than a minute Alicia's phone buzzed with an incoming mail. She opened the mail and nodded as she scrolled through the series of images and then finally the book vendor's name and address.

Alicia felt a sudden wave of exhaustion flow over her. She gently stroked the top of Bagel's furry head, leaned her head back and closed her eyes.

She had two hours before the next part of her mission, and before she could complete her train of thought, sleep claimed her.

CHAPTER SIX

Alicia stepped out of the Venice train station and breathed in the salty air. "Woah, you weren't kidding when you said this place is on the water."

Less than a stone's throw from the train station was a large canal at least one hundred feet wide. It seemed so strange to see boat traffic so close to a train station, but then again, it was what Venice was known for—its countless waterways.

"Come on, let's catch this *vaporetto* before it leaves." Tony motioned for her to follow as he rushed toward a crowded dock, carrying their suitcase and empty cat carrier.

Her earbud failed to translate *vaporetto*, and the world itself didn't really give her much clue as to its meaning. At least not until she saw some of the signs near the dock using the word in context... it was a water taxi?

It took all of a minute or so for them to get a weekly pass for the waterbus system and Alicia followed Tony's lead as she stepped onto the *vaporetto*, which in this case was a large single level boat that had seating for dozens of people in the covered cabin area and a large open deck at the front of the vessel.

Tony looked over his shoulder and said, "I'd rather not suffocate inside the cabin, let's get to the front so we can at least feel some of the breeze on our face." His gaze traveled down to Alicia's sling and asked, "Are you okay, Mr. Bagel?"

Alicia looked down at her furry companion and smiled.

Only the cat's face was visible, his nose was up in the air, and Bagel was sniffing at the new scents surrounding them. He let out a long, drawn-out meow as a response.

"Ah, such a pretty cat." A man called out from across the deck and smiled in Alicia's direction. "And I couldn't help but notice the beautiful smile attached to its owner."

The dark-haired man, who looked like he was in his twenties, approached and Tony immediately stepped in front of him and said, "That's very nice. My god daughter is busy."

Alicia felt her cheeks getting warm. She took a deep breath and let it out slowly. It seemed very strange to have Tony running interference for a guy who was seemingly trying to flirt with her. Or was he just paying her a compliment and not meaning anything by it? Either way, it was something her father, Uncle Vinnie, and Tony had warned her about. Italian guys could sometimes be a bit forward, at least compared to what she was used to.

The man's eyes widened as he took in all three-hundred-pounds of Tony and took a step backward. "Of course, *signore*. I meant no disrespect at all. Maybe I can call on your god daughter some time, with your permission, of course."

"That will be impossible." Tony shook his head, glowering at the would-be suitor. "We don't live in Venice."

"Oh..." the man took on a crestfallen expression. "That is too bad." As the boat departed from the dock he smiled and pointed in the direction they were going. "Since you are visiting, I can at least help describe some of what we're seeing. I'm a seventh generation Venetian and know these waterways better than anyone." He looked expectantly at Tony and the large man nodded. "Excellent."

Alicia smiled as the twenty-something-year-old walked to the front of the deck and cleared his throat. He had dark hair, a chiseled face with distinctly olive-toned skin. The man was handsome, without a doubt, and she felt a twinge of regret that somehow the circumstances weren't what they were. Dating was not something that was in the cards on this mission, especially under Tony's watch.

"As the boat gently pulls away from the station, we find ourselves cruising along the majestic Grand Canal."

"Hey!" A crewman walked up to the would-be tour guide and handed him a microphone. "Nobody in the cabin can hear you over the engines. Speak into this."

The handsome stranger studied the mic and tentatively said, *"Hello."*

His voice broadcast through speakers in the cabin.

"Ah, yes. Okay. As I was saying, the Grand Canal, often referred to as Venice's main street, is adorned with magnificent palazzos each telling a story of the city's opulent past. Notice the Ca' d'Oro on the right, a splendid example of Venetian Gothic architecture. Its name, 'Golden House,' hints at the golden decorations that once adorned its facade."

Alicia glanced at Tony who gave her a wink. This guy was definitely putting on a show as he grew more animated. A crowd began to gather as he talked excitedly about the landmarks they floated past.

"As we approach the Rialto Bridge, observe the vibrant market scene. The Rialto has been a bustling hub of commerce since the Renaissance, and the markets below offer a sensory feast. The bridge itself, with its sweeping arches, is not just a crossing but a symbol of Venetian grandeur."

Alicia shook her head and had trouble imagining how much work it must have taken to create a sturdy bridge with such an artistic aesthetic. The bridge had a half-dozen arches flanking each side of a larger central arch, and all of this was done before the invention of modern construction equipment. It was all constructed by hand.

"Venice's palazzos are not just buildings; they are living testimonials to the city's history. Look to your left at Palazzo Barbarigo, an exemplary display of Baroque magnificence. The

intricate detailing and elegant design showcase the wealth and taste of Venice's noble families."

More people exited the cabin and began crowding the front deck, a majority of the people on the boat were now listening to the eloquent narration given by the Venetian. Alicia remembered reading somewhere that Venice was a tourist destination, and from the various languages and accents she heard in the crowd, it was obviously true.

"*As we pass San Giorgio Maggiore and Giudecca, these islands carry tales of art and tranquility. San Giorgio boasts a captivating church with views to die for, while Giudecca offers a serene escape with its residential charm. Venice is not just a city; it's an archipelago of stories waiting to be discovered."*

Bagel meowed from within his sling. Alicia looked down at his furry face and nodded. "He'd make a good real estate salesman."

"*As we near St. Mark's Square, the heart of Venice, the Campanile and St. Mark's Basilica come into view. The square has been a political and religious center for centuries. The Doge's Palace, to our right, stands as a testament to the republic's once-mighty rule."*

The boat slowed to a stop as a crewman jumped to the dock, a rope in hand, securing the boat and extending a walkway for everyone to depart.

A loud bell rang, breaking the spell that the impromptu tour guide had over the crowd, and several people clapped and tried handing the twenty-something-year-old tips, which he declined with a look of embarrassment.

Tony nudged Alicia and said, "Let's go."

Alicia hesitated, and for a second wanted to approach the Venetian who'd entertained them for the last twenty minutes of the boat trip.

No. She chastised herself and followed Tony as he headed toward the dock. It seemed rude not to at least thank the man for the impromptu narration of what they were seeing, but it would probably give him the wrong impression.

"Have a good visit pretty woman." The man's voice broadcast through the cabin's speakers and Alicia hesitated as she stood on the walkway. *"Maybe we see each other in our dreams."*

Alicia sighed as she stepped off the boat, resisting the urge to look over her shoulder—he was probably staring right at her.

This was a part of her life, the whole dating thing, that she was terrible at. And this was *not* the time to work on it.

"Come on, Alicia, let's get to the Rialto Bridge." Tony turned right onto a narrow Venetian walkway called Rive del Ferro and looked over at her. "What'd you think of the boat ride? Pretty different than getting around in the city, eh?"

"I'll say." Alicia breathed a sigh of relief that Tony didn't mention the guy. Her father would probably have teased her incessantly. Ripping her thoughts away from the boat and the guy, she focused on her surroundings. It was a narrow path, and very unlike anything she'd encountered in her travels. There were a bunch of tiny shops lining the street to her right, and on her left was the

Grand Canal. "It's just weird having stores a few feet away from the water. Also, it's very strange not having any cars around."

"This part of Venice is really a pedestrian town." Tony grinned. "You'll see why soon enough. We could have actually gotten here by foot, but it would take longer." He pointed across the canal and said, "The Don's cousin told me about a place that we can use on the arm."

On the arm was a term she'd only heard a few of her father's associates ever use. "You mean for free? But why would—"

"Alicia, trust me, you want this favor. And besides, that bookseller of yours is near the apartment. The few places we could get on short notice in this part of town might rent us a room, but there'd probably be a communal bathroom that we share with the rest of the floor. You might be willing to live like that, but I'm entirely too set in my ways to live like a college student again."

She gave Tony a sidelong glance and smiled. "You went to college?"

"Bah!" He waved dismissively. "You know what I mean, smart aleck." Tony turned left onto the bridge and nodded in the direction of the shops that lined the span of the bridge. "Ignore these for now, we'll have time later to window shop. I'm sick of lugging this suitcase around."

Alicia felt like a tourist as she walked along the four-hundred-year-old bridge crossing over the Grand Canal. The bridge was teeming with tourists pausing every few seconds to look at something new, which made quick forward motion almost impossible.

Tony lost any semblance of patience he'd had and began plodding forcefully through the crowd, only pausing when faced with a white-haired woman who was making her way across the bridge with the assistance of a cane.

It took a couple minutes to cross what amounted to not much more than one hundred feet, but once they were free of the crowd, Tony glanced at his phone and pointed to the northwest. "We're almost there."

Alicia followed closely as they walked through alleyways so narrow that they wouldn't have fit two people standing side-by-side. "Okay, this is just craziness. How did they build these buildings so close to each other?"

"By hand," Tony deadpanned. It was as much of an answer as she would get, his gaze shifting back and forth from the map on his phone to their claustrophobic surroundings.

It was hard to tell exactly how old these buildings were since many of them were covered with a layer of stucco. Yet over time the rock-like coating had become pockmarked with age, revealing some of the building's underlying stone construction.

It took only a couple minutes for them to finally emerge from yet another alley into a plaza that was really nothing more than a thirty-foot square between a series of multi-story buildings. At its center was some kind of giant pottery structure filled with sand, and at the north, south, east, and west sides of the clearing were arched doorways without any obvious identifying markers.

"How does anyone find anything here?" Alicia studied the buildings with a perplexed expression.

The large mobster pointed north. "I think it's that one. The Don's cousin gave me the code."

"The code?" Alicia asked and as they approached the door her confusion vanished. "Oh, I get it."

Despite the obvious old age of the buildings themselves, the door on the north building had an electronic keypad.

She watched as Tony pressed a six-digit code onto the keypad. There was a beep following by a loud whirring noise. Lacking any obvious door handle, he pressed on the eight-foot-tall wooden door and it opened on well-oiled hinges.

Alicia stared wide-eyed as she walked through the door into an air-conditioned apartment. The atrium was a round two-story room with marble floors and a skylight that illuminated the interior with natural light. At the center of the tiled floor was a round five-foot patch of soil. Sprouting from it was a ten-foot-tall citrus tree, with clusters of tiny green and yellow-hued fruit strewn through and across its branches. A lemon tree? Inside an apartment?

She followed Tony and entered a small living room furnished with a leather sofa, recliner, and a flat-screen TV. To her left was a modern-looking kitchen gleaming with chrome fixtures with black and white accents. Attached to it was a dining area with a wooden table long enough to seat eight. This place was like nothing she'd have imagined from the outside.

Tony deposited the suitcase in the middle of the living room and walked over to the built-in double-wide refrigerator. Peering inside he asked, "You want a beer? Pellegrino? A snack?"

Bagel wiggled out of his sling and plopped onto the ground. He stuck his nose up in the air, sniffed at his new environment, and padded away to explore.

"I'm fine. How is it that this is—" She stopped herself and figured that this place was maybe a Mafia safe house or something. What difference did it make? "It's getting kind of late and we should probably go find this bookseller before he closes for the day."

Tony took a big bite from a large red apple and nodded. "You're probably right. Let's get going. Where did Mr. Bagel go?"

Hearing his name, the cat made a long, drawn-out yowl in response.

Following the sound of his vocalization, Alicia retraced her steps toward the atrium. Upon entering the circular room, she spied Bagel squatting next to the lemon tree, relieving himself. She pressed her lips tightly together, barely suppressing the laughter that threatened to burst out.

The loud crunch of Tony biting into his apple preceded his arrival as he took in the scene and chuckled. "When you have to go, you have to go. Good job, Mr. Bagel. Are we ready?"

Bagel appeared ready to leap into the tree as he reached upward, claws extended. However, he sank them into the bark and pulled downward, leaving tiny scratches in the otherwise pristine fruit tree. He then strolled over to Alicia, gazing up and signaling his readiness with a few calculated paw pats to her leg.

Alicia scooped him up in her arms and said, "Okay, let's get going. We've got Viktor Sokolov to hunt down and have a little chat with him about a secret society nobody seems to know anything about."

Alicia scanned the pockmarked walls of the buildings that lined the narrow alley, feeling a rising sense of frustration. "Who in their right mind would have a storefront hidden in some alleyway?" She glanced over her shoulder at Tony who was panning his gaze along the second-floor windows overlooking the alley. "Tony, are you sure this is Calle del Filosi?"

Tony frowned. "Honestly, I'm not one-hundred percent sure. I saw the sign on the front of this building." He slapped his palm on the stucco-covered stone wall to his right. "But that could mean it's this street, or maybe it's the intersection behind me?"

A peal of laughter erupted from the far end of the alley as two elementary-aged kids raced into the corridor, chasing each other.

"Hey!" Alicia yelled at the kids who immediately froze, as if caught doing something they weren't supposed to be doing. "We're a bit lost." She pointed at the ground. "Is this Calle del Filosi?"

The boy shook his head and pointed in Alicia's direction. "No, *signora*. Over there, behind the fat man."

"Fat man?" Tony protested.

The boys bolted in the direction they'd come and Alicia laughed as she walked back toward Tony. "I guess it's behind you."

They both retraced their steps and began looking for numbers once again.

"Alicia, your Italian is getting a lot better."

"What do you mean?"

"There's a number." Tony pointed near the roofline of the nearest building. "What I mean is that you spoke to those boys in Italian and you didn't even hesitate. The pronunciation was a bit weird, but good enough."

"Thanks." Alicia couldn't help but smile at the compliment. "I guess it's starting to sink in. To be honest, I didn't even realize that I did it until you mentioned it." She pointed at the door of the building they were approaching. "There it is."

"Are you sure this is it?" Tony's expression was full of doubt.

Alicia walked up to the eight-foot-tall wooden door, knocked, and tried opening it.

It was locked.

Tony stepped forward and pounded his fist loudly on the door.

The scarred door looked like it was hundreds of years old and it didn't even rattle as the big mafioso battered the wooden barrier. It almost seemed like it was fused into the stone doorway itself.

"Hey, you looking for the bookseller?"

Alicia turned back toward the voice and noticed an older woman peering out of a nearby building's second-story window. "Yes."

"He's not there," the woman shouted down at her. "Won't be until tomorrow."

"Do you know what time he's usually here?" Tony asked.

"He's a strange one," The woman said with a sour expression. "That Russian keeps early hours. He's almost always already there by the time I have my morning espresso, and he's usually gone by the time I'm having my midday *soave*."

Tony looked over at Alicia and said in a hushed tone, "Soave is one of the local wine regions."

"That's right, *signore*." The woman nodded; her hearing was obviously excellent. "The Garganega grape is one of the best for winemaking. Be careful with that Russian. He's not very friendly... it's a wonder the man does any business at all."

The woman made a vulgar gesture in the general direction of the store and vanished from sight.

Alicia stared open-mouthed at the vacant window for a

full few seconds before Tony tapped her on the shoulder. "I think you and I need to get some rest before we come back in the morning." He motioned for her to follow.

Alicia followed Tony as he began retracing their steps through the maze of alleys. "Any chance you'd be up for taking in some of the sights, maybe look at some of those shops?"

Tony smiled and shook his head. "I have something better in mind."

"Like what?" Alicia asked.

"You'll see. It should be relaxing."

Relaxing? Alicia had no idea what the big guy had in mind, but she was looking forward to exploring this unusual city.

With a gentle breeze wafting over the water, Alicia breathed in deeply, savoring the salty air as the gondola eased away from its dock. Bagel adjusted his position on her lap, choosing to stay mostly within the confines of the sling she carried him in. Nevertheless, he poked his whiskered face out of his hiding spot, rubbed it against her hand, and she obliged by giving him a gentle scratch on his cheek.

"*Buongiorno, signore e signora! I hope you enjoy what promises to be an enchanting journey through the timeless canals of my home city of Venice. If you have any questions or requests, feel free to ask. Venice, la Serenissima, has endless stories to tell, and I'm here to share them with you."* The gondolier's voice carried a warm tone, a speaker's voice that effortlessly prevailed over the sounds of the occasional splash or passing boat on the canal.

Alicia sighed contentedly, leaning back against the cushioned chair in the gondola. Initially when Tony proposed that they take the evening off to act like tourists, she wasn't sure it was such a great idea. However, now she found herself captivated by the sunset, the lights of Venice coming to life, all while the gondola peacefully glided down the canal. Glancing at Tony, she admitted, "You were right; this doesn't suck."

Tony gave her a wink as the middle-aged gondolier, who was at the back of the gondola, continued his narration.

"As we pulled away from the dock, I'm sure you caught a glimpse of the Rialto Bridge. It's the oldest and most iconic bridge spanning the Grand Canal. Built in the late 16th century, it has been a bustling center of commerce for centuries.

"But as we glide along, cast your eyes to the left, where you'll see the beautiful Ca' d'Oro, a splendid example of Venetian Gothic architecture. It was once a palace for a wealthy merchant family and it is now an art gallery that I recommend you visit if you have a chance.

"Ahead, the magnificent St. Mark's Basilica comes into view. Marvel at the stunning domes and intricate mosaics that adorn this symbol of Venetian opulence and power. The Campanile di

San Marco, the bell tower, stands tall beside it, offering breathtaking views of the city."

The gondola turned from the Grand Canal and entered one of the many smaller waterways that snaked between the one hundred or so islands that made up the city of Venice.

"Now, we're passing through the narrow canals where the hidden gems and charming corners of Venice are found. On your left is the famous Palazzo Contarini del Bovolo, known for its spiral staircase with panoramic views."

As the shadows lengthened and nighttime began to fall, the gondolier had no need for spotlights to show some of the attractions. So much of the city was geared to the tourist trade, it served as no surprise that the landmarks were illuminated by hidden lights.

As the gondola navigated into an even narrower canal, they departed from the vibrant atmosphere of the main parts of the tourist area. The only lights came from the single red light at the front of the gondola and the faint glimmers emanating from apartment windows situated two and three stories above the water.

Suddenly, the gondolier cleared his throat and began to sing an operatic ballad:

Ma il mio mistero è chiuso in me;
il nome mio nessun saprà!
No, No! Sulla tua bocca
lo dirò quando la luce splenderà!

. . .

Alicia was about to start clapping at the amazing performance when the gondolier said, *"I hope you lovers can enjoy Venice as a place—"*

"What!" Tony exploded and turned in his seat, a look of fury on his face. "This is my god daughter, you imbecile!"

Alicia reached over and put her hand on Tony's arm, more worried about what he might do to the gondolier than what the man had actually said. "Tony, he didn't know. It's okay."

Bagel let out a loud hiss, which caught Tony's attention.

Chaos erupted as a muzzle flash illuminated the shadows, only fifty feet away. A barrage of shots peppered the gondola, plunging the serene night into a symphony of violence.

"Get down!" They both yelled as Tony grabbed her and slammed her onto the floor of the gondola, putting himself on top of her as a shield from the deadly hail of bullets.

Amidst the turmoil, Bagel leaped from the boat into the murky water. The gondolier, quick to respond, also plunged off the gondola, disappearing into the canal's depths.

Alicia was about to put her head up to look in the direction of where she'd seen the muzzle flash when another burst of shots rang across the canal, accompanied by a stream of curses and the click of a jammed gun.

They were sitting ducks.

With her heart pounding, she screamed, "Get into the water!"

The gondola lurched as they both plunged into the filthy canal waters.

The moment Alicia surfaced, she heard Bagel's furious scream mingled with a matching yell, and the sound of something falling to the ground from an unseen presence lurking in the shadows.

The distinct sound of rapidly receding footsteps echoed through the darkness.

Why the hell would someone attack them?

Alicia turned to her left, saw Tony's profile and motioned silently toward the small dock where the muzzle flash had first appeared.

He nodded.

Keeping her nose and eyes just above the water, she swam toward the dock and noticed Bagel perched on the side of the dock, cleaning himself.

Panning her gaze across the pier, she saw nobody other than her furry companion, who was sitting next to a ladder.

Somewhere in the canal she heard the splashing of what she presumed was the gondolier, who was the least of her concern.

Alicia looked up again at Bagel. The cat's ability to detect something being amiss was uncanny, and he wouldn't be sitting there cleaning himself if the coast wasn't clear.

Just as Tony dog-paddled up to her position, Alicia

silently climbed up the ladder, crouched low and scanned the shadows for any signs of movement.

Her eyes locked onto a metal object sitting on the dock and she smiled.

The sound of the attacker's yell replayed in her mind and Alicia turned to the cat. "Did you attack him?"

Bagel yowled his response, which she took as an affirmative.

Tony grunted as he pulled himself up the ladder and asked, "What did you just say?"

Alicia walked over to the dropped magazine. "Well, the best I can figure is our furry friend scared the hell out of our attacker. So much so that he dropped the magazine to his MP5."

Tony's dripping wet form stared down at the curved magazine. "How do you know it goes to an MP5?"

Alicia rolled her eyes. "You don't even want to know how many thousands of rounds I've shot with one of these. I recognized the sound of that three-round burst before I ever saw this thing." Crouching next to the magazine, she noticed the half dozen or so spent casings littering the dock, and looked up at Tony. "Why in the world would someone shoot at us like this? Is this a mob thing?"

Tony's brow furrowed and he spoke with a low growl. "I don't know, but whoever did this is going to regret their actions."

Using the currently empty sling, Alicia carefully picked up the magazine by the edges of the base plate, looked up at

Tony and asked, "This thing probably has some fingerprints, if you know someone who can do something with this."

Tony winced as he dug his hand into his front pocket. His wet clothes made getting his phone a struggle. He turned his back to her for a second and Alicia gasped.

"You've been shot!" She rushed over to him and ran her fingers across two holes on the back of his suit jacket. Alicia's throat tightened and she felt a surge of emotions, mostly anger at the attacker.

Tony snorted. "Yeah, you don't have to tell me the obvious. I can feel it."

"But—"

"Don't worry." He gave her a crooked smile. "I've got a vest on. And besides, those weren't big bullets. Probably only a .38 or maybe nine-millimeter by the feel of it. A bit of a bruise and that's it. I've been hit by worse."

"Um, you saved my life." Alicia blinked away tears as the weight of what had just happened crashed down on her.

"I'm sorry, but it was probably me that put you in danger. Let me call a few folks back home, I'll get to the bottom of this." Tony put the phone to his ear, waited a couple seconds and said, "It's Tony. I need to talk to the Don, we've got a situation."

Bagel strolled over to Alicia and gave her leg a few purposeful paw pats. "All okay."

Alicia nodded. She wasn't sure if he was asking a question or trying to reassure her. "Everything's fine." She pointed at the sling that currently held the dropped magazine and said, "I'll have to carry you until we get things straightened out, okay?"

He yowled affirmation and returned to licking his fur.

"You got it," Tony said into the phone. "I'll make sure of it." He pocketed the phone, turned to Alicia and gave her a nod. "The cavalry is incoming."

CHAPTER
SEVEN

Alicia stared wide-eyed at what looked like a team of forensic specialists combing the dock for evidence. It was less than half an hour after the attack, and there already were a couple armed men stationed on a motorboat guarding the approach from the canal. On the dock itself there were two men with Benelli shotguns hanging loosely at their sides talking with Tony. One person who'd been combing the deck and picking up spent shell casings with tweezers had begun shining a black light across the wooden pier.

A thin, wiry man wearing surgeon's gloves approached her and asked, "*Signora*, you have some evidence I believe?"

"I do." She showed him the magazine.

Without touching it, he inspected it from a variety of angles and frowned. "It isn't empty." He turned to his partner and said "Carlos, bring the light over here and check this."

The other man walked over and shined the black light over the magazine she was still cradling in the sling that Bagel normally occupied.

Several smudges and what looked to Alicia like partial fingerprints glowed under the UV light.

"We should be able to pull those prints." Carlos affirmed and walked back to the pier to finish what he was doing. The man with the surgeon's gloves pulled out a clear plastic bag, carefully put the magazine inside, and sealed the bag shut. "Thank you, *signora*."

Tony walked over to Alicia, leaned close and whispered, "There's a crew coming to take us to a safe house."

"The apartment's not safe?" Alicia frowned. "I assume your guys think that's necessary."

He shrugged. "The local crew is being pretty cautious. They've got eyes and ears out on the streets, but we don't yet know two key things: who and why."

Alicia caught the sound of a motor boat's engine and one of the men on the dock whistled in their direction, motioning for them to come. "I'm guessing this is our escort?"

Tony put his arm around her shoulders and gave her a one-armed squeeze. "We'll be fine."

"Did the gondolier get taken care of?" The gondolier had been a total mess and she saw one of the crew take him aside to talk with him, but that's the last she saw of him.

"Don't worry." He nodded. "Him and his gondola are heading back to where we'd started the evening."

Despite what had just happened, she hadn't been all that worried. This wasn't the first time she'd experienced live rounds being fired in her general direction. Alicia gave Tony a sidelong glance and noticed his clenched jaw and furrowed brow.

Now she was worried.

Bagel walked up to her and she quickly scooped him up and he squirmed his way into his sling.

Alicia clenched her fists as they walked over to the dock. Keeping her eyes on the low-profile boat drifting toward them, she leaned over to Tony and whispered, "I'd feel a lot better if I had a gun on me."

He nodded. "I'll see what can be done about that."

Alicia walked to the end of the small pier just as someone on the deck of the sleek motorboat tossed a rope up to one of the mob crew members.

He gathered the slack and helped keep the nose of the craft pressed against the dock.

The boat looked like the cigarette boats she'd seen news reports of that were often used to smuggle drugs between the Bahamas and Miami. It was long, thin, and sleek—a luxury racing boat of sorts.

Standing on the front deck of the boat was a man whose face was covered with a ski mask. He was also dressed from head to toe in black fatigues and blended almost perfectly with the dark backdrop of the canal. He held up a gloved hand toward her and spoke in lightly accented English. "*Signora*, let me help you. The deck, she is slippery."

"I'm fine." She crouched and hopped down to the deck, letting gravity do most of the work.

Alicia turned just in time to see Tony attempt the same thing, but as he landed, one of his feet shot out from under him.

She lunged, barely catching hold of one of his arms.

"Woah, big guy." The hooded man laughed as he held onto Tony's other arm.

Were it not for her and the man in black catching him, Tony would probably have pitched over the other side of the boat and into the canal.

"I hate boats." Tony muttered as another identically-dressed man motioned from the rear of the boat. "Please, both of you go below into the cabin for your safety."

Alicia's brow furrowed, but she followed Tony to the back of the boat and climbed down into the cabin.

They both sat on opposite bench seats as the door to the cabin closed. A single weak light lit the interior of the cabin and Tony looked over at her. "The safe house is about twenty minutes away."

Alicia felt the vibrations of the boat's engines revving as the boat pulled away from the dock.

She nodded, feeling a rising level of anxiety. "I don't feel good knowing that I'm getting shot at and don't have a vest and side arm."

Tony nodded. "I'm sure something can be arranged, but understand that you packing heat in Italy isn't something that would be on the right side of the law. Let's find out if the guys can figure out who shot at us and we'll pick up from there."

"How long do you think that'll take?" Alicia asked.

"Not sure. Carlos and his brother Paolo are actually members of the *Carabinieri* and—"

"What's that?" Alicia's earbud translator blanked on that word, which usually meant it was some formal name instead of an actual word with meaning.

"It's sort of like the Italian version of the FBI. Those two are part of the RIS, the *Reparto Investigazioni Scientifiche*. Think of them as forensic analysts."

"Hold up, they're part of the Italian FBI *and* part of the Mafia?"

Tony grinned and shook his head. "I don't know what you're talking about. But hopefully those two can get us some data fairly quick."

Alicia leaned her head back against the wall, feeling the vibrations as the boat twisted and turned through the water at what seemed like reckless speeds.

The idea that the Mafia worked with a government agency seemed very odd. Maybe it was more that the Mafia had rogue agents who'd infiltrated the government... but was that much different than what the Outfit did?

She wasn't about to be conflate what roles the Mafia and the Outfit play in this world, but somehow knowing that things weren't as simple as they seemed validated some of what Alicia had observed.

She knew her father wasn't a criminal, at least not really... it was complicated. More complicated than she'd probably ever know, but confirming this little tidbit somehow made her feel a bit better about Tony and his cohorts.

They had a system... and she'd have to trust it to an extent.

"Tony, we still need to go visit the bookseller. You realize that, right?"

"I know." Tony leaned his head back and closed his eyes. "One thing at a time, there are priorities to this thing we're doing, and for the moment, my uncle will have to wait. The Don wants to make one-hundred percent sure you're safe, and so do I."

Alicia pressed her lips together. She didn't like the idea of waiting for an indefinite amount of time.

She closed her eyes and before Alicia could even think about the first sheep, the darkness claimed her.

Alicia startled awake as a man's voice called from outside the cabin.

"Antonio, *signora*, we are safe. Don Vianello wants to meet you both."

She looked over at Tony as he got up and watched him desperately try to wipe away the wrinkles from his canal-stained suit. "Vianello?"

"Shh." Tony put his finger to his lips and whispered, "He's the head of Veneto's... he's an important person in this city."

Alicia nodded and pet Bagel's head as it poked up out of the sling. She looked down at the cat and whispered, "Just relax and we'll get back to normal soon enough."

The cat reached out with his arm and smacked out a sequence of paw pats against her stomach. *"Hungry."*

"I'll see what I can do... get some rest."

Following Tony, Alicia climbed up from within the speed boat's cabin and took in their new surroundings.

The boat had driven directly into some kind of warehouse that had a pier with several boat slips. The area was illuminated by several evenly spaced street lamps and there were two men busily tying the speed boat to the dock. A large, barrel-chested man stood near the end of the pier, he was immaculately dressed and focused on the men working at securing the boat.

One of the boat's crew members lifted into place a gangplank that reached up to the dock and motioned toward it. "Please *signore e signora*."

Tony's gaze focused on the man wearing a suit at the end of the pier. "Dino?"

"Hey *goombah*, how you doing?" The big man spoke

English without an accent. He smiled as Tony walked up to the dock and the two men embraced like lost brothers.

As Alicia stepped onto the dock, Tony turned to her and patted Dino on the chest. "Dino, did you ever meet Levi Yoder?"

"Che dici?"

The man made the same pinched finger gesture Alicia had seen countless times and even though her ear buds hadn't translated those words, she knew it meant, "What are you talking about?"

"Of course I know Levi. Him and I did a few things for Don Marino back a couple years ago over at Virginia Beach. Why do you ask?"

Tony motioned for Alicia to come closer. "This young woman is his daughter."

"What?" Dino turned to Tony with a look of disbelief. "I don't..."

Alicia walked up to the large man and held out her hand. "Hi, my name's Alicia. Alicia Yoder. I know I don't look like my father, obviously I'm adopted."

"Oh, that makes more sense." Dino smiled, gently took her offered hand and patted it with his other. "Your father is definitely a man full of surprises."

"Surprise!" Alicia grinned. "I'm one of them."

The large man laughed and gave her a curt nod. "Well, I suppose so." He drew a phone from within his suit jacket, put it to his ear and after a second's hesitation said, "They're here. Montelaro and Levi Yoder's daughter."

Alicia couldn't make out what the other person was saying, but Dino's expression remained unchanged as he listened to the person speaking on the other end of the line.

After a moment's pause Dino said, "We're on our way," and ended the call. "We're going up to meet with the Don first thing, and after that we'll arrange for a place for you guys to bunk since I'm sure you both need some rest."

Sensing Bagel squirming a bit in his sling, she inquired, "Could we possibly get something for a cat?"

"A cat?" Dino asked, and Bagel stuck his head out of the sling, yowling in the big man's direction. Dino smiled and let out a chuckle. "I'm sure the kitchen can scrounge up something. I'll see to that after you guys meet with the don." He motioned for them to follow him and walked purposefully toward the less well-lit part of the warehouse.

As the mafioso led them through the warehouse, it became clear to Alicia that this was some kind of offloading facility. There were stacks of unmarked crates rising as high as the roof, which was twenty feet above them, and as they weaved through the towering stacks, she spied the occasional huge metal shipping container, whose presence defied logic. How could such a massive thing have been brought into this warehouse? This place had to be attached to some kind of major shipping port.

It was only after they'd walked almost the length of a city block inside the warehouse that they came to the far end where a few men in suits were waiting for them in front of a massive wooden door.

One of the men approached with what looked like a security screening wand, it looked like a flattened police baton and was almost identical to what Denny had used on her. "*Per favore, alza le braccia ai lati.*"

Her earbuds weren't working for some reason, but she raised her arms to the side, having understood the request. Maybe the whole Italian language thing was starting to sink in?

The man moved the black wand slowly along Alicia's body and as it passed over her front right pants pocket, it let out a loud squeal.

The man held out his hand and said in Italian, "Please empty out your pocket."

She took out her phone, glanced at it and noticed it had zero bars—no signal whatsoever down here—and handed it to the man.

He passed the wand along the other side of her body and it squealed yet again, this time the man jumped back and let out a curse as Bagel poked his head out of the sling. "Mother of God! I didn't expect..." The forty-something mafioso shook his head and laughed as he once again approached, waved the wand over Bagel and it squealed at the collar he was wearing.

Bagel gave the wand three rapid-fire smacks with his paw and ducked back into the sling.

The guard smiled and finished his scanning with Tony, who also ended up handing over his phone. "*Signore e signora*, I will keep your phones safe while you meet with Don Vianello."

Alicia felt a surge of curiosity at the screening they'd just gone through. This level of precaution meant that this encounter might give her a tiny peek into her father's world.

Her father might have a reputation with some of the Mafia families, and even though she was very familiar with the head of the Bianchi family, she never really experienced the mafia as a business entity. Her relationship with it and its members was more of a familial thing, all other aspects had been hidden from her. She had no idea what to expect when meeting the head of another Mafia family.

The two men led them through the door and into a long wood-paneled corridor. The lighting was subtle and coming from the occasional sconce on the wall. Eventually they entered another wing of the building, one that resembled a home. They walked past a large dining area that could easily seat thirty people.

This place was huge, dwarfing anything she'd ever been in in the US. As they walked through another open room, she spied on the far end an elegant piano, and beyond it were floor-to-ceiling windows that overlooked what to her looked like a commercial port on the edge of what likely was the Mediterranean Sea.

Finally, they entered a library. Books crowded the shelves from the floor to the fifteen-foot-tall ceiling, the higher ones accessible via an attached wheeled ladder that moved along a track.

One of the boss's men knocked on a heavy oak door that was partially ajar. The door was nearly half a foot thick and looked like it had come from a medieval castle.

A gruff voice sounded from within. "Come in."

The two men who'd escorted them stood on either side of the open door. Dino entered first, and Alicia followed Tony right afterwards. The boss's men closed the door behind them.

Don Vianello was a beefy man in his sixties. He was about her height, just a few inches shy of six feet, but likely weighed close to three-hundred pounds. Surprisingly, the man wore it well. He was thick-wristed and the epitome of what someone might have rightfully called big-boned. The same genetics someone would need to be a professional defensive lineman... or a leg breaker.

Dino motioned toward Tony and spoke in Italian. "Don Vianello, this is Antonio Montelaro. He's the friend of ours that I talked to you about earlier."

Tony nodded toward the boss. "It's an honor to meet you, Don Vianello. Don Bianchi sends his best."

"I talked with Vincenzo earlier today. If he truly sent his best, he'd be sending this young lady's father." He turned to Tony and gave him a wink. "No offense, *signore*."

"None taken, Don Vianello. Levi has earned his reputation." Tony motioned in Alicia's direction. "I suppose you already know this, but I'm here as escort for Levi's daughter."

Alicia stepped closer to the desk and held out her hand,

trying not to embarrass herself as she spoke to him in Italian. "It's a pleasure to meet you. I've heard a lot of good things."

The man erupted in an uproarious laugh and offered her a lopsided grin as he shook her hand. "I hope your lies are better in English, because they're not so good in Italian," he said, speaking almost accent-free English. "There's no reason for you to have ever heard of me before, but I appreciate the gesture."

The don looked over at Dino and made a shooing motion. "You and I will talk later." As Dino quietly left the room, Don Vianello motioned to the chairs arrayed in front of his desk. "Both of you, have a seat."

Alicia sat in an ornately carved wooden chair that reminded her of furniture she'd seen in museums.

"So," the don continued speaking in English and shifted his gaze to Alicia. "I was informed about the incident that had occurred earlier this evening and I've promised Vincenzo that I'd get to the bottom of things. We have people processing the... how do you say *forense* in English?"

"Forensics," Alicia and Tony both replied at the same time.

"Ah, yes, forensics. The forensics are being processed and hopefully that helps us identify who attacked you." He shifted his gaze to Tony. "And yes, it's likely that the target was, how shall I put it, *business* related. Nonetheless, both of you are under my protection, and I'll see to your comfort and safety until we can get the answers to some questions." He shifted his attention back to Alicia and asked, "I understand that Antonio is here as an escort for you, but can you share with me the reason why you're here? Vincenzo said something about your uncle—"

"Don Vianello," Tony interjected. "It's my Uncle Alessandro. He's a priest at the Vatican, and he's gone missing."

The don's eyebrows raised a bit and he held a troubled expression. "I'm sorry to hear this. Is there a ransom or is this truly that he's missing?" He glanced at Alicia. "And how does the young woman fit into this if it's your uncle?"

"Let me explain," Alicia said as her mind raced, knowing that she had to tread carefully. No lies... but certainly not the truth. "My father has trained me in many things since I was little, and since he's away, unable to help, I volunteered to help Tony with looking for his uncle."

The don frowned. "Young lady, I have the greatest respect for your father's reputation and skills, but I hope you understand that finding someone who is missing can sometimes lead into unexpected danger."

"Oh, I understand completely." Alicia nodded. "You're concerned that a seemingly frail girl like myself might be in over her head."

He shrugged. "What else am I supposed to assume, knowing little else."

Alicia grinned. "Would it be a big surprise if I told you I've trained extensively in Brazilian Jiu-Jitsu, Krav Maga, Tae Kwon Do, and Aikido? My father and some others have overseen my training and I've shot thousands of rounds through various weapons systems, including the standard Glock 17,

Sig Sauer P226, and the Heckler & Koch MP5. Also I've trained extensively in precision long range shooting, and have hit human-sized targets at over eighteen-hundred meters."

"That's impressive—"

"Also, I can break down an M4, swap components, and have it back together before most infantryman can finish breaking down their weapons. It's not just about pulling a trigger; it's about understanding the tools of self-defense inside and out."

"Don Vianello," Tony interjected with a sheepish expression. "I can vouch for what she's said on the martial arts. She's not nearly as fragile as she looks. And to be honest, I asked her to help because even her father sees her as a genius of sorts, and he's not one to lavish undeserved praise even on his children."

The don laughed as he held his hands up. "Okay, I give up. You're not as simple of a package as you seem, and I apologize if you felt insulted by my being skeptical."

Alicia shook her head. "No need for an apology. I actually see my harmless appearance as an asset."

The don put his elbows on his desk and jabbed a thick finger in her direction. "And you would be correct. Who'd believe that a Tasmanian devil lies inside such a pretty package?" He shifted his gaze and finger to Tony. "I've already asked my people to retrieve your belongings from the apartment. I'm going to ask you to stay here until we figure out what we're dealing with." Alicia cleared her throat and the don looked over at her. "Yes?"

Alicia felt a wave of uncertainty wash over her. She didn't want to push her luck, but she also didn't want to sit here and do nothing for an indefinite period of time. "Don Vianello, I hope it isn't too presumptive for me to ask, but the more time we wait on searching for Tony's uncle, the harder it will be to find him. I was hoping to ask for three favors, if it's okay."

Out of the corner of her eyes she saw Tony's wide-eyed expression. She was probably pushing her luck...

"Three favors?" The Don held a neutral expression as he stared at her. "And what favors are these?"

"Well, first and probably the most important is that there's a bookseller I wanted to visit in the morning who might be able to help with the search for Father Montelaro. I'd still like to visit with him and see if he has any useful information."

The don made a rolling motion with his hand. "What else?"

Alicia winced, not sure how to read the suddenly lifeless expression coming from the man who only moments ago seemed very engaged and even amused. "Well, I suppose if you know who might sell this to me, I'd like to buy some body armor and get a decent firearm, just in case we have a repeat of the evening's incident."

The don shook his head. "There will be no repeat of this incident, because you won't be going out in my city without proper protection." He pressed his lips together and was silent for a few long seconds. "I'll see what I can do about your requests. I'll need the address of this bookseller and we'll see what happens. I can make no guarantees. Understood?"

Alicia nodded. "Thank you, and I'm sorry—I didn't mean to impose. I'm really very—"

"Enough." The don gave her a lopsided grin. "You have spunk, young woman. What do the Jews call it... *chutzpah*. That's what you have mountains of." He slid a piece of paper across the desk and said, "Write down the name and address of the bookseller."

Grabbing the pen he handed her; she began writing out the address as the don flicked a switch on his desk.

Almost immediately the door to his office opened and one of their escorts entered the room. "Yes, Don Vianello?"

He gestured toward the two of them and said, "Get them situated and have Mario come see me. I have a project for him that needs to be done tonight."

"Of course."

Alicia and Tony both stood, thanked the don once again, and then followed their escort out of the office.

As they walked up a large spiral staircase, presumedly heading to their temporary quarters, all she could think of was, "What was the don going to do with that name and address?"

Alicia startled awake at the knock on her bedroom door. Blinking the sleep out of her eyes, she staggered out of bed as Bagel leaped up onto the dresser and let out his multi-syllabic yowl that could mean almost anything.

The knock repeated and she yelled, "One second," as she wrapped a robe around her and opened the door.

Tony filled the doorway, looked her up and down and shook his head. "You're still in bed?"

She let out a yawn and looked longingly over her shoulder at the most comfortable bed she'd probably ever slept in. "I guess I was more tired than I thought."

Tony turned to someone in the hallway and said, *"Un attimo. Si sta vestendo."*

She didn't have the earbud in, nor would it do her much good since her phone wasn't getting signal in this place. Luckily her Italian had become proficient enough for her to know that he'd just told someone she was getting dressed.

Tony motioned toward the suitcase laying near the foot of her bed. "Get dressed, one of Don Vianello's people is here and has something for you to get fitted for."

He closed the door and Alicia scrunched her forehead as she wondered what in the world she was being fitted for.

She shook her head, grabbed a few things, quickly changed into a new set of clothes, and opened her bedroom door, announcing, "I'm dressed."

Without warning an old man stepped into the room carrying a satchel and what looked like wide strips of cloth draped on a hanger.

Tony walked in as the man began removing scissors, measuring tape, white wax sticks, and a variety of other items from his bag. He pointed at the old man. "This is Gilberto, and he's going to measure you for a vest."

Alicia's eyes widened. "A custom-fitted one?"

"Yes, I have everything with me that I need. Now please lift your arms so I can take some measurements."

Alicia did as she was asked.

The tiny old man took the tape measure from around his neck and began measuring around her shoulders, her neck, around her bustline, and finally her waist.

In about five minutes, he measured, put marks on various strips of thick cloth, and displayed an amazingly deft hand with very sharp scissors before declaring, "I've got everything I need. Let me go to the sewing machine, and I'll be right back."

As the old man left, another person knocked on her open door and poked his head in. "*Signora*, the Don mentioned you might have need of my services. May I come in?"

"What services are those?" Alicia asked as she waved him in.

A dark-haired man walked into the oversized bedroom, leaning heavily on an elaborately carved walking stick. "I'm a weaponsmith, *signora*."

"That's great." Alicia smiled, feeling happy at the

prospect of once again carrying a gun. "You don't by chance have any Sig 229's, do you?"

The man stared at her for a moment and shook his head. "I'm sorry, but no. That's not going to be possible."

Alicia sighed. "Okay, then anything that's easy to conceal would work as long as I can get ammo for it."

The man chuckled and shook his head again. "I'm sorry, but I can't take the responsibility. You're a woman."

Alicia frowned. "Yeah, and what does that have to do with anything?" She noticed Tony shake his head and look away.

"*Signora...*" The man held an amused expression. "It's a well-known fact that women flinch when they shoot. This gun thing won't work."

For a moment Alicia was stunned into dumb silence as she stared at the man. He couldn't be serious. It had to be some kind of joke.

The man held up his walking stick but Alicia's self-control failed as she dropped a few choice curses at the man in Mandarin, a language she was fairly certain nobody in the room, other than herself, spoke. "Give me a goddamned break. I shoot guns all the time."

"Seriously?" The man tilted his head and stared at her. "Why would you need to be shooting guns anyway, young lady?"

With a building sense of frustration, Alicia blurted, "I hunt and kill aliens."

"You what?" The man gave her that stupid pinched finger gesture that all Italians seemed to make. "Aliens don't exist."

"Have you ever seen one?" Alicia asked, trying to keep her voice steady.

"No..."

"You're welcome!" She barked at him.

The man stared at her for a full five seconds and burst out laughing.

"Can we talk about the kind of guns you might have that I could get?"

The man gave her a warm smile and shook his head. "I'm sorry, *signora*. But you're also an American, and there's just no way legally for you to have one. The don has forbidden it." He held up the walking stick. "I hear you are a martial artist. Knowing that, I've brought something here that I think you might find useful." He held the walking stick horizontally and said, "This may look like a normal cane, but it is made of... I don't know the world in Italian, but the Australians call this 'bull oak.' It's the hardest wood in the world."

Alicia's mouth dropped open as the man switched between Italian to English and back to Italian. Him switching languages wasn't the shocking thing... it was her not even realizing that she'd been talking to him in Italian the entire time that sent a chill up and down her spine. It was as if something in her mind had switched gears and even though she had to work at sounding the words out correctly, Alicia had been thinking in Italian.

"And if you look at the handle," the man continued talking, showing her the intricacies of the stick he'd brought her. "Press the nub at the top of the handle and twist counter-clockwise and *voila!*"

The walking stick separated into two sturdy pieces, but one of those pieces had a razor-sharp thrusting dagger embedded on its end.

That caught Alicia's attention and the man handed her both pieces. It was definitely heavy for its size. Heavy enough to do a number on anyone who'd get smacked with it, but the knife was a nice added bonus.

Alicia twisted the pieces back together and felt them click into place.

With a quick press of the recessed button on the end of the handle, she almost instantly twisted the pieces apart, one stick in each hand, her arms raised and ready to strike or defend.

The separation was very smooth and the craftsmanship was excellent.

The weaponsmith's eyes widened as he took a few steps back. He smiled and gave Alicia a curt nod. "It looks like you might have trained with sticks before. Is that a karate thing?"

Alicia shook her head as she reassembled the walking stick. "No, sticks are more an escrima thing. A lesser-known martial art from the Philippines." She held the walking stick horizontally in both hands and gave the weaponsmith a quick bow. "Thank you for this. I appreciate it."

"Anything to help keep those aliens under control." The man smiled and gave her a wink.

The tailor knocked on her door, announcing his arrival just as the weaponsmith departed. He held up several hangers with finished Kevlar-doped vests in various colors. "All done."

Dino walked into the room and looked back and forth between her and Tony. "Are you guys ready?"

Tony hitched his thumb over at Alicia and said, "She's just getting finished. What's up? Did we get an ID on whoever tried to whack us?"

"Not yet, but there's a crew waiting downstairs for you. I think Mario said something about a bookseller. Anyway, they couldn't find him, but he's scouted a safe path to the store if you're interested in going."

"Oh, hell yeah." Alicia responded without hesitation. Not really caring about who saw her, she took her outer shirt off, grabbed a matching vest from one of the hangers the tailor was holding up and put it on. Despite the thickness of the material, it lay on her almost as if it weighed nothing at all. She looked over at the tailor and smiled. "It fits perfectly." Putting her shirt on over it, she looked over at Tony. "Are you ready?"

He nodded.

Alicia scooped up Bagel's sleeping form from the dresser, and practically shoved him into the sling as she looped it over her shoulder.

That Russian bookseller was her only real lead left to find Tony's uncle, and despite the pleasant surroundings, the longer they waited, the worse it would likely be trying to track him down. Alicia didn't like the idea of failing at anything, especially on a mission that was so personal to someone she thought of as practically family.

She walked to where Dino was standing in the doorway and said, "Well, let's get going. I've got lots of questions for our Russian friend."

CHAPTER
EIGHT

It was just an hour past dawn, and a faint chill lingered in the air as Alicia and Tony awaited the signal to proceed. Alicia had never been part of a security detail like this herself, but she had trained with those who had. It felt odd for her to be involved in one, especially since she wasn't tasked with security; she and Tony were the designated VIPs, while others attended to the protective measures.

One of the men that had accompanied them cupped his hand over his earpiece and said "understood" into his wrist mic. He turned to them and said, "The bookseller has arrived at his store." He motioned toward the narrow corridor. "It's clear for you to go."

Alicia and Tony walked past a beefy set of men stationed at the end of the alley, just two of a dozen or so mobsters who'd been assigned to scout the area, clear it of any danger, and ultimately monitor the vicinity around the bookseller's storefront.

The don was serious about keeping them safe, especially since they hadn't yet ascertained the reason for last night's attack.

As they approached the weathered door, Alicia glanced at Tony and whispered, "Let me handle this. Okay?"

He nodded. "The show is all yours."

Alicia knocked on the door and immediately felt the sting of the weather-hardened wood on her knuckles.

She paused, listening intently for a response, and after a few seconds tried opening the door. It was locked.

She turned to Tony. "Are we sure he's here?"

"He's in there, dear girl. Just kick the door," an older woman yelled down to them from her second-story apartment window. "The Russian's probably got his nose in one of his books and didn't hear your dainty knock."

Alicia glanced up at the gray-haired woman, who was sipping at her morning espresso. "Thanks," she yelled back. There were very few times in her life that anything she'd done had been described as dainty.

With a practiced movement, Alicia smashed the heel of her palm repeatedly into the door, causing a wooden thud that echoed across the alley, and was hopefully loud enough to get Viktor Sokolov's attention.

Almost immediately, the door swung open noiselessly and a thin older man greeted them in the doorway. He looked back and forth between Alicia and Tony. "Yes? Can I help you?" The man had a thick Russian accent when speaking Italian.

Alicia withdrew Uncle Alessandro's book from her backpack and said, "I was told by someone I trust that you can help me with something."

The man pursed his lips as his gaze unerringly shifted toward the book in her hand. He stood in the doorway, silent for a few moments, before finally pointing at the leather-bound tome. "I see you've brought a book." He motioned for them to enter. "Let's go inside and see what you have there."

Alicia walked into the dimly lit room and paused, surveying the twenty-by-twenty-foot space. Its walls were lined from floor to ceiling with shelves overflowing with books, scrolls, and even in the far corner, she spied a stack of stone tablets. She inhaled deeply, savoring the scent that could only come from books whose age far exceeded her own. It reminded her of certain sections of the main branch of the New York Library, but she suspected that many of the books in this room were much older than anything she'd find outside of a museum.

"Please, take a seat," the bookseller gestured toward a set of sturdy wooden chairs positioned next to a table loaded with half a dozen teetering stacks of leatherbound volumes in the center of the room.

The bookseller took a seat at the table and as Alicia sat next to him, she noticed several partially-unrolled scrolls behind one of the stacks.

She noticed the beautifully-written Chinese calligraphy and wondered what kind of place this was.

The middle-aged Russian turned to Tony, who was still standing near the room's entrance, and pointed again at one of the chairs, "You're making me nervous standing there. Please, have a seat."

Tony shook his head and said with a polite yet firm tone, "I prefer to stand."

"Fool," the man muttered in Russian as he turned to Alicia.

"He no fool," Alicia responded in broken Russian.

The bookseller's eyebrows rose. "You understand Russian?"

Even though Alicia's earbud translated what he'd asked, she shook her head. "Very little. My father's girlfriend taught me a bit of Russian. Mr. Sokolov, I'm here—"

"One second young lady." The man's thin face took on a troubled expression. "How do you know my name?" He asked in fluent rapid-fire Mandarin. "Come to think on it, how did you know to come here? Who sent you?"

Alicia's earbud struggled to keep up with the translation, but this time it wasn't necessary. She responded in Mandarin. "Why did you assume I could understand what you're saying?"

He waved the question away. "Don't be ridiculous, I can hear the tones in your voice, even when you're speaking in a non-tonal language. Your voice carries its own signature that marks you better than your epicanthic folds."

Alicia stared at the man, coming to the realization that he spoke her native language better than she did. Her earbud translated into English the word she'd never heard in Mandarin: epicanthic. And it was only a fluke that she'd stumbled upon that word and knew what it meant: referring to the fold of skin that covers the inner corner of the eye, creating the characteristic "slanted" appearance of East Asian individuals.

Sokolov leaned forward and asked, "Again, how did you know to come here and what my name is?" The irritation was obvious in the tone of his voice.

This man didn't seem to be a run-of-the-mill bookseller. He was suspicious, clearly private, and seemingly not used to dealing with the public. Alicia glanced at Tony, who understandably looked a bit perplexed, given that he didn't understand what was being said. She gave him a quick thumbs up and turned back to the Russian, switching to English. "It's not in my nature to do this, but I'll tell you the truth." She hitched her thumb toward Tony and said, "My friend's uncle is missing, and we believe he came to this city looking for something very specific. Are you familiar with the *Custodes Veritatis*?" She saw the flicker of a reaction on his face and didn't need him to verbalize the answer... this guy recognized the name.

"What makes you think I'd know about..." He paused for a moment.

"*The Custodes Veritatis*, it means Guardians of Truth."

"I know what it means, young lady." Sokolov frowned.

"Why do you believe I would know anything about such a thing?"

Alicia brought up in her mind's eye the scanned images that Denny had sent to her and recited a passage that some unnamed person had written long ago:

"The inception of this clandestine organization traces back to the seventh century when enlightened minds, inspired by the intellectual currents of their time, laid the foundations of the Guardians of Truth. Within the heart of the Serenissima Republic, these Guardians covertly established a hidden refuge, exploiting the labyrinthine water passages and concealed alcoves of the city to veil their endeavors. Amid opulent palaces and time-honored libraries, they meticulously assembled a repository of wisdom, accumulating rare manuscripts, artifacts, and revolutionary ideas."

Sokolov sat up straight, pursed his lips, and stared silently at her.

Alicia gestured around and said, "We find ourselves in Venice, don't we? My friend's uncle is an archivist for the Vatican. He's spent most of his life studying old texts that hold wisdoms from the ancient past. And we have reason to believe he came here, seeking this clandestine group. I asked some people I trust about who to talk to about rare books in

Venice and I was given your name. What might you know about this group?"

Sokolov shook his head. "That's the wrong question to start with Miss... sorry, you have me at a disadvantage. You seem to know my name, but I don't have yours."

"My name's Alicia. What question would you prefer that I start with, Mister Sokolov?"

"Please, call me Viktor. And Alicia, the question you should be asking is why your friend's uncle would have been seeking such a group. And before we even broach that subject, what makes you believe this man was seeking knowledge of this group?"

Alicia placed Uncle Alessandro's book on the table and said, "It started with this."

Viktor grabbed a pair of linen gloves from the table, ran his finger over the worn leather and nodded. "I recognize this book. The *Tractatus de bibliothecis mundi, praesentibus et praeteritis*. The Treatise on the libraries of the world, present and past. It's not a rare book, for it was printed not so long ago. Its first and only printing was in the early 1800s if I recall. It wouldn't surprise me if several hundred copies had been printed, mostly for academic institutions and scholars of the day." He carefully opened the book and nodded, his eyes darting across the yellowed paper as he flipped through the first few pages. "It is in fair condition. I've not had the pleasure of reading this, but I'm not sure what about this would lead you to—"

"Let me show you," Alicia interrupted as she leaned

forward and flipped through the pages until she got to the proper spot. "Here it is." She put her finger on the underlined phrase. "*Custodes Veritatis.* Guardians of Truth."

"Someone wrote with ballpoint pen in this." Sokolov looked at her accusingly, made a clicking sound with his tongue and shook his head. "It's practically a sin to put marks into books, even relatively common ones such as this." He continued flipping through the pages. "Tell me again how you came to possess this book and why those two words were explicitly marked."

Not wanting to walk the man through the entirety of the story, Alicia took some liberties with the details. "The book was sent to us from my friend's uncle with no explanation. He's an older man, and it's not within his character to leave his duties at the Vatican nor to worry his family like he has."

"Wait a minute, you say he works at the Vatican. Is he a priest? What is his name?"

Alicia nodded. "He *is* a priest. Father Alessandro Montelaro."

Sokolov's eyes widened and for a split second he bore an angry expression. "I had a priest visit me last week. He too was asking questions of a very similar nature."

"He did?" Tony blurted the question in English.

Sokolov looked over at Tony. "Ah, you're probably the American he talked about." He shifted his gaze back and forth between Alicia and Tony. "Your uncle visited me last week. This is true. He was a very interesting person. Much more spirited than is typically found in someone of his age."

"What did you guys talk about?" Alicia asked and hitched her thumb toward Tony. "And how did he come up in the conversation?"

The Russian made a sucking noise through his teeth, his attention drifting elsewhere for a few long seconds before responding. "He asked me about the Guardians of Truth. I relayed what I will share with you: they're a covert group of scholars with what they consider to be a sacred mission dating back to the Roman era, which I'll have you know collapsed during the fifth century AD. Long before your claim of a seventh century origin to the group. I won't feign familiarity with the entirety of their history, but what I can attest to is that those scoundrels have escaped with many of the items I've spent months pursuing. Numerous times, I've been on the trail of an artifact for a client, only for it to vanish from my grasp at the eleventh hour. Are the Guardians of Truth real? Undoubtedly.

"He told me that he was on Vatican business. He was trying to track down an ancient artifact, which of course piqued my interest. He wouldn't share with me the details of what he was seeking, but he did share with me some interesting tidbits of data."

"Such as…" Alicia made a rolling motion with her hand.

"One second." Sokolov walked over to one of the shelves on the far end of the room, reached up above his head and plucked a dusty old tome from the upper shelf, and returned with it. He flipped it open and within seconds placed his finger on a passage. "It was interesting, my encounter with the priest. He had recited something from memory that morning when we talked, wondering whether I could help him unravel the mystery behind it. The words he'd spoken left me troubled. I knew that I had heard that same turn of phrase before, or more appropriately I'd read these same words in the past, but it took me several hours to recall where I'd seen them written down."

"What words?" Tony asked.

Sokolov tapped a gloved finger on the book he'd retrieved. "Even though this particular book is only about two-hundred-and-fifty years old, it contains transcriptions of ancient scrolls that scholars of the time wanted to preserve. Your uncle's words were identical to something I'd read in this book." Putting his finger on a passage in the middle of the page, he read, *"In the land where the river's gift meets the sun's eternal gaze, beneath the guardian palm's shade, the hidden words shall find sanctuary."*

Alicia gasped, realizing that those were the same words she'd read on the scrap of parchment. "He'd sent us those same words. Were you able to help him decipher its meaning?"

"No." Sokolov shook his head. "He was supposed to meet with me the next morning, but never returned." He shifted his attention back to the book. "What he'd memorized was only a fragment of a longer message. The rest of the passage should have read, '*In the shadow of the Great Library's remnants, where the Nile's waters caress the city's edge, seek the sacred sigil carved into the stones of the temple ruins. There, you may seek the truth. Amidst the cradle of wisdom, the hidden words shall be revealed.'"*

"Great Library." Alicia repeated the words as her mind raced. "The Nile... is that talking about the library at Alexandria?"

"Very good." Sokolov smiled. "The guardian palm refers to the ancient and iconic Egyptian date palm tree, which of course was highly regarded in ancient Egypt for its shade, fruits, and various uses. I find that some of these ancient passages are heavy with symbolism, and need to be interpreted with care. Certainly, palm trees were commonly associated with protection and sustenance, making them symbolic of security and life. In the context of this passage, it symbolizes a specific place or location in Alexandria, Egypt, where something of great value is hidden." He looked over at Tony and said, "I suppose the thing that frustrates me a bit is that your uncle almost certainly got that fragment of information from somewhere other than this compilation of ancient scrolls. He may even have an idea of what this hidden treasure might be, which is definitely intriguing and worrisome."

"Worrisome?" Tony asked. "Why would that worry you?"

The Russian sighed. "I sensed that your uncle was a bit unaware of the dangers involved in so openly seeking the Guardians of Truth. Very few are aware of their existence, and it's for good reason. I asked him who else knew about his interest in them, and he mentioned an American..." he glanced at Tony and nodded. "That part of the puzzle is solved."

"Wait a second." Alicia felt her skin prickling, almost as if with a mild electric shock. "You said these guardians are scholars, why would that pose a danger to someone asking about them?"

Sokolov shook his head. "The danger is not from them. In my opinion, they are thieves, but they are not criminals."

A strange distinction that made little sense to her.

"It's more an issue of other groups who are attracted to what the Guardians might seek. Anyone speaking of them may attract unwanted attention.

"These groups are also known to me... they have less scruples and operate with a different intent. Operating mostly in the shadows, the group I'm thinking of has no formal name that I know of, yet they are organized. I knew one member many years ago who once referred to belonging to a brotherhood known as the Dark Schemers. He was looking for a special book and said that his 'family' would pay handsomely."

Alicia's eyes widened. The term Dark Schemers didn't ring any bells, but in her mind she saw the word *Obscura Machinare*, which was the Latin equivalent to Dark Schemer. She snatched back Uncle Alessandro's book and began rapidly flipping through the pages, finally landing on page 238. Her finger landing on the reference. "They're mentioned in this book."

. . .

In the annals of bibliographic lore, a dire tale harks from the year 1625, when Biblioteca Ambrosiana in Milan bore witness to a brazen heist, bereaving its hallowed halls of the sole extant Codex Atlanticus, a compendium of Leonardo da Vinci's erudite treatises and sketches. Spanning myriad subjects and brimming with the polymath's profound ruminations, this magnum opus comprised thousands of pages, yet only a scant fragment remains within the Milanese repository's grasp. The remainder, alas, has slipped from the public's purview, presumed ensconced within private collections. This nefarious deed was ascribed to a clandestine cabal known as the Obscura Machinare, whose shadowy machinations continue to shroud the fate of this priceless relic in obscurity.

"That is *quite* interesting." Sokolov held a surprised expression. "Maybe I should acquire a copy of this book... anyway, my concern for your uncle is that no matter how highly I think of myself, the information I possess is not exclusive to me. If your uncle does possess knowledge of a hidden artifact, there are those who might take advantage of that information."

The buzzing sound of a phone vibrating echoed through the chamber and Tony put his phone to his ear. "Yes?"

Alicia focused on Sokolov and asked, "Do you have any contacts that we might pursue regarding either of these groups?"

"For the guardians, I'm sorry, I do not. If you give me a contact number, I can see what I might be able to learn regarding the Dark Schemers. I have little love for either group." He gave her a crooked smile. "After all, in many ways they're my competition. Anyway, the reputation of the schemers is not one I'd trust my elderly relative with, if you understand my meaning."

"Alicia, we have to go." Tony's gravelly voice had a no-nonsense tone to it. "Last night's person of interest has been found."

Alicia stood, gave the Russian bookseller her phone number and then shook his hand. "Thank you for the help, and I hope maybe we can talk again soon."

Sokolov nodded and pointed at the book she'd scooped up. "If you're interested in selling that, I'll be a buyer at two-hundred euros."

"I'll have to think about—"

"Three-hundred euros," Sokolov blurted.

Tony opened the front door and as Alicia turned to leave, the bookseller said, "Five-hundred euros, it's my final offer."

Alicia tossed the bookseller a smile and shook her head. "Maybe, but not right now. Call me if you find any contacts for me." She walked out of the cramped one-room store and whispered to Tony, "The don's guys found the shooter?"

"Evidently so. He's being taken to a safe place so information can get squeezed out of him."

"Please tell me that he's going to be kept in one piece so I can question him," Alicia whispered fiercely.

"You want to question him?" Tony paused in the alley and gave her a concerned look. "Are you sure about that?"

Alicia took a deep breath and let it out slowly. "Tony, don't mess with me on this. I'm actually trained to do this. I want to be the one who interrogates him."

Tony glanced at the men at the far end of the alley and held up his index finger, telling them to wait. He pulled out his phone and said, "I'll call and see what I can do."

She poked the big man's arm. "I also want his name, family, known acquaintances, anything we can get. We also might need to make a trip ahead of the interrogation."

He gave her a look and she said, "Trust me, I know what I'm doing."

Alicia pulled out her own phone, dialed a number and put the phone to her ear.

She felt the tension rising within her as the second ring went unanswered. On ring number three, she heard someone pick up and felt a sense of relief as she heard Denny's voice.

"What's up?"

"Denny, I've got a favor to ask, and I sort of need it ASAP."

"I'll see what I can do. What do you have in mind?"

"Denny, I have an idea, but it'll need you to work some magic for me."

CHAPTER NINE

Alicia glared at the large mobster standing in front of the closed door. "I said let me in."

The mobster looked past her and said, "Antonio, you know how this is. It's not right for a woman to see such a thing. She's not... I mean..." he shook his head, "You understand, right?"

Anger bubbled up within her as she stepped closer to the man blocking her from the interrogation room. She poked him in the chest and growled, "Didn't Don Vianello tell you to let me handle this?"

"No *signora*, he did *not*. He said you are a respected man's daughter and to allow you courtesies we normally wouldn't give to anyone outside the family. But this—"

"Mario, listen to me." Tony interjected. "I'm the one who got shot by this bastard, believe me, I understand and agree with everything you're saying. This situation is a little different. I trust her, and do me a favor and trust me when I say it's okay."

The tall, thick-necked mobster frowned and stared at Alicia for a few seconds before shrugging and stepping to the side. "This is on you, Antonio. I take no responsibility, understand?"

Tony clapped his hand on the big man's shoulder and said, "I appreciate this, Mario. Is everything we arranged for inside?"

Mario nodded. "Yes. And the piece of garbage has been softened up a bit already."

Alicia steeled herself for whatever it was she was going to see. Tony had warned her that the shooter had not come willingly and had been worked over a bit. Given what Mario had just said, it was clear that the suspect had been beaten, but how badly... well, there was only one way to find out.

Tony opened the door and Alicia walked into a dank, dimly-lit corridor that reminded her of a scene she'd seen in a movie about walking into death row.

Alicia breathed through her mouth as the acrid smell of old urine permeated the air.

"You okay?" Tony asked.

Alicia nodded as Bagel squirmed in his sling and she felt more than heard a growl coming from him. "I don't think Bagel likes this place." They walked to the end of the corridor and were greeted by a mobster wearing a blood-spattered sleeveless undershirt. "Is Mr. Guani conscious?"

The man stared wide-eyed at Alicia, a look of surprised etched on his face. He shifted his gaze to Tony and then back to Alicia. He nodded. "He's in and out. Our guy... he's not a talker. I swear, had I not pried his mouth open myself to look, I'd have thought his tongue had been cut out at its root." With an icy grin he leaned closer, the dank smell of his body odor wafted from him. "You must be a specialist. I'm curious... how are you planning on making him talk? He doesn't seem to care about pain or broken bones, as you'll see."

As a child she'd seen horrendous things done to others on the streets. She'd had terrible things happen to her before her father took her away from that life. The man staring at her was no different than those who had taken pleasure in abusing her.

That was then... this is now.

A wave of calm washed over Alicia. On the streets, you never showed fear or exposed your true emotions. Whatever she was thinking about this man or the situation she was in, she smothered it and smiled, patting the man's stubbly cheek. Her voice was calm and she felt like ice was flowing through her veins. "Everyone has their weak points. It's only a matter of finding them."

The man's smile faltered and he nodded. "Is there anything you need from me?"

"No." She waved him away. "I've got this."

Alicia peered into the room beyond the corridor. About fifty feet ahead she spotted the back of a metal chair with the attacker slumped forward, seemingly unconscious. Even from this distance, she noticed the dark stains of pooled blood on the floor at the base of the chair.

As soon as the torturer was out of earshot, Tony turned to her and shook his head. "As you can tell, this is a dirty business... you sure you're up for it?"

She nodded. "Go ahead and get yourself situated. If it comes to it, you know what you need to do, right?"

With a grim expression, he nodded. "This isn't the way your father would handle things, you realize that, right?"

"I'm not my father," Alicia responded with a sense of finality. She hitched her thumb toward where the torturer had departed. "You heard what Don Vianello's guy said. Our guy isn't a talker. It's a good thing that we've come prepared. I'm willing to do what's necessary, and I presume you will as well."

Tony nodded. "This isn't right or natural." Tony shrugged. "I'll do it if it comes to it, but I don't have to like it."

"You'll be fine." Alicia gave him a lopsided grin. "Just remember, no matter what you hear in that room, I want you to keep your place. You've got your job, and I've got mine. You have everything you need?"

Tony held up his hands and wiggled his fingers. "As long as these are working, I think I'm good. I'll go get myself set up and just yell if you need me to go through with it."

Alicia nodded, took in a deep breath and let it out slowly as Tony walked into the room. He slowed as he came alongside their attacker, and smacked the side of his head, which lolled to the side.

He continued past the shooter, turned the corner and vanished from sight.

Despite the serious nature of the situation, Alicia felt surprisingly calm as she walked into the room. As a kid on the streets, she'd learned to numb herself to everything around her so that nothing could truly harm her. It had been almost fifteen years since she'd left the streets, yet she wore the cloak of numbness as easily as if she'd never left the streets.

The Outfit never trained their agents to torture people, none of the government branches were allowed to do that. Yet Alicia knew that if it came to it, as it might in the next few moments, she was capable of almost anything.

Alicia walked into the room, pulling in another deep breath, taking in the coppery-scent of blood that lingered in the air.

Next to the steel chair, which was bolted to the ground, there was a table with all variety of devices that would have seemed proper in a torture museum. Metal corkscrews, a car battery with naked wires hanging from it, razors, hammers, and a variety of other tools to assist in causing various levels of harm.

Alicia walked over to the table, grabbed a pair of latex gloves and slipped them on. "Luca, are you awake?"

She turned to face the shooter and he remained motionless. His arms, legs, and chest were tightly strapped to the chair, while his head hung loosely, facing the floor. An occasional drip of blood splashing to the ground from a wound she couldn't yet see.

"Mr. Guani, do I need to wake you up?"

No response.

Bagel yowled and hissed, wriggling out of the sling and leaped onto the table. His eyes flashed as he directed his hisses toward the shooter.

"It's okay. He's not in any position to harm anyone at the moment," Alicia reassured, but the cat's response was only a low growl and repeated hisses, with his tail swishing spasmodically back and forth.

Alicia walked over to a couple of metal tripods and switched on the spotlights, directing blindingly bright beams of light at the shooter.

With the room flooded with light, she reached for a capsule from what appeared to be a candy dish filled with other such capsules. Next to the dish was a blood-spattered hammer. The blood spatter was red and still had a sheen to it. It was fresh and hadn't yet dried.

Walking over to Luca Guani, she grabbed his hair, lifted his head roughly, then squeezed the capsule of smelling salts under the shooter's nose.

The unconscious man lurched away from the sharp smell of ammonia, straining against the leather bindings that held him to the metal chair bolted to the floor.

Bagel hissed yet again.

Following the man's movements, Alicia kept the capsule directly under his nose until the man's eyes opened wide.

"Rise and shine," Alicia said sweetly as the man squinted against the bright lights aimed directly at him. "I have a few questions for you. You answer them, and you're free to go."

It was a lie, but maybe he was the gullible type.

The man strained against the loops of leather once more and spit at Alicia. "Fuck you, you whore. Where's that godfather of yours? I'm sure he's around here somewhere."

A chill raced up Alicia's spine as she studied the man's bloodied face.

His nose was crushed and shifted slightly to the side from a recent blow. It was oozing blood and likely the key contributor to the blood spatter in the room.

In addition to the horribly damaged nose, his right eye was practically swollen shut, he had a series of angry red scratches across his face, and yet he looked familiar.

"Where's that godfather of yours?"

His voice replayed in her mind... it was unmistakably one she recognized.

"Have a good visit pretty woman."
"Maybe we see each other in our dreams."

. . .

The guy from the boat who'd tried to flirt with her.

Bagel let out a low growl that became louder and more high-pitched, ending in a scream.

The shooter spit in Bagel's direction. "Stay away, demon."

Smacking the tabletop with his paw, Bagel growled as the seemingly random pattern spelled out a simple message to Alicia. *"Bad man scratch."*

Alicia grinned at the shooter, with his attention focused on the angry cat. "Luca." He turned to her and grinned.

His smile revealed blood-streaked teeth and he immediately spit in her direction.

She launched a stinging open-hand slap across his face, rocking his head violently to the side with a loud smack.

Luca's eyes widened and his face turned red with anger. "Whore!"

Bagel launched himself at the man's face, claws extended, and Alicia barely caught him in mid-air, almost falling over as she fought to regain her balance.

"Keep that demon away from me, whore."

Alicia kissed the top of Bagel's head and whispered to her furry friend, "Let me handle this."

"You can't handle anything, you whore."

Alicia laughed. "I've been called so much worse; you can't even begin to imagine." She studied his face and barely recognized the handsome man. His prior day's flirtation was obviously a ruse... "Why did you shoot at us?"

Luca's eyes narrowed and he shook his head.

She walked over to the table, grabbed the ballpeen hammer and walked back over to her would-be assassin. Alicia took in all of what the torturer had done. The damage to his face was the most obvious, but as she twirled the carpenter's tool, she noticed the bruised and swollen right hand. Probably smashed by a larger profile object, maybe a mallet or a brick.

"Listen, this doesn't have to be this way. I have a few questions that I need answers to. That is all. I can make this all go away. No police. No more beatings. Just answer a few questions."

Luca looked up at her, squinting past the bright lights, and made a hocking sound as he got ready to spit.

Bagel launched at him with a scream, claws extended and teeth sinking into the man's cheek.

With a swift motion, Luca whipped his head to the side, sending Bagel flying to the floor. Blood dripped from the fresh claw marks and the bite wound on his face.

Bagel gathered himself for another assault.

Alicia swiftly scooped him up, hushing the growling furball, and placed him back on the table, giving him a frown. "I said let me handle this."

"Keep that demon away from me!" Luca yelled, his eyes wide and spittle dripped from the corner of his mouth. He stared at Bagel and yelled again, "Demon!"

"Demon!" He repeated even louder than before. "Demon!"

With a blur of motion, Alicia's open hand connected with Luca's face, knocking his head back against the chair. "Enough!"

Her hand throbbed from the impact. She'd always practiced closed-hand strikes against people and heavy bags, and her fists had never hurt, but Alicia's attempt to avoid causing Luca any serious damage had backfired on her.

"Your yelling is pointless," She reminded the man as she opened and closed her fist.

The man was now staring daggers at her. Bagel growled and he focused again on the cat, his lip curling up with disgust.

It seemed odd that he was having such a visceral reaction to Bagel. "Believe me, nobody can hear you scream down here."

Swapping the hammer into her dominant hand, Alicia made a few practice swipes in the air, and Luca growled, "Go ahead, beat the shit out of me. I'll remember you fuckers and my family will avenge me."

"Your family will?" Alicia smiled. "What family might that be? Your parents lived near the Spice Merchants' Street, if I recall."

Something flickered behind Luca's mask of hatred, but he remained silent.

"Your parents can't seek revenge since they're both dead. Luca," Alicia's voice took on a sultry purr as she emphasized his name, "what family are you referring to, my dear?"

Luca's eyes narrowed, and his breathing slowed while Alicia watched the horror of a man strain against the thick leather straps binding him to the chair.

Alicia let out a girlish laugh and moved closer to Luca.

The man's gaze shifted to the table as Bagel growled.

"Don't worry about the cat," Alicia reassured him with a toothy grin. "He's the least of your worries."

She trailed the business end of the hammer across the top of his thigh, then swiftly stepped back as he spat at her, managing only to let a glob of bloody phlegm dribble down his chin.

Tucking the hammer's handle into her pocket, Alicia picked up some gauze from the table, unfolded it into a single layer, and grabbed a spool of duct tape that happened to also be on the table.

"Enough of the spitting," Alicia declared, moving behind the chair and wrapping the gauze around his head. She adjusted some of the gauze to leave his eyes exposed and sealed it all with the tape.

After retrieving the hammer, she took a few practice swings in the air before facing the prisoner again.

Satisfied with her preparations, Alicia nodded—any further attempts to spit would now be thwarted by the gauze, yet he could still breathe through his mouth. She needed him conscious and able to speak.

"Who sent you to intercept us?"

He stared back at her silently.

Alicia stepped closer, offering an affectionate smile. "My dearest Luca, you have no idea what I'm prepared to do to get the information I want."

Luca's eyes conveyed his murderous intent as he replied, "There's nothing you can do to make me talk."

Alicia burst into laughter, fully embracing her street persona, a role in which she felt completely at ease—void of emotions, devoid of pity, driven by pure animalistic cunning.

"Oh, Luca, I'm inclined to agree with you," she said, tapping his knee lightly with the hammer. "Given how resilient you've been, I could probably break every bone in your body, keep you alive with a transfusion, and even bring in the batteries to employ some electric shock therapy—yet, I doubt you'd speak." Alicia then tapped his other knee a bit more forcefully. "You're a strong man, not a 'weak woman' like me, or like your sister—"

A flicker of something flashed behind the man's smoldering eyes.

"Yes, your sister Bianca," Alicia continued, crouching to meet his gaze. "Did you really think I was unaware of her? Indeed, she no longer bears your family name but Fontanelli, correct? She married three years ago. Her husband vanished under mysterious circumstances, and she returned to live in your parents' house. You didn't imagine that I'd do my homework on you, did you?"

A drop of blood fell from his chin, adding to the mess below. Luca's blood now seemed to seep through the gauze more quickly, and Alicia could almost sense his heart pounding. His lack of verbal response contrasted with the involuntary reactions of his body, revealing truths he couldn't conceal.

"Tony!" Alicia called out, locking eyes with Luca. "Are you ready?" she asked in English.

"Tell me when and I'll remove her gag." His deep voice projected loudly even though he was in another room.

Luca's eyes widened and he turned toward the source of Tony's voice.

The street version of Alicia continued to smile. Luca was off balance. This wasn't something he'd expected.

In the adjacent room, with its door ajar and preparations made in advance, she was ready to do whatever was necessary to uncover why this man had targeted them.

"Go ahead, Tony. Let her say 'hi' to her brother for a moment."

Instantly, a woman's voice shrieked, *"Luca! Luca! Help me, I'm—"*

Her voice was abruptly cut off, and Luca's eyes grew wide as he stared at Alicia. "Let her go!"

"Of course," Alicia replied, her smile sweet, her head tilting in a gesture that looked almost tender, caring. "But first you need to answer my questions. Who sent you to intercept us?"

"I don't know what you're talking about," Luca growled.

"Why did you shoot at me and my friend?"

"I don't know what you're talkin—"

Alicia slammed her fist onto Luca's already injured hand, feeling the broken bones grind against each other. "Lies!" She spat in his face and stood. "Fingerprints place you at the scene. Those day-old scratches on your face match the ones my cat gave you today. You can't lie your way out of this." She turned slightly. "Tony! Her right hand... break it."

"You got it."

A heavy thud sounded from the next room, followed by a muffled cry. "No!" Luca cried out.

"Tony, tell her that her brother is withholding information. Once he shares what we need, she can go. See if she can persuade her brother."

After a moment, the sobbing of the woman became more distinct. *"Luca... please... my hand... it hurts. I'm scared, Lucino. I'm sorry if I'm causing trouble—"*

"No, Bianca, it's okay!"

Her voice was quickly muffled again.

Alicia cleared her throat. "Ready to talk now?"

Luca, tears in his eyes, growled, "I hate you. I wish I'd never heard of Alicia Yoder or your accomplice, Antonio."

"Who told you to look for us?" Alicia probed as Luca's expression darkened.

She crouched down once again to meet the gaze of a physically broken man. "Believe me, I find no joy in this. Your sister, an artist—her hand will heal. But unless you answer my questions, Antonio will start removing her fingers, one by one. This is your last warning. Do you understand?"

Luca closed his eyes for a long moment before finally nodding. "Please, no more harm to her. I'm as good as dead either way, but I'll answer your questions if you promise to release my sister."

"You will answer my questions, and only after I've verified their truth will your sister be set free. Understand?" Alicia's expression was as unyielding as stone, revealing nothing of her thoughts.

He nodded again. "I'm part of a brotherhood known as the *Obscura Machinare...*"

Holding her breath, Alicia poured the liquid onto a bundle of cloth, then walked behind Luca's chair and shoved the chloroform-soaked rag against his nose and mouth.

Luca struggled for a few moments before his body went limp.

She kept the rag in place for an extra thirty seconds before discarding it.

Exhaling deeply, Alicia made her way to where Tony was waiting. The session with Luca had drained her, both physically and emotionally. Upon entering the room, Tony leaned forward, placing all four chair legs back on the ground, and asked, "Did you find out why he shot at us?"

Alicia nodded. "Believe it or not, it has to do with that group that bookseller told us about."

"What? The *Obscura Machinare*? That one?"

She nodded.

"So, this wasn't just a random attack; it's connected to my uncle?"

"It seems to be, but our guy didn't seem to know much of anything about your uncle. Luckily, this guy was devoted to his sister, which means we now have some leads to follow."

"Do we?" Tony asked.

Alicia nodded. "Thanks to your help."

Tony shook his head, offering a crooked smile. He gestured towards the table, which held a small set of speakers and Alicia's phone. "I bet your dad wouldn't have handled this the way you have. This... AE stuff—"

"AI," she corrected, "it stands for artificial intelligence."

"Yeah, well, it's just not how things are supposed to be done. I was probably just as surprised as our shooter when I used that app of yours and heard that girl's voice coming out of those speakers."

Alicia laughed almost maniacally as a wave of mixed emotions threatened to overwhelm her. The emotional numbness behind her street facade began to crumble. She took another deep breath and exhaled slowly, trying to steady herself. "Now you see why I needed those voice samples of his sister."

"Sure, but it doesn't add up. She never said any of that stuff you had me make that AI voice say. His sister said none of that when we delivered flowers to her. Yet, your phone made it sound exactly like her."

"At school, I took some linguistics classes as part of my neuroscience curriculum, so I figured it would be possible. I'm just glad it worked well enough." With the voice samples of Luca's sister, Denny's help with the new app he remotely installed on her phone, and some Bluetooth speakers they purchased at a local electronics store, she had engineered a convincing deception. "Are you actually complaining about not having to resort to violence for answers?"

Tony grinned. "Don't act all innocent on me young woman, I heard you give him a smack or two. Mr. Bagel did his part as well, just like I'd expect of a Yoder."

The cat squirmed, poked his head out of the sling and gave Tony a long multi-syllabic yowl in response, as if recounting to the mobster what had transpired.

Tony nodded at the cat and leaned forward with his fist extended. "I agree, he totally deserved it."

Bagel paw-patted the mobster's fist and Alicia rolled her eyes. "Do you two have some kind of secret cat language I'm not privy to? Anyway, are you complaining that we didn't have to beat on his sister to get him to talk?"

Tony opened his mouth to respond, hesitated, then simply shook his head. "It just doesn't sit right. Your father wouldn't have approved."

"He'd have tortured some innocent girl to get the information he needed?" Alicia refused to believe her father was capable of that.

The mobster frowned. "Well, no... but..." he seemed at a loss for words. "I don't know. It's just not natural."

"It's a new world, Tony. Things change." Alicia picked up her phone and gestured for him to follow. "Let's move. Our guy said he took some notes when he got the call from his handlers. He claimed only to know that you and I were trying to stop them from a big score, and he didn't know anything about what the big score was about. It also wasn't obvious that he was told about or knew anything about your uncle. Either way, someone put him on our trail, and the only way Luca knows to get ahold of his handlers is through a dead drop."

Tony got up and asked, "A dead drop? Does that mean what I think it means?"

"How am I supposed to know what you think it means?" Alicia gave him a sideways glance and grinned. "Luca told me about a dead drop he uses just outside his apartment. He puts a message inside a special envelope that he's got at his apartment, dumps it into a specific garbage can, and someone calls him later in the day."

"Got it, more of your dad's spy stuff." The mobster nodded. "I guess we've got an apartment to visit."

Alicia led them past the still-unconscious form of their shooter, and headed toward the room's exit. She hitched her thumb back toward Luca, leaned close to Tony and whispered, "I don't need much imagination to figure out what's going to happen to him, but I just wanted to make sure he's not somehow going to be found in some alley somewhere for at least a day or so while we follow this trail."

Tony chuckled as they walked out of the torture chamber. "Don't worry about. I'll talk to Don Vianello's guys. I'm sure it'll be handled discretely."

Alicia checked her phone, and noticed that she had full signal. "Okay, you go do that while I wait here. I need to make a few calls. When you're done, just come get me."

The mobster nodded. "Okay, whatever you say." He glanced at his watch. "It's still early in the day."

"Roger that," Alicia responded as she pulled up Denny's number. "When you get back, we'll be heading to the shooter's apartment."

"Do we need any backup?"

Alicia shook her head. "No, but do you know where I'd be able to get my hands on a lockpick set?"

"What, you didn't pack one for the trip?" Tony winked. "I'll see what I can find, but I hope you're not thinking I know how to use one of those things, because I'm all thumbs when it comes to that stuff."

"No, I think I can handle it." The countless hours Alicia had spent practicing on locks replayed in her mind. "Go." She motioned for him to leave. "My phone call probably won't take long, so I don't want to waste any more time. Your uncle's out there somewhere."

"Gotchya, boss." Tony turned and quick-walked toward the nearest set of stairs.

Alicia put her phone to her ear, heard someone pickup and said, "Denny, do you mind brainstorming something with me? I have an idea, but I'm not sure if it'll work."

"What do you mean?"

"Well, before I get to the brainstorming part, let me be blunt and say that I need something like a wiretap, but I don't even have a clue how to begin something like that in a legal manner, much less in a foreign country."

The bar owner and electronics whiz chuckled for a few seconds before responding. *"Alicia, I don't know how to tell you this without sounding condescending, so I'm going to be blunt right back at you. Some things in life we don't ask for permission, we just seek forgiveness at some later date."*

Chapter
Ten

Alicia crouched in front of Luca's door, casting glances down the dimly lit hallway as Tony kept watch. Beside her, Bagel sat with his tail twitching spasmodically.

She inserted the flat metal pick into the lock, twisted it slightly, the same way she'd turn a key. With her other hand, she inserted a long, thin pick with a slight upward bend on its end and felt for the pins in the tumbler. She proceeded just as she'd practiced countless times, feeling for one of the pins in the lock. As she maintained upward pressure with her pick, she slowly scraped forward until she heard a satisfying click.

The sound was the first sign of success and helped Alicia focus on what she was doing. The two picks were soon extensions of her fingers. It was almost like when she worked on solving puzzles or deciphering a tough math problem—everything else faded away and it was just her and the object of her attention.

Maintaining pressure with one of the clips, Alicia searched for the second pin, found it, and pressed it into position. Again, she was rewarded with a click. She repeated the process four more times, and when she heard the final click, the mechanism rotated, and the lock disengaged.

The apartment door swung open and Bagel strode inside like he owned the place.

Alicia's senses heightened as she entered the dark apartment, inhaling the mingled scents of body odor, cologne, and the mustiness of the building's aged walls.

Tony walked into the apartment, shutting the door behind him. "I can't see crap in here." His eyes were wide open as he swiveled his gaze and whispered, "Where's the light switch in this place?"

Ever since she'd recovered from a false cancer diagnosis, her senses had improved beyond anything she could have imagined possible. It seemed like a lifetime ago, but it was no more than a few months since a new world had opened up to her. New scents, new sights, and new sounds... and as her eyes adjusted to the darkness, she patted Tony on the shoulder and whispered, "Wait here."

Alicia cautiously advanced into the apartment, her eyes swiftly adapting to distinguish the various shades of gray in the compact fifteen-by-ten-foot living room. Approaching a rolltop desk, she turned the knob on a gooseneck lamp, casting a warm glow throughout the space.

Tony approached as Alicia rifled through the desk Luca had mentioned in their "discussion." Beside a vintage beige pushbutton phone lay a notepad, its pages scrawled with notes detailing her and Tony's arrival, including age, weight, hair color, and style.

15:00 Stazione di Venezia Santa Lucia

Antonio Montelaro
  54 anni.
  130 kg.
  Capelli corti scuri.

Alicia Yoder
  25 anni.
  60 kg
  Capelli lunghi scuri.

Alicia continued searching through the contents of the rolltop desk's center drawer when Bagel yowled from a nearby room. She looked over at Tony and said in a hushed voice, "Can you go see what he's gotten into?"

She opened the right-hand drawer and smiled as she spied a small stack of black envelopes. Thankfully, Luca's affection for his sister had ensured the accuracy of his information.

"Alicia," Tony called out. "You might want to see this."

Grabbing the stack of envelopes, she put them in her fanny pack, and upon entering the adjoining room her eyes widened.

It appeared to be a bedroom, but Alicia's gaze focused on the cat, tapping at a picture of the Pope hanging above a set of dresser drawers. The framed picture was knocked partially askew, revealing the corner of a metal object embedded in the wall.

Tony walked up to the dresser and carefully lifted the framed picture off its mount. "Look what Mr. Bagel found."

Bagel yowled, sat under the now-visible wall safe, and returned her gaze with a self-satisfied feline smirk.

Tony focused for a long moment on the cat, who'd begun grooming himself. The mobster looked over at her and asked, "How in the world did he know to look for a safe?"

"I'm sure he wasn't specifically looking for it," Alicia shrugged. Bagel was unquestionably smarter than any cat she'd ever heard of, but sometimes that golden-eyed feline reminded her of just how unusual he was. "Who knows, maybe there's some tuna sandwich in the wall," she joked.

Alicia walked over to the safe, a sense of curiosity washing over her. The front panel of the safe was about one foot square, with a round dial and lever handle. She looked at the cat and asked, "Do you know what's in there?"

Bagel rubbed his shoulder against her belly and gave her a sequence of pats that translated to, "No."

She rubbed his cheek with her thumb and said, "There's only one way to find out." Alicia tried the lever, but it didn't budge. "I guess we'll have to open it the hard way."

"You can crack safes?" Tony asked.

She made a so-so gesture with her hand. "Have I done it before? Yes. Can I open this one? That remains to be seen." Alicia swept her gaze across the room and said, "Given that this guy wasn't exactly living the high life, maybe we'll get lucky and this one will be cheaply made and not be too difficult."

Rubbing the tips of her fingers against each other, Alicia whispered, "Let's see what we're dealing with here. This model has a common circular lock mechanism, with a relatively low number count of fifty, which implies less expensive."

"That's good, right?" Tony asked.

"Maybe." Alicia shrugged. "First thing I need to do is 'feel' the lock, listen to it. These older models are all about the touch and sound."

"How can you tell which one it is just by listening?" Tony asked as he hovered nearby, watching intently.

Alicia grinned. "This is going to sound a bit melodramatic, but I learned some of these tricks from a strange little old man who contracted with the FBI to train some of their agents. I think he was a second-story guy in his youth, and I guess had a screw loose, because he talked about locks like they were people with personalities.

"He said every lock speaks to you if you know how to listen." Alicia rubbed her fingers against the smooth metal face of the safe and said, "Let's see if this safe and I can become friends. First, I'm going to apply light tension to the dial, getting a feel for its motion, and how it's sitting in the lock mechanism itself. I'll rotate the dial slowly, listening for clicks or any change in resistance. Those clicks, those subtle changes, they're the lock's language."

"And that tells you...?"

"Each click, each pause, they narrow down the combination." Alicia made a hushing sound as she put her ear to the safe. "Now, I'm spinning the dial right, carefully...You can hear the mechanism inside... there it is. It was a faint click, but it's there." She glanced at the dial and put her ear back against the safe. "That's the first number in our sequence. Now, gently in the opposite direction...

"This takes patience. I had a former Olympic competition shooter once tell me when it comes to aiming that slow is fast, fast is slow. The same applies here. If I rush things, it just slows things down and I have to start over. It's about understanding the mechanism. Every safe, every lock has its quirks." Alicia carefully turned the dial. "This isn't one of the more sophisticated locks. It's good, but they took shortcuts in its manufacturing. I can feel the resistance changing slightly just as—there it is." She glanced at the dial. "That's our second number. For higher-end safes, I'd never be able to hear what I'm hearing unaided, so we're in luck. Now, back the other way for the third..."

"How many numbers do you need?" Tony asked.

"It really depends on the lock. Three, four, sometimes more. Ah, there's our third number. You feel that?" Alicia snorted and shook her head. "Of course you can't. I think I know why that old man went nuts, talking to too many safes. I can feel the dial moving slightly smoother now. We're close. I think this will be the final turn..."

Alicia's senses were so focused, she heard Tony's breathing and smelled the garlic he'd eaten last night. Her heart thudded as she slowly turned the knob and... "There it is. It was a click, but deeper than the others. That's the sound of the tumblers aligning, a sign that the mechanism unlocked."

"Are you sure?" Tony asked.

"You can never be completely sure, but," Alicia twisted the handle on the safe and they both heard a loud metallic click as the safe opened. "Now I'm sure," she smiled.

The mobster grinned from ear-to-ear. "Like father like daughter. You Yoders never cease to amaze."

"As the crazy old dude would say, 'Every safe tells a story, you just need to know how to listen.'" Alicia pulled on the lever, the safe yawned open, and her eyes widened at the sight of rubber band-bound stacks of euros that nearly filled the interior, along with a couple of baggies filled with a suspicious white powder. "It looks like Luca might have been a bit of a drug dealer on the side."

"*Madonna mia!*" Tony extracted the bundles of cash and sorted them by denomination. "This guy was not fooling around."

Alicia picked up one of the twenty-euro bundles and riffled through the bills, counting as she went. "It looks like one hundred bills in each of these bundles."

Tony shook his head as he straightened out the pile of fives, twenties, and hundred-euro bundles.

Alicia did some quick math in her head and gasped. "Tony, I think we have something like one hundred and fifty thousand euros here. What in the world can we do with—"

"I have an idea," Tony interjected, his expression was light and airy. "We might need some supplies. I'd like to kick up most of this to Don Vianello, if you're okay with it. I think it'll be to our advantage. It accomplishes a few things at once, but I think most importantly it'll buy us a few favors."

"Accomplishes a few things?" Alicia smiled, fully aware that for Tony, this would put him in good standing with the local mafia boss. Yet, her friend wasn't wrong. Having favors owed was certainly better than owing them. "It's not *my* money, so I'm totally fine with whatever you do with it," she said, pointing at the baggies of white powder still in the safe. "However, I'd rather not have anything to do with that stuff. Can we pretend we didn't even see it?"

Tony pocketed a couple of the bundles of cash and said, "You and I won't do anything with that stuff. I'll keep ten percent for our expenses, and put the rest back." He then began putting the money back into the safe.

"But I thought you said we're giving it to the don?"

"We are, but we've got stuff to do and it's not like I like the idea of carrying around a sack of cash with me." He put the last bundle back into the safe and asked, "Since you've opened it, do you remember what the combination is?"

"Sure." Alicia nodded. "It's 13, 7, 23, and 38."

"Okay, great." Tony closed the safe and put the picture back up on its mount. "After we're done here, I'll call this place in. We'll let Vianello's guys gather what's in the safe and our hands remain clean."

Alicia pulled out one of the black envelopes from her fanny pack, held it up and said, "This is one of the envelopes Luca mentioned he uses to make contact with his brothers in the *Obscura Machinare*. All we need to do is write a phone number on a scrap of paper, seal it in the envelope and dump it in a garbage can that's one block away."

"Wait a minute," Tony frowned. "We're supposed to wait for a call? What good does that do us?"

Alicia grinned. "I have some friends that can help us trace the call."

"Yeah, but what if the call is coming from a cell phone and the guy calling is on the move? What good does that do? Why don't we stake out the garbage can and see who ends up taking the envelope?" Tony asked.

Alicia frowned. "Even if it's a cell phone, there's going to be an account associated with it. We'll know who it is—"

"Not if they're using a burner phone you won't," Tony interjected.

"Oh damn," Alicia felt a wave of embarrassment wash over her. "You're right, I didn't think about that."

"Don't worry about it." Tony scratched the top of Bagel's head. "This is my world we're dealing with. You'll catch on quickly."

"Okay, fine." Alicia nodded as her mind raced to either affirm Tony's idea or come up with an alternative. "The garbage can is on a busy street, but for all we know it's being watched. Anyone dropping off the envelope can't exactly hang around without raising some level of suspicion."

Tony's expression turned pensive and he remained silent for a few seconds. "If this is the only lead we have to my uncle, I don't like how risky it is to just wait for a call and maybe the trace ends up being useless." He pulled out his cell phone and said, "I have an idea. Let me make a call to the don's people." He tilted his head at the hanging image of the Pope and said, "Maybe we can pull a few favors sooner versus later."

Tony put the phone to his ear and Alicia listened to one half of a whispered conversation that made utterly no sense.

"Hey Dino, I got a serious score to kick up."

Alicia strained to hear the other side of the conversation, but to no avail.

"It's about one hundred G's, so don't send any *stunads*."

Alicia's ear bud mistranslated the slang word into "crazy" but having been around her father and his friends for long enough, she knew in context it was Italian slang for someone who was an idiot.

"Yeah, a standard cleanup crew." Tony shook his head as someone on the other end of the line talked. "No, it's portable—about ten pounds or so. Also, do we have any shadows that are reliable? I need to borrow at least one for a thing I'm doing."

Shadow? What could that even mean?

"Yeah, we're still looking. When you talk to the big man, tell him I appreciate the help." Tony looked at his watch and nodded. "We'll wait just inside the building."

As soon as Tony took the phone from his ear, Alicia asked in a hushed tone, "What's going on?"

"Let's get downstairs, some guys are going to be here to pick stuff up in five minutes." Tony motioned for her to follow.

Alicia followed Tony to the front door as she typed up a quick text to Denny and hit "send."

Change of plan. Don't need the wiretap for the moment. Thanks.

As Alicia closed the front door behind her, she asked, "What's the cleanup crew and shadow thing?"

Tony glanced at her as they walked down the hallway. "The cleanup is just to make we don't leave behind any prints. As to the shadows... you'll see soon enough." He gave her wink and said in a terrible cowboy accent, "This isn't my first rodeo, darlin'."

CHAPTER ELEVEN

Alicia's gaze followed a pair of Don Vianello's men as they walked down the hallway toward the stairs. One of them carried a suitcase, while another had a duffle bag slung over his shoulder. It was the cleanup crew.

The front door to the apartment building opened once again, and two short, wiry men with glasses walked into the lobby where Alicia and Tony had been waiting. They both scanned their surroundings and the one with a mustache looked to Tony with a neutral expression. "*Signore*, you needed our services?"

"Giuseppe?" Tony asked.

Mustache shook his head. "I'm Franco." He hitched his thumb to his clean-shaven partner and said, "That's Giuseppe."

Were these the so-called shadows that Tony was talking

about? Both men were dressed in street clothes and to Alicia, they looked like any normal Italian might look. Not intimidatingly large like Tony or some of the other mafiosos she'd met. Dark hair, dark eyes, nothing in particular about either of these men stood out. Very much like a shadow wouldn't want to draw attention to itself. Was that the point?

Tony patted Alicia on the shoulder and spoke to the men in a hushed tone, "Alicia's calling the shots on this." Turning to her, he added, "Tell them what you need and we'll come up with a workable plan."

"Right here, in the open?" Alicia glanced up and down the corridor flanking the building's tiny lobby. "Okay, you're right. We can't waste time." She pulled out one of the black envelopes from her fanny pack, explaining, "There's a dead drop at the Piazza San Marco. This envelope," she held it up, "needs to go in a garbage can beneath the sign for a place called Caffè Florian."

"One moment, *signora*." Giuseppe pulled out his phone and, with a few quick swipes, displayed a map of the vicinity. "Here we are." He scrolled to the famed Piazza San Marco and pointed out, "And here's the café you mentioned. I see it, but the garbage can... ah, there it is. It's nestled among the tables in the plaza. Is this the one?"

Alicia peered at the screen, where, thanks to Google, there were detailed images of tourists seated around numerous tables scattered across the plaza. The garbage can was prominently positioned next to a pillar in front of Caffè

Florian. "It looks right, though I was informed that this particular can has a lid that operates on a hinge."

"A hinge?" Giuseppe echoed, examining the image with a puzzled look. "So, you're saying I need to lift the lid from its base to insert the envelope, rather than simply dropping it in through an opening at the top?"

"That's what I was told," Alicia confirmed with a nod.

Franco nudged Giuseppe. "It's possible that someone is looking out for that specific action. It makes sense, considering only sanitation workers typically mess around with the garbage, and they're uniformed."

"Okay." Giuseppe seemed satisfied with that as a response and glanced up at Alicia. "*Signora*, we can easily do this. I assume you want us to watch who picks up the envelope and follow them?"

"Exactly—"

"Wait a second," Tony cut in, switch to English. "Don't we also want to follow that guy so we can... have a *talk* with him?"

The way Tony said 'talk' suggested an obvious double meaning. Talking could imply a friendly chat, or like the talk Alicia had with Luca. Very different things, and probably all within the realm of possibilities.

The idea of roughing someone up to extract information should have bothered her more than it did, and Alicia knew that this was something she'd have to get right with God over at some point.

Alicia responded in Italian, so the other two could understand. "Tony, yes we need to talk to whoever ends up picking up that envelope but they might very well know what you and I look like. If we suspect that there might be somebody watching that dead drop, us being anywhere in the vicinity during the drop off might make them not come."

Franco cleared his throat and smoothed his mustache. "*Signora*, I have an idea. It is our intent to have Giuseppe go first, and place himself within sight of the garbage can. When he is ready, he will give me a signal and I will come to drop off the envelope as you instructed. I would then just walk away, and Giuseppe will watch and follow." He took off his glasses and handed them to Alicia. "However, if you put these on, you will see what I would have seen. You tell me when to go, and I'll go. Afterwards, you can follow Giuseppe when he's on the move, if you understand what I mean."

Alicia raised her eyebrows in surprise and put on the glasses, realizing they weren't prescription lenses as she had initially assumed. She scanned the room and caught a very faint reflection of herself looking around the room. Turning to Giuseppe, who was watching her intently, she noticed what seemed like a ghostly mirror image of herself in the lenses she wore.

She was observing what Giuseppe saw through his glasses reflected in her own pair. Ingenious.

Giuseppe raised a thumb, eyeing it closely. "This will be my ready sign."

"How far apart can we be for these glasses to still function?"

"Up to one kilometer," they said simultaneously, confirming the impressive range of their neat gadget.

That was a little bit more than half a mile. "We're already closer than that to the plaza."

"Glasses work?" Tony asked. "Alicia, what are you talking about about?"

"I'll explain in a bit." She put her hand on her partner's shoulder and gave it a light squeeze. "Okay guys, I think this will work."

Franco held out his hand. "The envelope, *signora*."

She handed the mustachioed shadow the black envelope, he tucked it away and gave Giuseppe a nod.

The clean-shaven man turned and left the small lobby.

Franco walked closer to Alicia and Tony and whispered, "You keep watch for Giuseppe's signal, but in the meantime, let's talk about what you need to be done once Giuseppe latches onto your target."

"I hate tourists." Giuseppe grumbled into his phone as he sipped his double espresso. He grimaced at the burnt flavor and looked at his upward-pointing thumb.

"She's telling me you're in position. Any questions on what to do with the target?" Franco asked.

"No, I'm good. See you in a bit." Giuseppe hung up and muttered a curse under his breath. He had paid six euros for an espresso that should have cost no more than half that amount, and it tasted like charcoal. Whoever had bought the beans or had been operating the machine didn't know what they were doing.

He took another sip and shuddered.

It was a beautiful day as he sat at one of the tables in the open space of the Piazza San Marco. At least half a dozen languages were being spoken all around him, tourists from other parts of Europe, a Chinese couple, and about half a dozen English-speaking people at a nearby table laughed uproariously, drawing attention to themselves in a manner typical of most Americans.

Not being a fan of tourist areas, this wasn't exactly his idea of a good time, especially given his current task—staring past the crowd of tourists and focusing his attention on a garbage can.

He continued to sip the espresso, despite his dissatisfaction with both the quality and price, he needed the jolt of caffeine while he waited for Franco to make his appearance.

It had only taken him four minutes to walk from the apartment building and as he finished his mental countdown, he spotted Franco enter the Piazza San Marco at the same spot he'd entered from, arriving exactly on time.

His mustachioed partner walked past his table without a glance in his direction. Dodging the occasional tourist or baby stroller, he made a beeline for the garbage can. He pulled up on one end of the lid to no avail, switched sides and the lid tilted upward on its unseen hinge.

He only caught a dark-colored blur as Franco deposited the envelope, lowered the lid, and continued across the Piazza and disappeared from sight.

Giuseppe pulled out his phone and even though it may have looked to others like he was reading something on it, he'd actually started videoing.

Even though he was only in his mid-thirties, he was old enough to appreciate the relatively recent technology advancements. The idea that he could surveil a target while seemingly staring at something in his hand would have seemed impossible just ten years ago.

He hit the "3x" on the touchscreen and the phone zoomed onto the garbage can.

If someone came by, he'd have a record of it, just in case they somehow managed to give him the slip.

To his surprise, only two minutes had elapsed when Giuseppe noticed from out of the corner of his eye someone wearing a street cleaner's uniform.

He had seemingly appeared out of nowhere. Maybe from inside one of the shops?

The man was carrying an empty trash bag as he walked directly toward the garbage can Giuseppe was surveilling.

The target flipped the garbage can's lid up on its hinge, and through the camera image Giuseppe noticed something that made him nod with understanding.

A black box was attached to the underside of the lid, with wires leading from it to the unseen hinge.

It must be some kind of transmitter.

That would explain how the so-called street cleaner had arrived so quickly.

The target grabbed the half-filled bag of garbage and replaced it with the empty bag he'd brought.

Knowing that the Asian girl was seeing what he saw, he finished his espresso and began following the target.

Alicia quickened her pace as she followed Giuseppe through the narrow streets of Venice.

"Do you see him?" Tony asked in a hushed tone as they walked along the busy store-lined streets north of the Piazza San Marco.

"No, but from the image in the glasses I can tell we're about half a minute behind him."

It was a strange sensation for Alicia as she saw the faded image of what Giuseppe was seeing in her borrowed glasses.

All the while, her contact was randomly popping up translations for any text it saw that wasn't in English.

It constantly felt like Alicia was on the verge of visual overload and wondered if there was a way to pause the contact's translation.

Giuseppe stopped suddenly as their target, who was wearing a street cleaner's uniform, looked through the garbage bag he'd been carrying, and pulled out a black envelope.

The street cleaner pocketed the envelope and deposited the half-filled garbage bag into a nearby garbage can

Alicia quickened her pace, passing tiny boutiques and local shops, turned on Salizada San Lio, which was a wider brick-paved street with many of the shops having small awnings that advertised their wares.

This was a pedestrian's city, and probably the first city Alicia had ever been in that mostly didn't have the concept of street cars or taxis. It would have been impossible given the narrow streets and canal system.

She let out a click with her tongue and caught Tony's attention. Alicia pointed ahead and he nodded as they both slowed.

Giuseppe was about one hundred feet ahead of them.

Alicia watched as their hired shadow was waiting on their target. The man had stopped at a small café, talked with someone behind the counter and then was once again was on the move.

The target turned right into a narrow alley and Giuseppe paused for a moment... was he listening for something?

Alicia saw the back of Giuseppe's head as he replaced his glasses with a set of goggles and turned into the narrow alley.

Giuseppe strode down the narrow alley, his gaze lowered as he pressed an old-style flip-phone to his ear.

"Maria, why didn't you tell me this earlier?" he protested vehemently into the inactive phone.

The target had paused at a door, fumbling with his keys.

As Giuseppe sensed the man's glance in his direction, he escalated his loud complaints into the phone. "You know I don't like going to your parents' home for dinner. That means I have to get dressed—yes, I know that!" While continuing his faux conversation, he subtly fingered the tube-like injector in his pocket.

Just as the apartment door began to creak open, Giuseppe lunged at the man, smashing the target's head against the doorframe.

He clamped his hand over the man's mouth and pressed an autoinjector into the side of the man's neck.

With all his strength, Giuseppe only managed to pull them both into the apartment's interior hallway as the target fought back fiercely, almost sending him flying off the man's back.

But then, the paralytic took effect.

Giuseppe felt the fight quickly drain from the man and the target collapsed.

CHAPTER TWELVE

A chill raced down Alicia's spine as she looked down at the unblinking man splayed on the floor. Giuseppe was busily hooking him up to various wires as Franco turned the knobs on what looked to her like an old-school polygraph that likely belonged in a museum. "Is he dead?"

Giuseppe laughed and shook his head. "No, just paralyzed."

Her eyebrows nearly shot up into her hairline. "Really? What did you use to do that?"

"It's something called sux. The dose he has in him will only last a few minutes, and I've got four more injectors I can plug him with."

Alicia nodded, recognizing the name of the drug. It was a shortened version of succinylcholine, a neuromuscular blocker that is often used as a paralytic in anesthesia. More commonly sold in the US as Quelicin. As a former graduate neuro student, she'd learned about various drugs and their effects on human cognition. If there was a drug she'd recommend giving someone so that their mind remained awake but they couldn't move, this would be the one. It was specifically not a sedative, and these shadow guys the don sent clearly knew what they were doing.

This target wouldn't be able to hide some physiological responses to carefully crafted questions.

Very smart.

Realizing that she was working with professionals in the criminal world, pangs of guilt washed over Alicia. She watched the men working on the unnamed target, the empty black envelope lay discarded only a few feet away along with half of the man's clothes.

There was little doubt that Alicia was an active party to the wrong end of the laws at the moment. Working for the Outfit, she had less qualms about twisting things, because she knew that the actions she'd be taking were sanctioned in one way or another. Even if it was wrong, the Outfit would cover her tracks.

Now... not so much. She needed to be careful.

Then again, this guy had likely arranged for Luca to try and assassinate them. Almost certainly, this man was no angel. But did he deserve what was happening? Alicia felt uncertain about the whole thing.

Tony walked back into the small living room where they'd gathered and shook his head. "This apartment is clean as a whistle. There's nothing here to even give us a clue who he is."

"What about his fingerprints?" Alicia asked.

Franco shook his head. "Already tried. I did a quick search of the fingerprint hashes in the Interpol database and there was nothing."

Alicia maintained a neutral expression as she listened to the unassuming man talk, but was impressed with the way he spoke. She'd taken him as a lithe bruiser type of guy, a miniaturized version of Tony, but evidently not. This guy seemed to have some technical background that she wouldn't have expected from a typical street tough.

"He doesn't seem to have a criminal record." Franco continued as he adjusted the knobs on his box-like device. "The eu-LISA folks didn't have his prints on the entry and exit system either, so no recent passport database entries. He's evidently a ghost."

Alicia's gaze swept over the man stretched out on the floor of the sparsely furnished living room.

Giuseppe gently closed the target's unblinking eyes with a brush of his fingers. He looked at Alicia and shrugged. "He can't blink right now."

Alicia nodded, fully aware of the drug's side effects. The paralyzed man appeared to be in his late thirties or early forties, with a puckered scar trailing along his jawline—a likely souvenir from a crudely healed knife wound. "I hate to stereotype, but this guy looks like he's nothing but trouble.

Let's see what I can dig up." She took out her phone and launched her facial recognition app.

The app was one of the goodies Denny had installed on her phone. The way he'd explained it to her was that it leveraged the facial recognition technology inherent to her phone and was able to turn a person's 3D facial image into some stream of bits and bytes. She didn't quite understand some of the computer jargon he'd used, but evidently the app would convert the image into some form of data it would use to search the world's databases for a match.

As Alicia pointed her phone at the unnamed target, Tony asked, "What are you doing?"

"Let's just say my father taught me some tricks..." Alicia responded.

In fact, Dad knew nothing about this stuff, he was somewhat of a luddite, but Denny... she now totally appreciated why her father had someone like Denny in his life.

Her phone beeped and she turned to look at what it was doing just as it began flashing several progress messages on the screen.

Searching Interpol (International Criminal Police Organization):
   complete

Searching Europol (European Union Agency for Law Enforcement Cooperation):

complete

Searching FBI (Federal Bureau of Investigation):
 complete

Searching IOM (International Organization for Migration):
 complete

Searching UNHCR (United Nations High Commissioner for Refugees):
 match found -- Luciano Ferrini, age 35.

"Looks like I've got something. Our friend is named Luciano Ferrini."

Alicia stared wide-eyed at the prompt the application had displayed.

A psychiatric evaluation report has been found. Display?

She motioned for Tony to come over and showed her phone's screen to him.

"Are you going to press 'yes' or am I?" Tony asked.

She pressed the "yes" option and the app filled the hand-held display with the first page of the report.

Alicia and Tony both leaned closer to her phone's tiny screen as she began slowly scrolling through the extensive report, which seemed to read like a cross between a patient's medical chart and academic record.

Psychiatric Evaluation: Luciano Ferrini

Patient ID: LF-1985
    Age of Evaluation: 17
    Evaluator: Dr. Alessandro Vitale, State Psychiatrist
    Location: Venice, Italy

Luciano Ferrini presents a complex psychological profile characterized by high intelligence and adaptability, contrasted with a propensity for manipulative and antisocial behaviors. Raised in an orphanage following the death of his mother during childbirth and with an unknown father, Luciano's early life was marked by instability and a lack of familial bonds. This environment, while providing basic needs, failed to offer the emotional support crucial for healthy psychological development.

Behavioral Observations:

Luciano has demonstrated a remarkable ability to influence and manipulate those around him, often to his benefit. Despite a troubled youth filled with minor criminal activities, he exhibits a charm and charisma that endear him to both peers and authority figures, allowing him to often evade the full consequences of his actions.

Criminal History as a Child:

Documented incidents of theft, vandalism, and fraud. It is noteworthy that Luciano's record abruptly becomes unblemished upon reaching adulthood, suggesting a calculated effort to conceal activities or a shift in tactics to avoid detection.

Psychological Assessment:

Tests indicate high cognitive function but reveal concerning patterns consistent with antisocial personality traits. Luciano displays a lack of empathy, difficulty forming genuine emotional connections, and a pragmatic view of morality tailored to his immediate needs.

Recommendations:

Given Luciano's intelligence and potential for rehabilitation, a structured environment with emphasis on ethical development and social integration is recommended. Close monitoring and continued psychological support are imperative to mitigate the risk of further antisocial behavior.

Edited Notes by State Members:

Update 1 [Patient Age: 22]:
   Note by Dr. Carla Rossi, State Psychologist:
   Luciano Ferrini was presumed dead following a boating accident. Legal death declared. Psychological support and monitoring were consequently terminated.

Update 2 [Patient Age: 27]:
   Note by Inspector Marco Romano, Venice Police Department:
   Rumors persist in the criminal underworld of a figure resembling Ferrini's description, suggesting he may have faked his death. Investigation ongoing; no substantial evidence found.

Update 3 [Patient Age: 32]:
   Note by Agent Sofia Ricci, Italian Intelligence Service:
   Intelligence suggests Luciano Ferrini is alive, operating under an assumed identity in Rome. Activities appear to have a focus on the exfiltration of ancient artifacts from the area, with biometric detection having occurred several times within the borders of

Vatican City. Efforts to gather concrete evidence are in progress. Recommend re-opening psychological profile to anticipate behaviors and potential motivations.

Update 4 [Current Date]:
Note by Dr. Giovanni De Luca, State Psychologist:
An alert has been given by the Tourism and Antiquities Police (TAP) out of Egypt for a man matching Luciano's biometric signature. The man is suspected of murdering two shopkeepers in Khan El-Khalili. Given recent developments, it is advised that Luciano's file be updated to reflect his presumed activities and current psychological state. The transformation from a troubled youth to a figure of significant danger warrants a reassessment of initial recommendations and poses significant challenges for intervention strategies.

"That's a lot to digest." Tony's nostrils flared as he looked down at the paralyzed man.

Alicia crouched and looked over at Franco. "Is your box ready to go?"

He nodded as Giuseppe sat cross-legged next to the man's head. "Just remember, the questions need to be phrased so that I can detect deception. Make what you say a true or false statement."

"Can he hear me?" Alicia asked.

Franco pointed to one of the meters whose signal seemed

to bounce somewhat erratically. "Of course. I'll give you this sign," he gave her a thumbs up, "if he agrees. And this sign," he switched to a thumbs down position, "if he doesn't agree."

With an autoinjector laying on the floor in front of him, Giuseppe leaned forward and tapped on a spot near Luciano's eyebrow.

It was the same spot that had the supraorbital nerve running across it. It seemed like the enigmatic Italian knew that tapping it would have normally caused the blink reflex to kick in, but nothing had happened. A reasonable test to see if the paralytic was still doing its thing.

Alicia sat cross-legged next to Luciano and said, "Your name is Luciano Ferrini."

From her periphery she saw Franco give a thumbs-up.

Relief washed over Alicia at the confirmation that the data her app had dug up was evidently accurate.

Bagel climbed out of his sling, sat next to her and put a paw on her knee as if trying to encourage her.

She gave the cat a scratch on the top of his head as her mind raced, trying to formulate the right questions to ask, all the while knowing that time was of the essence. She took a deep breath, let it out slowly and felt a blanket of calm envelop her. Focused on her target, Alicia asked the first critical question:

"You gave Luca Guani a task recently."

A heavy silence, reminiscent of a tomb, hung in the room

for a few tense seconds before Franco signaled with a thumbs-up.

"You meant for him to kill two people."

Several seconds elapsed and she glanced at Franco who shook his head and made a rolling motion with his hand.

"You sent Luca to stop two people from doing something."

Thumbs-up. Stop *us* from what? Finding Tony's uncle?

"You have never met Father Montelaro."

Thumbs-down.

Alicia inhaled deeply, struggling to contain her excitement. This man knew Tony's uncle!

She pressed on, maintaining a steady voice, "You know nothing about Father Montelaro's current location."

Thumbs-down.

Alicia and Tony exchanged excited glances.

"You sent Father Montelaro somewhere outside of Venice."

Thumbs-up.

"You sent other people to accompany Father Montelaro."

Again, thumbs-up.

Tony pulled out his cellphone and began typing something on it as Alicia pressed her lips together, worrying about his uncle's situation.

The priest could be held hostage, but if so, where? The world was a pretty big place outside of Venice.

Her mind was racing as she pondered what type of true or false questions she could ask that would get her the answers she needed when Tony leaned over and show her his phone.

"Didn't the Russian bookseller say something about Egypt?"

Alicia shot Tony a thumbs-up and nodded as she replayed in her mind the conversation. The Russian had read from a book the phrase, *"In the land where the river's gift meets the sun's eternal gaze, beneath the guardian palm's shade, the hidden words shall find sanctuary."*

The same words that had been written on that scrap of parchment Tony's uncle had placed in that book.

And then the bookseller continued reading beyond what the scrap had spelled out, *"In the shadow of the Great Library's remnants, where the Nile's waters caress the city's edge, seek the sacred sigil carved into the stones of the temple ruins. There, you may seek the truth. Amidst the cradle of wisdom, the hidden words shall be revealed."*

The reference to the Nile River, and the Russian had said that the guardian palm referred to the Egyptian date palm...

Giuseppe tapped on Luciano's eyebrow, it flickered, and the so-called shadow plunged an autoinjector into the man's neck.

Alicia looked over at Giuseppe as he pulled out another of the injectors.

He gave her a nod and motioned for her to go on.

Focusing back on Luciano, she asked, "Father Montelaro was sent to Egypt."

Alicia looked over at Franco who stared at the panel of dials on the wire-laden box.

It took a few seconds before the man nodded and tossed her a thumbs-up.

Tony pumped his fist in the air and held a determined expression.

The priest was in Egypt... with people from this *Obscura Machinare*—oh wait, was that really who they were dealing with?

"The *Obscura Machinare* is holding Father Montelaro prisoner."

Alicia looked expectantly at Franco for a few long seconds and he made a so-so hand motion and shrugged.

A maybe?

"The *Obscura Machinare* is with Father Montelaro."

Thumbs-up.

Alicia nodded. Okay, that made sense, but was he a prisoner or not?

"Father Montelaro is free to return to the Vatican whenever he wants."

Thumbs-down.

Alicia and Tony both glanced at each other with grim expressions.

This was very ominous. How were they going to find him? If he wasn't free to go, it likely meant he wasn't wandering around in the public. If only...

"There are records of Father Montelaro's travel destination in this apartment."

Alicia prayed to all that was holy that—thumbs-up. A large smile bloomed on her face.

"The records are hidden."

Thumbs-up.

Alicia pursed her lips as she pondered where they might be.

"It is in a safe."

Thumbs-up.

Alicia pulled out her phone and typed up the question, *"Did you see a safe anywhere?"* She showed it to Tony and the other two.

They all shook their head.

Alicia panned her gaze across the living room. "The safe is in the living room."

Thumbs-down.

"The safe is in the bedroom."

Thumbs-up.

Tony hopped up from the floor and bolted for the bedroom.

Something crashed to the floor with a dull cracking sound, it didn't sound like glass shattering, maybe ceramic?

Something heavy scraped across the floor.

The sound repeated several times before she heard Tony laugh.

More loud, heavy scraping and just as Alicia was about to get up to go look, Tony came back and showed her a picture.

It looked like a safe had been hidden behind a tall set of dresser drawers, but it didn't look like any safe she'd ever seen. The metal square embedded in the wall had no dial, and no obvious handle to pull it open. Was it even a safe?

Alicia looked at the small pile of items that had been stripped from Luciano. She grabbed the key ring and shook her head. They all looked like regular keys. She motioned for Tony to lean down and whispered, "There's no key hole anywhere?"

Tony shook his head.

She turned back to Luciano. "The key to the safe is hidden in the apartment."

Thumbs-up.

She held his key ring, which only had three keys on it. "The key is on your key ring."

Thumbs-down.

"The key is in the living room."

Thumbs-down.

"The key is in the bedroom."

Thumbs-down.

Alicia frowned. "The key is in the kitchen."

Thumbs-up.

Tony strode toward the small alcove attached to the living room that served as a kitchenette.

He started rifling through the drawers, each time upending their contents onto the floor with a resounding clatter of silverware.

Reaching the last drawer, he paused for a moment before

extracting a small stack of papers and spreading them out on the counter. Among what looked like a collection of assorted newspaper clippings, Tony's expression brightened as he picked up a small chain, akin to those used for military dog tags. Dangling from it was something that looked like a single-button garage door opener.

Alicia turned back to Luciano and said, "The safe is opened with a remote control."

It took a few seconds but Franco nodded, tossing her a thumbs-up.

Alicia sprang to her feet as Tony tossed the remote her way.

She approached the bedroom, her eyes widening at the disarray left in the wake of 'Hurricane Tony,' who had managed to turn the room upside down in the mere moments he'd searched it.

Entering the bedroom with her, Tony watched as she pressed the remote's button. They were greeted by the sound of the safe clicking open, its door swinging wide with an inviting yawn.

Inside the safe Alicia spotted the butts of several handguns, at least a dozen magazines, boxes of ammunition, some stacks of cash and a notebook.

Alicia retrieved the notebook and began poring over its contents while Tony pocketed a few bundles of cash and began emptying the safe.

Her brows furrowed as she began flipping through the pages of handwritten notes.

It seemed to be a log of recent transactions having to do with ancient artifacts.

Euphronios Krater – ~515 BC – ~~sold,~~ repatriated - VG
  Intact fresco of Herculaneum – 79 AD – sold, customer R32
  Cerveteri Sarcophagus #1 – ~520 BC – sold, customer G13
  Cerveteri Sarcophagus #2 – ~520 BC – sold, customer W8
  Cerveteri Sarcophagus #3 – ~520 BC – ~~sold,~~ repatriated - VG

"Lookie here." Tony pulled out a red passport, flipped it open and shook his head in frustration. He showed it to her, displaying his uncle's picture, and said, "Why the hell would these bastards take an old man's passport?"

"I have no idea." Alicia felt a rising sense of frustration. "This book seems to be a log of ancient artifacts that this guy either sold or I'm guessing maybe retrieved for—"

"Damn it!" Franco yelled from the other room.

Alicia's heart pounded as she bolted out of the bedroom, the moment of silence was broken only by a loud yowl from Bagel as he paced back and forth, his tail twitching spasmodically. The scene that unfolded before her was one she could never have prepared for. There, sprawled across the cold, unforgiving floor of the living room, lay Luciano, his chest still, his face an ashen mask. Franco and Giuseppe hovered over him; determination etched into every line of their faces as they administered CPR.

"Luciano!" Alicia's voice cracked as she stumbled forward, her mind racing with the gravity of the situation. The man who had been the key to unraveling a web of deception and danger now lay motionless.

Franco, with his hands positioned over Luciano's sternum, pressed down rhythmically, counting under his breath, his brow furrowed in concentration. Giuseppe, meanwhile, tilted Luciano's head back, trying to clear his airway, his eyes darting to Alicia as she knelt beside them, her hands trembling.

"What happened?" Alicia's voice was barely a whisper, fear gripping her throat.

"He stopped breathing," Giuseppe responded, his voice strained. "The paralytic... I suppose maybe it was too much for him."

Alicia's gaze fixed on Luciano's still form. The paralytic—a calculated risk that had spiraled into their worst nightmare. They had believed they could control the situation, which didn't exactly work out as planned. The weight of the miscalculation bore down on her.

Franco paused, his hands stilling as he checked for a pulse, the seconds stretching into eternity. Alicia held her breath, hoping against hope for a miracle that would snatch Luciano back from the brink. He was certainly not a good person, but she didn't need his death on her conscience.

"Anything?" she asked, her voice a thread of hope in the thick air of despair.

Franco shook his head, the finality in his gesture a blow

that knocked the wind out of her. "I'm sorry, *signora*. He's gone."

The words hung between them, heavy and irrevocable. In that moment, the room seemed to close in, the walls bearing witness to the tragic end of a man whose life was almost inevitably going to end in a bad way—but she hadn't ever intended to be a party to his demise.

Alicia closed her eyes, a silent prayer escaping her lips for the soul, good or evil, they had just lost. As she opened her eyes and met the gazes of Franco and Giuseppe, a new resolve hardened within her.

Alicia's mind was a whirlwind of confusion as she re-entered the bedroom, the weight of a person's death pressing down on her like a physical force. The bedroom now felt like the epicenter of a mystery that stretched across continents.

Whatever they had in this apartment was the only thread they had to finding Tony's uncle.

The safe, left gaping open, was a testament to the secrets it had relinquished: on the bed were handguns and ammunition, stacks of money, a log book that hinted at a clandestine network dealing in ancient artifacts, and, most damning of all, Father Montelaro's passport.

These bastards had taken the man, evidently to Egypt, but even that wasn't certain.

Her fingers trembled as she picked up Father Montelaro's passport, the reality of the situation sinking in. Luciano was deeply entangled in this web; he had dispatched an assassin after her and Tony, and now, the discovery of the priest's passport in his safe pointed to a more ominous plot. The mention of Egypt in connection with Father Montelaro's recent movements only added layers to the mystery. What was he doing in Egypt? And why was his passport hidden away in Luciano's safe?

Turning her attention back to the log book, Alicia flipped through the pages with growing urgency. The list of artifacts, some sold, others repatriated to VG, was extensive. "VG... what the hell is that?" The initials meant nothing to her, a frustrating unknown in her quest for answers.

It was Tony, who had been quietly observing over her shoulder, who broke the silence. "VG stands for Villa Giulia," he said, his voice low. "The National Etruscan Museum in Rome."

Alicia looked up at him, startled. "You're sure?"

Tony nodded, a grim expression on his face. "Positive. My family has been a patron of museums for years. It's a thing for us Montelaros. Villa Giulia houses one of the most extensive collections of Etruscan artifacts. If these items were destined for or came from there, then this..." He gestured to the log book, "...is bigger than we thought. The items would be practically priceless."

Alicia delved deeper into the notebook. Her fingers traced the edges of the pages as she flipped through the book, each entry pulling her deeper into a world shadowed by the enigmatic *Obscura Machinare*.

She continued flipping through the pages of handwritten notes desperately looking for anything that would lead her to finding Tony's uncle when suddenly a particular entry caught her eye— "A lost gospel"

Lost Gospel – date unknown – pending, Fr. Montelaro

A chill went down Alicia's spine as she saw the priest's name.

This told her nothing but everything at the same time. It directly linked Tony's uncle with something the Obscura Machinare cared deeply about. Almost certainly it meant that the priest knew something about an item that to these people was worth a lot of money.

What did "Lost Gospel" even mean? Was it a piece of art? It couldn't actually be referring to an actual gospel... a missing part of the bible? Impossible. Or was it?

She continued scanning the pages and found herself in a new section of the logbook. This seemed to be enumerating various assignments.

It was a roster of names, all unmistakably Italian, each paired with an ancient artifact designated for retrieval. The methodical list painted a vivid picture of a network sprawling in its reach and ambition. Alicia's pulse quickened as she realized she was peering into the operational heart of the *Obscura Machinare.*

But it was one entry, in particular, that drew Alicia's focus—a mission involving the "Lost Gospel." Unlike the others, this entry listed two names, and instead of the task of "retrieval" both men were tasked with an unusual role: "escort."

Tony, who'd been staring over her shoulder at the same logbook, suddenly pointed at the bottom of the page. "There it is! They chartered a goddamned boat."

Her finger traced the lines that detailed their assignment further. It mentioned a boat, chartered specifically for this mission, set to leave Venice and make its way to Egypt. "It looks like Port Said is where they went to."

"Do you know where that is?" Tony asked.

"It's in Northern Egypt along the Mediterranean." Alicia carried a rough mental image of many parts of the world, including Northern Africa. "It's a main port on the north end of the Suez Canal. From there, you can get to just about anywhere you need to." She turned to Tony and said, "The lost gospel... this sounds like the kind of thing that a historian type might give his—"

"His right arm for," Tony interjected and shook his head. "I know what you're thinking. You're thinking he's just gone rogue and wants to relive his past by taking one last adventure, and maybe the folks at the Vatican told him 'no.'"

"That's not what I was thinking, but it's certainly possible. It's not like your uncle's boss was particularly forthcoming with helpful information. I don't think it matters why he's there or what motivated him." She tapped on the logbook and said, "These people are up to no good, these *Obscura Machinare* types. Even if they're helping him now, I don't think your uncle realizes what kind of people he's involved with. If they find whatever it is that they're looking for, they almost certainly intend to profit, and probably have a buyer in mind already. I mean, imagine if it's some lost artwork by Da Vinci, or even something from the earliest times of Christianity. Can you imagine how much money a holy artifact would bring to the right buyer?"

"My uncle would rather die than ever let a holy artifact—"

"Exactly. And that's why I don't care why your uncle is with these people." Alicia put her hand on Tony's shoulder and gave it a squeeze. "We've got two named escorts, a priest in a foreign country with no travel documents, and a date of arrival at Port Said that's only five days ago. It's a major commercial port with lots of traffic and likely lots of cameras. I'll pull some strings and see if I can get access to any of the security footage from the port."

Tony pulled out his phone and put it to his ear, "I'll book us a flight into Cairo," he pointed in the direction of the living room and said, "I'll also make sure we get some cleaners coming to take care of things."

Alicia's mind drifted back to the dead body in the living room and felt a jittery mix of emotions. She was undoubtedly mixed up with the death of someone, yet the man had sent a killer after them. Pulling in a deep breath, she let it out slowly and retrieved her phone.

She had some of her own phone calls to make.

CHAPTER
THIRTEEN

Alicia gripped the arms of her first-class seat as the plane's landing gear hit the runway with a reassuring thud, signaling their arrival in Cairo. The cabin erupted in the soft dings of the seatbelt sign turning off.

She turned her phone on and it immediately buzzed with a received message.

Still working on it... making headway. Will get back to you with everything as soon as I'm done.
-D

Denny's text had been sent nearly an hour ago. "Making headway" was a good sign, and she silently prayed that it turned into something actionable.

Bagel meowed from within his cat carrier, located under the seat in front of her.

"I agree, it wasn't too bad of a flight," Alicia said as she unbuckled her seatbelt, grabbed the carrier and met Tony in the aisle as he retrieved their carry-on.

Alicia grabbed her walking stick from the overhead compartment, its etched grip feeling very comfortable in her hand. Despite assurances from the don's weaponsmith, she was still surprised that it had managed to get through the airport security X-ray, knowing that there was a blade embedded within it.

She opened the cat carrier, and Bagel emerged, his golden eyes blinking up at her and the others assembling in the aisle. He hopped onto her seat and stretched languidly as she adjusted his travel sling so it rested against her stomach. He then slipped into his sling, curled up into a furry ball, and she felt the vibrations from him purring.

"Did you nap at all?" Tony asked.

"I didn't expect to, but I slept like a baby." She'd rarely ever been more comfortable flying, and since Tony had 'liberated' the funds for their tickets from Luciano's safe, it was a luxury she didn't feel too guilty over.

It took only a few moments for airplane doors to open and Alicia, Tony, and Bagel joined the queue shuffling towards the customs checkpoint of Cairo International Airport. The atmosphere was charged with the impatience and anticipation of international arrivals, eager to step into the embrace of the ancient city.

Alicia had never been here before, so the sights and sounds were interesting. She recognized the snatches of various languages being spoken as her earbud did its best to translate from the fragments of Arabic and French she was hearing.

As they neared customs, Alicia felt Tony's tension, his eyes constantly surveying their surroundings, alert for anything out of place. She glanced at him and asked, "Ever been here?"

"Nope." He shook his head. "Italy and the good ole U S of A is about it. You don't by chance speak Arabic, do you?"

Alicia grinned. "I understand it." She really didn't, but Tony didn't need to know that. "And nowadays your phone can automatically translate lots of things if we need to. I wouldn't worry too much about it."

As they approached a customs officer, Alicia reached into her fanny pack, her fingers brushing against the veterinarian-prepared documents for Bagel, who was probably going to charm his way through the Egyptian bureaucracy.

"Purpose of your visit?" the customs officer asked in accented English, his face an impassive mask as he scanned her passport.

"Tourism," Alicia replied with a confident smile, the lie smooth on her tongue.

The officer's gaze then fell to the cat peering out from the sling, his golden eyes bright and curious. "And the animal?" he inquired, reaching for the papers Alicia handed over.

"A companion pet," she said. Bagel, sensing the scrutiny, did what he did best—charming. He let out a soft meow, tilting his head as if understanding exactly what was needed in that particular situation. The officer, perhaps a cat lover himself, couldn't help but crack a smile, his professional demeanor slipping for a brief moment as he handed back the documents.

"All seems in order," he conceded, marking her entry with a decisive stamp. "Welcome to Egypt."

She nodded, stepped forward and waited for Tony to repeat the process, and they passed through customs, stepping into the arrival hall where the sounds and smells of Cairo enveloped them—a mix of diesel and jasmine, of dust and the distant hint of the Nile. The airport was a gateway to finding Tony's missing uncle.

Alicia's phone buzzed once more.

"Tony, one second." Alicia paused as she retrieved her phone. Her eyes narrowed as she read Denny's message. His words appeared on the screen, stark and urgent:

I combed through the Port Said dock footage.

In the Port Said Marina, at Dock A, a forty-four foot trawler arrived at 0400 under the cover of night.

Security cameras caught sight of three people disembarking from the boat at 0400. They rushed from the marina, one person clearly slower than the others, and I managed to capture an image, included below, of all three men as they passed near one of the security cameras. I enhanced it and am fairly certain the man in the middle is Father Montelaro.

Alicia stared at the image and knew Denny was right. "Looks like one of my folks dug up an image from the Port Said Marina."

She showed Tony the picture and he cursed under his breath. "I'll make these bastards pay." He clenched his fists and his knuckles made a popping sound. "What else did *your people* dig up?"

At this point, there was no hiding the fact that Alicia was using third party helpers. They both continued reading Denny's message.

They didn't linger. Footage ends at the edge of the marina. Unfortunately, the security cameras at the port are either offline or otherwise out of service.

It wouldn't surprise you to hear that all three of them bypassed customs, because the port customs office cameras were working and nothing resembling our guys show up there.

I ran a trace on the two names you gave me.

I found their birth records, I can tell you where they live, their education, all that normal stuff, but it seems like these guys are purposefully making themselves hard to track.

Neither Stefano Moretti or Marco Rossi seems to have credit cards. They both have bank accounts in UniCredit, which is a large multi-national bank based out of Italy, but neither have withdrawn money in over a month, and that withdrawal was for nearly 5,000 euros each out of the San Marco branch in Venice.

That's why it took me a bit longer than usual to get back to you. I had to expand my search to their family and see what kind of call records I could find.

Luckily, I managed to hit upon something that you might find interesting. Two days back, Marco Rossi's mother, who lives in Manhattan, got a call. The Utah Data Center had a full transcript of the call, and after I waded through it all, it was nothing other than a son calling his ailing elderly mother to check on her and she managed to keep him on the phone long enough for a solid trace to occur.

The call originated in Alexandria, Egypt. It came from a residential block of apartments on the west side of the city, and even though the phone systems over there are seemingly from the stone age, I managed to triangulate which apartment it came from.

Next text will contain the transcript I pulled from the UDC, the originating address, and the name of the current renter.

Hopefully this helps. Let me know if you need anything else.
- D.

. . .

Alicia clicked on the next text, which at the top had the originating phone number and address. She looked over at Tony and said, "I guess we have our destination. Alexandria is about three hours west of here." Alicia pointed to one of the signs in the distance, the Arabic automatically translated in her contact lens and said, "There's a place where they have rental cars. How about we rent a car and on the way, I'll see if I can do a bit of research on the target address. It's not like we can reasonably expect to just knock on the door and say 'hello, where's my uncle?' to these guys."

"You want to bet?" Tony growled. "That's fine, and while you're at it, we'll need to deposit our stuff somewhere and have a home base of sorts. I'm feeling pretty naked without a piece on me."

Alicia sympathized with Tony's sentiment. It felt weird not having a gun on her somewhere. She held up her walking stick and joked, "Don't worry, I've got this, if things go south, I'll just throw it at them."

"You're not fooling anyone." Tony chuckled and shook his head. "I know what you can do with a bo stick, I've seen it a dozen times before. I'll feel a bit better if I can get my hands on something, anything."

"I understand, we'll see." Alicia led them to the queue in front of an Avis rental car counter and whispered, "I'd feel better with you being armed as well, but first, let's get ourselves closer to where we need to be."

Alicia took a deep breath, the air filled with the rich scents of spices and the smoky allure of charred meats, as she immersed herself in the boisterous energy of commerce that animated one of Alexandria's vibrant bazaars in the waning afternoon light.

She followed Tony as he wound his way through the marketplace, the sights and sounds were all very far removed from her own experiences in the Far East. The sun beat down mercilessly, casting a golden hue over the sea of stalls, each brimming with treasures and trinkets. A host of things to distract the tourists, but this too was where the locals shopped, as they likely had since the Roman era and probably even before that.

Tony was navigating the foreign landscape with a sense of purpose. His eyes, sharp and calculating, he made his way to a stall displaying all variety of forged items. His gaze settled on a set of knives, their blades gleaming under the makeshift lighting of the stall.

The narrow shop was a trove of shimmering steel, each blade a silent sentinel awaiting a worthy hand. Amid the array of weapons, a quartet of knives demanded Tony's attention.

The mobster looked across the table at the shopkeeper, who was a short man whose thick, muscular forearms reminded Alicia of the exaggerated arms of the cartoon version of Popeye.

Tony pointed down at the blades in front of him and asked in English, "May I pick one up?"

"Of course, my friend." The shopkeeper spoke with a warm Middle Eastern accent. "My blades are of top quality, that I can assure you."

Alicia approached the display and asked, "Did you forge these yourself?"

"Of course. I'm one of the last masters of hand-forged metalwork you'll find in all of Alexandria."

The blades were artworks, rippling with the distinctive Damascus patterns that spoke of skilled craftsmanship. The shopkeeper watched, a flicker of pride in his eyes, as Alicia looked over the display.

Tony nodded as he looked at the dagger in his hand from all angles. "Impressive."

"These look nice," Alicia pointed at the identical copies of what Tony was looking at, her voice a blend of admiration and skepticism. "But true Damascus steel isn't just skin-deep. May I?"

The shopkeeper nodded, a silent assent to the unspoken challenge.

Having spent a lot of time with her father at the forge at her grandmother's farm, he'd taught her a lot about forging and metallurgy. Alicia drew her fingernail across the flat of the metal, her gesture both delicate and probing. A true Damascus blade would show layered construction even at the edge, not just a superficial façade to fool the tourists. The shopkeeper held his breath as her nail came away clean, the surface unmarred, revealing the integrity of the metalwork.

"What's the carbon content?" she inquired, eyes not leaving the blade. "And the mix of metals? There should be a balance of toughness and flexibility."

The shopkeeper cleared his throat, stepping closer. "I used a blend of 1095 and 15N20 high carbon steels, folded over a thousand times for that pattern. It should prove to be incomparably resilient and maintain a keen edge."

Alicia nodded, approvingly, her fingers tracing the undulating patterns where the different metals married into a single, harmonious whole. Her eyes then shifted to the hilt. "And this? It feels like it could be walnut wood, but in this climate..."

"Ah, you have a good eye," the shopkeeper replied. "It is walnut, but treated with resins to resist moisture and warping. And here," he said, pointing to a subtle inlay, "is camel bone, dyed and polished."

"Young woman, you seem to know your way around blades." He handed Alicia a piece of softwood. "Test the grip, see how it feels when you carve into the wood. You'll feel the balance and the bite of the edge."

Alicia clasped the handle, feeling the natural fit of the knife in her hand. She brought the blade to the wood, and it bit into the grain as if slicing through water, leaving a smooth, clean groove. It took all of her self-control to not show what she was thinking. Just how well this blade cut and felt in her hand. She *needed* this blade.

"Impressed yet?" Tony asked, his voice carrying a playful edge.

She gave him a half-smile, "It's the real deal."

Tony turned to the shopkeeper, "How much?"

The shopkeeper began with a price that would have made a pharaoh blink.

Alicia watched as Tony began haggling with the shopkeeper, and she was shocked at the skill and dramatic flair the mobster exhibited as he got into the negotiating process.

Tony balked at the price, began walking away, to Alicia's dismay, but the shopkeeper called him back, and the two went through several rounds—a theatrical dance of negotiation, which resulted in the price plummeting.

"For quality, I'm willing to pay," Tony conceded, but his tone brokered no further attempts by the shopkeeper at inflating the price. "But let's not pretend we're at the Khan El-Khalili."

Alicia's brows furrowed—Khan El-Khalili—what in the world was that?

Numbers tumbled and egos parried until, at last, an agreement was struck. Four blades, two for each of them, at a price that made both the shopkeeper and Tony feign disappointment—a sure sign of a fair deal in the bazaar's unspoken rules.

The shopkeeper included a simple sheath for each of the

blades and Alicia and Tony left the shop with their new purchases.

She looked over at Tony and asked, "What in the world is Khan El-Khalili?"

Tony waved dismissively. "Ah, that's a place I looked up on my phone when I knew we were going to Cairo. It's supposed to be a famous bazaar where there's a bunch of goldsmiths. I thought it might be nice to visit if we get a chance, I've got a wife and kids to buy souvenirs for."

Alicia laughed and shook her head. "That was some masterful haggling, my friend. I'm impressed."

"Well, there's a leather shop not too far away, I'm sure we can get something that's the equivalent of a shoulder holster or something to hold our new toys."

Alicia looked to the west as the shadows lengthened and said, "We probably only have another hour or two until sunset. Let's finish up here and get back to the hotel so we can plan our next steps."

CHAPTER
FOURTEEN

Under the cloak of an unusually dark Egyptian night, Alicia and Tony found themselves in the silent, deserted streets of old Alexandria. Bagel had balked at the idea of being left behind at the hotel and was done with being carried around, at least for the moment. He walked alongside the two of them, his tail held up high as the group approached their destination.

The street lamp at the corner of the block, where their target's apartment building loomed, was conveniently out, casting the area into deeper shadows. The city that buzzed with life during the day had transformed into a silent, foreboding maze.

Having already scouted the area during the day, Alicia and Tony had strategized a solid plan that she hoped would go off without a hitch.

The apartment, located on the second floor of a decrepit building, showed signs of neglect, with its façade pockmarked with gaps between bricks—a clear indicator of decay. Alicia was sure that if this building was in the US, it would have been demolished long ago. But this building was no different than many of the other buildings in the area, they all seemed to be actively falling apart as evidenced by the crunch of mortar underfoot as they walked alongside the base of the building. The entire structure of the three-story building seemed to be held together with baling wire and miracles.

Their mission was clear yet perilous: to infiltrate the building undetected, overpower any resistance, and rescue Tony's uncle from his so-called escorts. The air was thick with tension as they approached the darkened entrance of the building, the weight of their task pressing heavily upon them.

With Alicia leading the way, they stepped inside the building, the eerie quiet within the structure enveloped them. It was as if the building itself was holding its breath, awaiting the unfolding drama. She turned to Tony and motioned from her eyes toward the stairs. He nodded and with her better than average ability to navigate through darkness, led them into the darkened stairwell and emerged on the second floor.

The hallway was surprisingly well lit, and as she led them toward the apartment, she jabbed her walking stick at each light as she passed it, the bulb shattering with a dull pop, plunging the corridor into an ever-deepening darkness.

Tony put his hand lightly on her shoulder and whispered, "It's dark-dark in here, can you see where you're going?"

"I'm good." She returned the whisper. "About twenty paces forward."

They moved unseen, their steps silent on the worn carpet.

Alicia watched as Bagel confidently strode ahead, somehow knowing which apartment it was, and as she caught up with the furball, she confirmed it was in fact the right apartment.

She heard a faint sound of a television or radio seeping through the crack under the door—a sign of life in the otherwise ghostly silence. Alicia retrieved her lockpicking tools from her fanny pack, and with deft fingers worked quickly, not needing to see what she was doing, she picked the rudimentary lock in less time than it took for her to put the lockpick set back where she'd retrieved it from.

Tony was crouching next to the door, his eyes wide, trying to gather any hint of light from the darkened hallway.

She leaned close and whispered. "Ready?"

He drew a knife from the shoulder harness he wore hidden under his shirt and nodded.

Alicia tightened her grip on the heavy walking stick and with a soft click, the door swung open, revealing the unsuspecting occupants.

They both rushed in, the scene inside was far from what they'd anticipated.

Instead of a den of villains with an imprisoned priest, they stumbled upon a young woman and an unfamiliar man in a compromising situation on the living room sofa.

The man jumped up from the sofa, and before confusion could take root, Alicia acted with swift precision, using her walking stick to sweep the man's legs out from under him.

His head smashed onto the ground with a loud thud, knocking him unconscious.

Tony rushed to the sofa faster than Alicia would have imagined possible for a man his size, held the knife against the half-naked woman's throat and signaled for silence.

The woman stared wide-eyed at Tony and nodded, not uttering even a peep as she tried to cover the lower half of her naked body.

Alicia drew her own knife, and searched the rest of the tiny apartment, confirming that they were alone.

She walked toward the sofa and motioned Tony away. "Are you Fatma?"

The woman nodded; her eyes focused on the knife in Alicia's right hand. "I'm sorry, I don't know what I did." The woman spoke English with a strong but understandable accent. "Whatever it was, I'll never—"

"Get dressed." Alicia cut her off and snapped her fingers, pointing at the woman's discarded undergarments lying on the floor. "We need to talk."

The flickering blue light of the old television was the only light in the cramped apartment, casting long shadows over the tense scene within. Alicia stood firm; her posture unyielding as she locked eyes with the woman seated before her. The air was thick with the tension of unspoken threats and recent violence, underscored by the presence of a large stranger hovering over the unconscious man slumped on the floor.

"Marco Rossi," Alicia began, her voice low and steady, "When was he last here?"

The woman, a mix of defiance and fear in her eyes, hesitated. "A couple of nights ago," she admitted reluctantly, "Just for the night, like always."

"And how does he contact you?" Alicia pressed, every word sharp and calculated.

"A call," the woman replied, a tremor in her voice betraying her composure. "He calls me."

Bagel yowled and let out a hiss as the still-unconscious man groaned.

Alicia's eyes narrowed, "Do you have his number?"

There was a pause, a flicker of calculation behind the woman's eyes before she nodded slowly. "It's on my phone." She glanced at the small table in front of the TV.

Without a word, Tony picked up the phone, brought it over to her and said, "Show it to her."

With trembling hands she unlocked the phone, brought up the contacts app and showed the entry for someone named "Marco."

Alicia noticed the "39" country code, the correct value for dialing any number in Italy. She wouldn't need to write it down, just seeing the phone number was enough for it to be engrained in Alicia's mind. She nodded and said, "Delete his number."

The woman hesitated for a second and then deleted the contact, showing both Alicia and Tony that she'd done as asked. Tony dropped a few one-hundred-euro bills into her lap. "That's for cooperating so nicely with us."

He dropped a few more bills in her lap and tilted his head in the unconscious man's direction, "This is for any inconvenience caused by our interruption." Tony crouched down so he was eye-to-eye with the woman, and with a quiet voice that promised unspeakable violence, he dropped several more bills into her lap and said, "That's for your silence regarding this incident. We were not here, and I promise you, if you break your silence, I'll know—and I'll be back. Do you understand me?"

The woman cringed and nodded vigorously. "I promise." Her hands shaking, the woman frantically gathered the pile of money, some of which had spilled to the floor. "I will not say a word. Thank you."

For the first time she saw a side of Tony that sent a chill up her spine. Despite knowing him as a good man, a family man, there was this other side to him. Probably like her father... the other side that friends and family didn't normally see.

She was glad Tony was on her side.

Bagel stretched up against Alicia's leg, letting out the tiny mew that she'd learned was the equivalent of his "pick me up" command.

His sudden shift from wanting to walk on his own and be involved with whatever was happening to wanting to be picked up was a sure sign that Bagel thought any danger had likely passed. Given his typically reliable instincts regarding such things, Alicia felt oddly comforted by his change in attitude. She lifted the purring cat into her arms, and he quickly nestled into his sling. There, he curled into a ball, began sucking on his tail and contentedly rested against her.

Leaving behind a stunned prostitute, with an unexpected cash windfall and an unconscious customer, Alicia and Tony exited the apartment with a valuable lead—a phone number that promised to bring them closer to their elusive target.

As Tony drove them back to their hotel, Alicia put her phone to her ear as it rang once... twice... and just before the third ring, Denny's voice blasted through the phone's tiny speaker with a bunch of other background noise.

"Hello?"

"Hey, Denny. It's Alicia."

"*One second, I can barely hear you, it's the dinner rush.*" Even though it sounded like Denny had put his hand over the receiver, his muffled voice came through, "*Rosie, I need to take this. I'll be back in a bit.*"

Alicia heard the sound of a beep, and then the background noise of the bar fell silent and Denny's voice came back on the line.

"*Okay, I can talk now. What's up?*"

"I sent you a text with the number to what I believe to be the cell phone that Marco Rossi is carrying. I know in the US there's ways to get the location of a phone if it's on, but it usually requires a warrant and other stuff. You don't by chance—"

"*You want to know if I have sneaky ways of doing the same stuff in Europe?*" Denny said as she heard him typing.

"Well, yeah." Alicia braced herself as the squeal of an oncoming car's tires filled the air, nearly slamming into them as it took a turn too quickly. In the darkness, she saw the first hints of a police car's lights flashing as it raced in the opposite direction.

Tony shook his head. "Those cops are never going to catch that guy."

"*I got the number you sent; it last pinged a cell phone tower in your general vicinity about seven minutes ago. Hold on, I have to hack into the Vodaphone system and see if I can get triangulation data for you.*"

Alicia turned to Tony, who was growing more and more frustrated sitting at a red light in the middle of the night with no other cars on the road. "Tony, that phone number we got is active and somewhere in the area."

He looked over at her just as the light turned green. "Just tell me where we need to go, I figured we weren't going to get any sleep tonight anyway."

"*Okay, I'm in,*" Denny announced, the rapid tapping of keys echoing over the phone connection. "*Yup, I've got the triangulated data for that phone. It turns out you have a decent number of cell towers in the area, so based on the various signal strength values received by each tower, I can put you within three-hundred feet of the phone. I'm sending you an address, but realize that's just getting you in the right area.*"

Alicia's phone buzzed with a received text.

"*Give me a second, I just thought of something. I don't immediately see anything about what protocol the phone is connecting with to the cell towers, but let me see if that phone is enrolled in the locationInfo-r10 opt-in for the LTE protocol. If so, the received packet information might give us some GPS data, which means I can get you within sixteen feet of where the phone is located.*"

"Sounds great," Alicia responded, looked at her text and showed her screen to Tony. "We've got an address that'll get us within three-hundred feet of the phone."

"Awesome, let's do this." Tony pulled the Land Rover over to the side of the road and typed the address into the SUV's navigation system.

"*Sorry, Alicia. No GPS information. But I just refreshed the data and we have some fresh pings to the cell tower as of less than a minute ago, meaning the phone is on, and it doesn't look like it's moved, at least not in the last five minutes."*

"You're a life saver, Denny. This will more than do. Get back to Rosie before she ends up killing you for leaving her alone at the bar."

"No worries." Denny laughed. *"As always, ring me if you need something."*

Tony pressed on the accelerator as the navigation plotted their course, it was only ten minutes away. He glanced at her with a puzzled expression. "Was that Denny from the bar?"

"Yikes." Alicia winced. "It was, and if you don't mind, I need you to keep that to yourself. I don't think Denny wants anyone to know that he's anything other than a bar owner."

Tony laughed and shook his head. "I sort of already knew that. Most of the family does."

By family, the implication being the Bianchi crime family based out of New York City. The same one her father was a part of.

"How so?" Alicia asked.

Tony turned left just as the navigation spoke to them, *"Turn left on Al Imam Al Azam"*

"It was a couple years back at least, but your father recommended to the don that Denny was his tech guy, and that 'bartender' ended up upgrading all of the security systems in the apartment building. Why do you think so many of us hang out at Gerard's?"

"It's got good food and drinks?" Alicia shrugged.

"Sure, but it's a safe place. We know there isn't anything

in there that's listening to things that they shouldn't be listening to, if you know what I mean. No bugs, no feds..." he glanced in her direction, "well, no feds we don't otherwise know about and trust."

Alicia felt a surge of emotion that tightened her throat. She wasn't sure why, but knowing that she was in on a shared secret that only some members of the Bianchi organization knew made her feel closer to Tony... and to her father. It wasn't as if she was becoming part of the mob or anything, but it still gave her a sense of camaraderie that touched on her somewhere deep inside.

"We're five minutes out from our new target." Tony said, his expression grim.

Alicia took a deep breath and let it out slowly.

They were close.

Everything rested on what was about to happen in the next handful of minutes.

CHAPTER
FIFTEEN

In the early hours past midnight, Alicia and Tony arrived at the address provided by Denny. The SUV's navigation had brought them to an unexpected open space in the heart of the bustling metropolitan city of Alexandria. This area, a stark contrast to the city's usual crammed streets, was flat and expansive, clearly an archaeological site.

The darkness enveloped them like a shroud, with only a dim glow emanating from the depths of the dig site.

They were greeted by the eerie silence of history that hung thick in the air. The moon, a slender crescent, offered very little light, casting ghostly shadows upon the ground strewn with what undoubtedly were fragments of relics from of a time long past.

Her eyes easily adjusted to the darkness, and the outline of ruins emerged from the shadows.

Alicia imagined herself expanding her senses, taking in whatever she could from her surroundings.

The quiet was profound, broken only by the occasional hoot of an owl or the distant bark of a dog. She could smell the earthy scent of the exposed soil mixed with the faint, musty odor of decay that seemed to seep from the ancient stones themselves. The air was cool and tasted slightly of salt from the nearby Mediterranean Sea, mixed with the dust of ages that seemed to have settled upon this place of antiquity.

Alicia's gaze swept across the rubble before her. She could make out the base of what looked like a monumental pillar, its limestone surface bleached pale in the moonlight. It had to be Pompey's Pillar, though its historical significance was mostly unknown to her, she remembered a lone pillar being described in one of the articles she'd read about Alexandria. The pillar stood solitary, a testament to the grandeur of civilizations that once reigned supreme.

Nearby, she spotted two sphinx-like statues, laying as silent guardians of the site. Their features were worn, but the craftsmanship was unmistakable, the remnants of majestic leonine bodies and human heads peering into the night as if waiting for dawn to return them to glory.

The cool breeze carried the scent of the sea and whispered of secrets buried beneath her feet.

In the distance there was a soft glow of light.

Bagel squirmed and poured himself out of the sling, the tip of his tail wet from having sucked it like a pacifier. The tail whipped spasmodically as he sniffed the air and let out a low growl.

Alicia secured her walking stick on her back and, alongside Tony, unsheathed their knives, ready for what lay ahead.

Even though he was only a cat, or at least that's what the golden-eyed furball pretended to be, she'd begun to trust his reactions.

If there was trouble about, Bagel was awake and ready to hiss, and possibly more, at the source of danger.

Tony glanced at her, she made a forward motion toward the faint glow in the middle of the excavation site, and he nodded.

The air was cool, carrying the hushed tones of Italian banter, a language Alicia now recognized well enough. Tony's hand rested on the hilt of his knife, a silent promise of violence should it come to that. They had braced themselves for confrontation, ready to rescue Father Montelaro from the clutches of the *Obscura Machinare*.

Stealthily, they made their way toward the light, the murmurs growing clearer.

Alicia crept closer, the night's stillness making the men's voices carry. She peered over the edge of what amounted to a wide hole with rough-hewn stairs descending into the ground. The two so-called escorts stood next to another set of downward steps, and whatever was down there was the source of the light. The men were unaware of her presence as they spoke in hushed, frustrated tones.

"*Should have been back by now,*" grumbled the first man,

her earbud started to translate, sputtered and paused, having trouble with the man's thick, gravelly voice. Alicia popped the listening device out of her ear and pocketed it. She didn't need it for Italian anymore. *"How long does it take to read a few etchings?"*

The second man spat on the ground; his silhouette outlined by the faint light. *"That stubborn old man, always with his nose in the dust. If he thinks I'm going down there to fetch him, he's crazy."*

Alicia exchanged a glance with Tony, who was crouched beside her. They stayed silent, absorbing every word.

"The old man's lost his mind," the first man continued, *"and so has Luciano. I don't know what either of them are thinking. This crazy man thinks he's going to find some lost gospel, bring glory back to the church or something."*

"Glory?" The second man scoffed. *"Luciano has other plans, but the old fool is chasing ghosts. And we're stuck here waiting for him like a bunch of idiots."*

Alicia's grip on her knife tightened, the pieces coming together.

Bagel walked up to the edge of the hole in the ground, stared down at the men and a rumbling growl bloomed in his throat.

"What a mess... This priest, he could be down there until sunrise, porca miseria," one man cursed under his breath.

The other scoffed, *"You know how he is, stubborn as an old mule. He says the spirits speak to him through the relics."*

"Ha! Spirits...more like the whispers of madness," the first snorted. *"Maybe you should fetch him before he turns into a ghost himself."*

Before the second could reply, Alicia and Tony sprang into action, surging from the shadows. They pinned the men against the wall, the cold steel of their knives against the escorts' throats.

"Where is he?" Alicia's voice was a deadly whisper, her blade a silent promise of violence.

The men's eyes widened in fear, but before they could stammer a response, an irate voice boomed from the depths of the catacombs.

"Stop it! You fools are disrupting the whispers of history! My concentration needs silence!"

Tony's eyes lit up with recognition. "Uncle Alessandro?" he yelled into the darkness.

There was a moment of stunned silence before the priest responded, his voice tinged with disbelief. *"Antonio? Is that really you?"*

Footsteps echoed from the depths below, and soon Father Montelaro emerged, his appearance disheveled, dust clinging to his clothes, his face marked with astonishment. "Antonio?" he uttered, his voice tinged with disbelief.

Tony fixed the man he had just held a knife against with a lethal stare, and whispered a threat so chilling it prompted the man to hastily make the sign of the cross. He pocketed his knife and turned to face his uncle.

The priest's face broke into a wide smile, and he walked over to his nephew, gave him a bearhug and said, "My boy, what are you doing in this ancient place?" He shifted his gaze to Alicia, who'd stepped away from the escort she'd nearly skewered with her dagger, and asked, "And who is your companion?"

"This is Alicia." Tony started speaking in English. "She's been... well, I've been her escort on this crazy journey to find you. We've together been trying to piece together your last message," Tony explained, his tone a mix of frustration and relief. "Uncle Alessandro, we've been looking everywhere for you. The family thought you were missing. The Vatican... they had no clue where you were." With a frustrated tone, Tony said, "Why is it that they don't know where you are? We even talked with Prefect Russo, he had no idea where you went."

The priest grumbled and made a dismissive motion, which seemed very unpriestlike to Alicia.

"To be honest, I think the Prefect Russo is more a politician than a good—no, I shouldn't disparage a fellow man of the cloth, even though I might want to." The priest's weary face broke into a smile. He spoke English with only a slight Italian accent. "He tried to claim that I'm too old to pursue where I believe God has meant for me to go, and I must at some point soon seek confession for the things I said in response. I followed the clues where they led me, regardless of the prefect's wishes."

"But, won't you get in trouble? I mean, isn't he your—"

"Nonsense." Tony's uncle shook his head. "I'll admit that for a while, I might have been stymied by the prefect, and I was planning on—God forgive me—going rogue. I'd made all my arrangements, but at the last minute, the Cardinal overseeing the archive as well as other things came back from a trip. I explained the situation, and he gave me his blessing to proceed, given the special circumstances. I won't bore you with the details of Vatican politics, but I was also assured that you were going to be notified of my..." the man snapped his fingers a few times, looking for the right word. "... being occupied for a while, and otherwise out of reach. I'm guessing such a message never was sent?"

"No, we were told nothing." Tony said it emphatically. "In fact, the prefect said absolutely nothing. He feigned total ignorance."

"No, I never informed Russo. He's... let's just skip talking about that man, I don't want to speak ill of him since I'm sure he means well." The priest looked accusingly at the two men from the *Obscura Machinare*. "I was told by Moretti and Rossi that my family had been properly notified of my travels."

Tony shook his head. "Nothing reached us other than the clue you left in your last message to me. Alicia and I tracked down Father Lombardi, which eventually led us to Venice, and finally to here."

The priest smiled. "Ah, Father Lombardi. How is Giuseppe? Doing well, I hope. Still with his nose in the books?"

"Um..." Tony hesitated. "When we last saw him, he was doing well."

Alicia noted how Tony avoided the subject of Father Lombardi's death. He didn't lie to his uncle, but he probably wanted to spare the older man some heartache, at least temporarily.

Tony dug something out of his pocket and handed it to the priest. "You might want to have your passport, since it seems you left Italy without it."

"How..." The man's eyes widened as he flipped open the red passport and said, "This is not a new copy, it's the one I lost. An urchin on the streets of Venice bumped into me and ended up stealing it, how in the world did you find this?"

Alicia glared at the so-called escorts. Their boss had possession of the passport, and probably arranged for it to go "missing" as part of an elaborate scheme—a scheme that these two had been a part of. Possibly unwittingly, possibly not.

Tony's jaw tightened as he too glanced in the escorts' direction. "It's a long story." He pointed at their surroundings and asked, "What are you doing here, of all places?"

"Do you know where you are?" Father Montelaro asked.

"Some ruins in the middle of Alexandria?" Tony shrugged.

The priest clucked disapprovingly. "Bah. Antonio, you need to read more. You're standing in the Serapeum of Alexandria, a place as steeped in history as it is in mystery.

"The Serapeum of Alexandria, established in the 3rd

century BC, was initially conceived as a temple dedicated to Serapis, the Graeco-Egyptian god of the afterlife." The priest grew more animated as he described their surroundings. "This magnificent structure evolved into a part of the larger Mouseion, a center of learning and scholarship, akin to a modern university. Over centuries, it became a repository of knowledge, housing part of the great Library of Alexandria.

"Back in the early days, the Serapeum was expansive, featuring a grand temple and a complex that included storerooms, lecture halls, and living quarters for scholars. Excavations have unveiled its considerable size and the extent of its influence as a cultural and religious hub. Like I said, this place transitioned from a center of worship to a beacon of learning, housing a significant portion of the Library of Alexandria's scrolls. Its decline began in the Roman period, with its eventual destruction marking the end of an era of unparalleled intellectual exchange.

"Beneath us, the catacombs hold secrets that have slept undisturbed for centuries."

Alicia, intrigued, leaned in. "What kind of secrets, Father?"

The priest's eyes sparkled with excitement. "Hidden texts, lost gospels, relics of a time when the world was young. We're on the cusp of unraveling mysteries that could redefine our understanding of history. The Serapeum is just the beginning."

Alicia watched as the old man enthusiastically spoke of ancient treasures and forgotten lore. The so-called escorts from the *Obscura Machinare* looked on, holding expressions of confusion. She too was uncertain about what the next steps might be.

They'd found Tony's uncle. Mission accomplished. Or was it?

Father Montelaro motioned for Tony and Alicia to come closer, and he spoke in a conspiratorial tone. "Antonio, Alicia, I know how this all must sound, and you have to understand, this is something that could change our understanding of early Christianity," the priest began, his voice barely above a whisper. "Antonio already knows that my job involves translation of ancient knowledge to modern text so that other scholars can research things from such ancient sources.

"But it was not too long ago that something happened. It was as if God himself had intervened, sending a small earthquake, and with such things you'd expect damage to buildings or heaven-forbid, people... but no, it was a revelatory thing. A long-hidden cache of early relics was uncovered in a cave near the walls of the Vatican. It pointed to a contemporary testimonial of something I'd never imagined. It hinted at the existence of a lost gospel. The lost gospel of Mark."

Tony, eyebrows raised in skepticism, interjected, "You mean Mark? As in the biblical Mark? The evangelist?"

"Exactly," the priest nodded. "I held in my own hands a recently uncovered scroll that documented its existence. Can you imagine, a contemporary testimonial of an unknown gospel, purposefully hidden for a future time. The gospel was hidden away to protect it from being destroyed. They were initially kept hidden in a cave near the present-day Vatican, but evidently it needed to be moved in the earliest years of Christendom to evade Roman scrutiny. Its destination was Alexandria, which if you think about it, was a logical place. Back then, this place was the largest repository of knowledge, both modern and ancient, in the world.

"I went to Venice to visit a fellow priest and historian at St. Mark's Basilica, a logical place to seek any hints of such a lost gospel. I found nothing there that confirmed or dissuaded me from believing what the ancient scrap of parchment hinted at. After having lost my passport, I despaired at the delay such a thing would have caused to my search." The priest motioned toward the two escorts. "But I luckily encountered these men who helped me get here, with what I admit might have been unusual methodologies."

"And you think the gospel ended up here, in the Serapeum?" Alicia asked, her curiosity piqued.

"Yes," Father Montelaro replied. "This place, once a grand temple and library, became a repository for items of immense importance. And within these walls," he gestured around them, "there are carvings, symbols that hint at something precious being hidden here, only to be moved later to a safer location, away from Roman eyes."

"Where do you think—one second." Tony turned sharply and walked over to the escorts, his voice firm. "Your services are no longer required."

Alicia saw Tony hand each of them a wad of cash.

Tony leaned closer to the two men, towering over them.

"Go back to Italy. And if I find you're still in Egypt by tomorrow, I will hunt you and your families down and end all of you. I promise you this on the soul of my mother. Now leave."

Alicia barely heard the whispered threat, but the reaction was clear.

One of the men again made the sign of the cross and they both scurried up the stairs and vanished into the night.

Tony turned back to his uncle and asked, "Where do you think the lost gospel is?"

Father Montelaro smiled, a twinkle in his eye. "The answer is closer than you might think, Antonio. But realize what this place was like back then.

"In the second century AD, Alexandria was under Roman control and was one of the most significant cities of the Roman Empire, second only to Rome in size and wealth. The city was a hub for cultural and economic activity, having been founded by Alexander the Great and later becoming the seat of the Ptolemaic Kingdom. During this period, Alexandria was known for its great Library and as a center for learning and scholarship. However, the era also experienced unrest, including tensions and riots between different ethnic groups and between pagans and Christians. Christianity was growing, but it faced persecution from Roman authorities, especially under emperors like Nero and later during the Diocletianic Persecution.

"This location we're standing in wasn't safe. Certainly

not from the Roman authorities. Even then, under threat of persecution, there were guardians of holy relics. It was only a few generations since the life, death, and resurrection of our Lord and savior. There were those who'd taken vows to protect any holy relics. To conceal them from the authorities. And from the reading I've done, it seems that the secretive relocation of holy treasures was underway." The priest hitched his thumb toward the downward-facing stairs behind him. "I deciphered a passage down there that talked about the dangers of the era. It also spoke of a new site, a hidden one that was roughly six thousand feet from here. A place to safekeep that which the Roman authorities found unacceptable. Perhaps even a lost Gospel." The priest's eyes sparkled with life as he spoke. "In this era of chaos, a new sanctuary was carved from the earth, intended as a safe haven for these sacred relics. This place, conceived in the second century AD, was an architectural feat, blending cultures and traditions, serving as a final resting place for the elite, and it was only rediscovered in the early 20th century. Its purpose evolved, yet it remained a silent witness to history. Today, it's an archaeological site, revealing our shared past. This sanctuary, known as the Catacombs of Kom El Shoqafa, holds the echoes of those ancient guardians. And it is only three kilometers from here. Just about six thousand feet. It *has* to be where these items were taken."

"Father Montelaro," Alicia tried to speak with a neutral tone, but she was highly skeptical. "If these catacombs were discovered nearly a century ago, wouldn't the lost Gospel have been recovered already?"

"It is possible," The priest admitted. "However, there are many unexplored areas in these catacombs. That much I do know. It's something that I have to follow-up on. I cannot rest until I've done what I can."

Alicia exchanged a glance with Tony, who simply shrugged. "Father Montelaro, don't we need permission to explore there?"

"Ah, but I have already secured it," Father Montelaro responded, extracting a folded piece of paper from his dust-coated jacket and showing it to them. "This is an official permit from the Egyptian Ministry of Antiquities, allowing us to investigate this site and several others, including the previously mentioned catacombs." He gestured towards the staircase. "The men Tony threatened," he glanced at Tony with a slight frown, "helped obtain this document. It's fortunate I met them when I did. Obtaining such authorization often requires influence from the Holy See."

"Uncle Alessandro," Tony pointed at the stairs leading deeper into the excavation. "Are you done at this site?"

The priest nodded. "I am." He glanced at the stairs leading up and said, "I presume you have some kind of transportation? Those two might have inspired my ire more than a time or two, but I still owe them my thanks for having gotten me here. And besides, we're in an apartment not far from here. I need to reclaim my things."

"What things do you have there?" Alicia asked, not believing a visit was a good idea.

"Mostly clothes, that is all."

"Uncle Alessandro, trust me when I tell you this, those two are not good people." He motioned for the priest to follow him. "Let's go, we'll get you to a hotel. I'll get you a room and I'll replace whatever clothes you're missing."

"But—"

"Trust me," Tony spoke emphatically, "not everyone's motivation is as pure as you might think it is."

The priest approached Tony and patted him on the cheek. "Antonio, I've been a priest for nearly as long as you've been alive. Trust *me* when I say I know what evil lies within men's hearts. I'm not blind to it. But I'd rather not burden you—"

"Father Montelaro, please listen to your nephew. And trust me, you are a burden to nobody. We'll arrange for whatever it takes. Let's just get into a hotel room, we could all stand to wash up and have a good breakfast in the morning. I'm too tired to go traipsing around the city in the middle of the night trying to reclaim someone's clothes."

"I'm sorry, young lady." The priest pursed his lips and nodded. "It is late, and I need to be more conscious of other people's needs. Fine, let's go to the hotel. And tomorrow we'll explore the Catacombs of Kom El Shoqafa. Understand that what we might find is something from the earliest days of Christanity. The effects of which could sweep through Christendom like nothing else has in millennia."

The priest's words hung in the air as they exited the archaeological site.

Alicia knew that just because Tony had potentially scared off the escorts, the danger was likely not over. The *Obscura Machinare's* shadow loomed large, but Father Montelaro's resolve was larger still. The elderly man was a force to be reckoned with. He would not leave, not with a 2000-year-old mystery to solve—the potential discovery of a lost Gospel of Mark, a treasure for all of Christendom.

Despite Alicia's extreme doubt of finding anything, the priest's faith and enthusiasm was contagious.

What if they found something?

Could they possibly uncover one of Christianity's oldest mysteries, hidden deep within the heart of Alexandria?

As they left the Serapeum under the cover of night, Alicia, Tony, and the priest crammed into the Range Rover, setting their sights on the sanctuary of a hotel. Tony's uncle opted to sit in the back seat and Tony asked, "Uncle Alessandro, I'm not sure what's available, but have you eaten?

"I'm fine, Antonio. Maybe if there's a piece of fruit at the hotel or something, I'll be fine until the morning. You don't have to fret over me, I've been taking care of myself for a very long time."

Tony put the car into gear and Bagel squirmed, climbing

out of his sling and perched on the center armrest, facing the priest.

As the priest's gaze fell upon Bagel, he exclaimed, "*Mamma mia!* Where did you come from?"

"That's Bagel." Alicia responded with a smile. "He's usually asleep, but I guess he's curious about you."

"Is he friendly?"

She glanced at Bagel and shrugged. "He's not hissing, so that's a good sign."

The priest's surprise quickly turned to admiration as he noted, "Did you know that in ancient Egypt, cats like this were revered, symbols of protection and honor."

Suddenly a voice from the past replayed in Alicia's mind.

"In my time, cats were seen as guardians of a sort. I rather think the one you now call Bagel makes a good match for you. Keep him close. He will be with you throughout your days."

The memory of Narmer left Alicia with some regret. She never got a chance to sit down and talk with him the way she'd have liked to. He'd prophesied things about her that had become true, and having the priest repeat fragments of what Narmer had said sent a chill down her spine.

Tony's uncle affectionately stroked Bagel's fur, and the cat responded with a loud, motor-like purr. "Your presence here, my little friend, might just be the good omen we need for our search." The warmth in his voice conveyed a deep respect for the cat's serendipitous arrival, as if Bagel himself was a blessing on their quest.

"Turn left on Amood Al Swari" the navigation system commanded.

As Tony turned, merging onto the aforementioned street, Alicia noticed through the passenger side-view mirror, the sudden illumination of headlights.

"Um, Tony... I just saw a set of headlights turn on somewhere back near where we'd parked."

Tony glanced at her, his brow furrowed. "I didn't think there was anyone else in the parking lot."

Alicia shrugged as she turned in her seat and looked out the rear window. "I didn't see anyone, but nonetheless, that car just left that parking lot and looks like it's following us."

"We'll see about that. Mr. Bagel, Uncle Alessandro, hold on. We're about to make some quick turns."

Alicia scooped up the cat and held onto him as Tony floored the accelerator.

"Turn right on Al Imam Al Azam"

"Make a U-turn on El-Ezz—"

"Shut up," Tony growled at the navigation as it began complaining incessantly.

Alicia braced herself as Tony took several turns so fast that she worried that the SUV might flip.

"Antonio," the priest gripped the seat in front of him and held a surprisingly calm expression for someone who was being bounced around the inside of the vehicle. "Is this really necessary?"

Tony pushed the SUV into a series of swift, evasive maneuvers, darting through intersections and weaving their way through the urban labyrinth that was Alexandria.

After a minute or so of wild driving, Alicia peered through the rear window and shook her head. "Tony, I don't see anything."

Tony slowed a bit, taking a few more side roads and glancing occasionally at the navigation, which had been muted. "Okay, I'll wind our way back toward the hotel."

Sitting on Alicia's lap, Bagel yowled in Tony's direction.

"Understood, Mr. Bagel." Tony nodded as if he totally understood what the cat had said. "We'll find you a treat when we get to the hotel."

Alicia's gaze was fixed on the passenger's side view mirror, looking for anything that seemed out of place.

Her mind raced, pondering if the vehicle that lurked in the shadows belonged to the *Obscura Machinare's* emissaries or if another unseen adversary had somehow marked them. The ambiguity of the threat, compounded by her inability to identify the make of the car only fueled her unease.

In the world of covert operations and shadowy figures that Alicia navigated, paranoia was not a weakness but a survival instinct. Much like Bagel's unerring sense of danger, Alicia's vigilance had often steered them clear of peril. The unidentified car who'd been watching them at the Serapeum was a stark reminder that their journey was far from unobserved.

Or it might all be an over-developed sense of paranoia.

Either way, she had to trust her instincts, and her instincts were telling her that their adversaries, whoever they might be, might still be just a few steps behind.

CHAPTER SIXTEEN

Alicia took her seat at the round dining table, Bagel purred as he adjusted himself in his sling, having just eaten his fill of fresh, locally caught sardines that they'd gotten from the nearby market.

Tony and his uncle sat as a waiter filled their glasses with water and said, "Welcome my friends, I hope you've brought your appetites, because the first course will be arriving at any moment."

The priest was dressed in his newly acquired street clothes, and despite his secular dress, Alicia felt a clerical aura about the man. Something about the way he talked, his mannerisms, or maybe how he held himself left her with the undeniable impression of his being a priest. A thing that she supposed was natural after nearly fifty years as a leader in the Church.

Father Montelaro looked wide-eyed at their surroundings and shook his head. "Antonio, this is a very nice place. How are you able to afford such an extravagance?"

"Uncle Alessandro, unlike you, I've not taken a vow of poverty. Just relax and enjoy, it's not often I get a chance to spoil one of my favorite relatives."

The priest stifled a smile as he wagged his finger at Tony. "Now, that's not something one should have, a favorite amongst your relatives. They are all equal in God's eyes, and so should they be equal in yours."

Tony grinned at his uncle as a waiter approached, carrying a large tray.

"My friends, let me produce for you the first course." The man spoke English very well, with an easy-to-understand Middle Eastern accent. "I hope you will find these delightful Middle Eastern cold *mezzeh* items to your liking. They emphasize fresh ingredients and unique flavors, offering our diners a tantalizing preview of what's to come."

The waiter placed small plates in front of each of them, filled with what looked like a festive dip of sorts.

"This first dish is something we call Mutabbal. You should experience the smoky richness of this velvety purée of grilled aubergines blended with creamy sesame paste." He put another plate on the table filled with sliced lemons "May I suggest that each bite be brightened with a squeeze of fresh lemon. You will notice that the purée is garnished with ruby-red pomegranate seeds, adding a jewel-like finish to the dish. It's a traditional dish that I hope you find is a harmonious blend of earthy flavors and vibrant accents, perfect for spreading over warm pita or simply enjoying as a sumptuous dip."

Alicia looked at the dish and wondered if it was the same as *baba ganoush*. It too was made from eggplant and something she was fond of the few times she'd tried it.

Another waiter placed in front of each guest a steaming basket of fresh pita bread as the other waiter placed a bowl filled with what looked like a salad in front of each of them.

"This is our restaurant's famous Fattoush salad. You'll find that the crisp vegetables meet the tangy zing of sumac and the sweet depth of pomegranate syrup. Fresh mint leaves infuse this salad with an aromatic freshness, while shards of crispy pita bread add an irresistible crunch. This salad is a lively celebration of textures and flavors, beautifully dressed in our house-made pomegranate dressing that I hope it will leave your palate dancing."

The waiter placed three more plates on the table with another dip that Alicia immediately recognized.

"And it wouldn't be a proper selection of *mezzeh* if it didn't include a beautifully-made hummus. Our hummus is a smooth, rich purée of chickpeas, elegantly combined with creamy sesame paste and enhanced with a splash of lemon. This classic dish is the epitome of simplicity and sophistication, offering a creamy texture and a balance of flavors that resonate with every bite. I find that most of our customers enjoy this as presented, consuming it as a dip with the fresh pita, or even saved for later courses as a companion to any of the upcoming dishes. Hummus is the ultimate invitation for you to savor the essence of Middle Eastern culinary artistry." The waiter panned his gaze across the table and asked, "Is there anything else I can get you while you enjoy the first course?"

They all shook their head, but Alicia smiled and pantomimed a silent applause. "If the food is half as good as your descriptions, this will certainly be a fantastic meal. Thank you."

"You're most welcome." The waiter bowed his head and quickly left them to their food.

Tony had a pleased expression and dug in.

All three of them were starving, and Alicia could have made a meal of the pita just by itself. It was so warm, luscious, and fresh—something she never actually imagined herself giving as a description for the traditional bread. If she didn't control herself, she'd probably eat the entire basket, it was so good.

The priest held up a piece of the pita with a smear of the hummus on it. "I must say, this is as good, if not better, than anything I had when I was last in Jerusalem. You two made an excellent choice."

Alicia pointed at Tony. "This was all your nephew's doing. He found this place." She focused her attention on the priest and asked, "What do you know of these catacombs that we're going to visit. I know what I've read on the internet, but in all seriousness, we're looking for a scroll of some kind, right?"

"I believe so." The priest said with his mouth full of a forkful of salad. "But I don't want to presume anything. Anything is possible. Maybe the information was transcribed onto a stone tablet. I've found such things in the past, where I was looking for one thing and found it, but not in the form I had expected. I have faith that this will be a fruitful search."

Tony scooped a bit of the eggplant dish with the pita, tasted it, and his eyed widened. "Wow, I didn't think I liked eggplant. This tastes so different than anything I've had back home."

Alicia nodded. "This tastes like *baba ganoush* to me. I love it."

Father Montelaro nodded. "The blending of flavors reminds me of the unity we seek in our own quest. Divine, isn't it?"

Tony chuckled, "Only you could make a connection between our food and our upcoming little expedition."

"It's not just any expedition we're undertaking." The priest looked back and forth at the both of them and lowered his voice to just barely above a whisper. "This thing we're about to embark on, if we're successful it could change everything. You realize that, right?"

Alicia and Tony nodded, though to be honest, she still held a lot of doubt about all of it. This would probably be just be another instance of opening Al Capone's vault, an incident that occurred before she was born, but was made famous as a giant waste of time that had been perpetrated on the world. In other words, a wild good chase. In modern parlance that the younger kids would understand, this expedition was probably going to be the equivalent of click bait.

But Alicia kept her doubts to herself. It would be rude to do anything else.

Just as they were finishing the first course, the waiter reappeared with a large collection of steaming dishes.

"My friends, may I introduce the second course, which will consist of a selection of grilled delights that I hope will tantalize your palates."

Two other waiters swooped in and cleared their table as the main waiter, who Alicia thought of as the Food Talker, deposited the first set of dishes.

"This is known as Shish Tawook. It's a dish that consists of succulent boneless chicken pieces, marinated in a blend of garlic, rich tomato paste, and aromatic spices, then grilled to perfection for what I hope you'll find to be a flavorful experience."

As the small steaming dish was laid in front of her, Alicia caught the aroma of garlic and cinnamon and other warm, Middle Eastern spices. Her mouth began watering as the waiter continued doling out more dishes.

"This is our Grilled Kofta, which I hope you'll find to be a mouthwatering mix of finely minced lamb, combined with the freshness of onions and parsley, seasoned with a select blend of spices, and grilled to create a juicy, savory dish." The waiter pointed at the tiny plates of hummus, chopped vegetables, and new baskets of hot pitas that other waiters were placing on the table. "Many people enjoy making sandwiches of a sort with the meat, and the provided accompaniments."

The waiter laid even more plates on the table and continued with his descriptions.

"Here is a Shish Kebab. Tender cubes of meat, marinated in a zesty mix of tomato, onion, and exotic spices, skewered and grilled to bring out a symphony of flavors."

Alicia pointed at the skewers, eyeing them with a bit of suspicion. "What kind of meat is this?"

"It's a young goat meat." The waiter answered matter-of-factly. "If you're unfamiliar with goat, I believe you'll find that it tastes very much like a mild form of beef. Most people who enjoy beef find goat to be a delightful alternative, and this is a most traditional staple in our country. I hope you enjoy it."

As the last of the dishes were arrayed on the table, Alicia speared one of the cubes of meat, swirled it in the juices it had come in, popped it in her mouth and chewed.

Her eyes widened as the flavors hit her tongue.

"What do you think?" Tony asked.

"Oh," Alicia gushed. "It's *so* good." She tried a bit of everything that she'd been given and her mind focused on her meal.

This was undeniably the best meal she'd had in ages.

"Be careful," Tony warned as he looked back and forth at Alicia and his uncle. "We have two more courses coming."

"Are you kidding me?" Alicia exclaimed as her stomach already felt like it was hitting its limits.

"Antonio," the priest said in a tone that would normally be reserved for an adult trying to talk reason to a child. "What are you thinking? I can't eat so much. Certainly not in one sitting."

"It's okay." Tony made a calming motion with his hand. "Just taste and enjoy, both of you. Thank God, Uncle Alessandro is safe, and we can have a good meal and have a small celebration, before our day starts in earnest. I suspect we'll be too busy to have another proper meal for a while."

Alicia struggled not to gorge herself on the rest of dishes that came out in the subsequent courses. Between the Salmon Harrah, the Shakriah Bel Lahm, and the Kofta Bel Sahn, she couldn't decide what she liked the most. Some of it was spicy, which she wasn't expecting, but enjoyed, others had a creamy sauce with vermicelli rice and the spices... oh the spices were all just so quintessentially Middle Eastern. It was an experience that she would likely never forget.

They ended their meal with a very simple rice pudding that was still a bit warm, had a touch of cinnamon sprinkled on it and felt a sense of contentment as the waiter arrived with a small silver tray.

"My friends, I have a special delivery from someone who wishes to remain anonymous." He picked up a long white feather from the tray and placed it on the table. "The man said this is for the older gentleman at the table, and he wished him luck."

"Woah," Alicia turned to the waiter. "Excuse me, but did you get a look at this man?"

"I'm sorry, but I didn't." The waiter shook his head. "I can bring over the person who received it, if you wish."

"Please."

The waiter left and both Alicia and Tony looked at the priest who picked up the feather, and studied it with a puzzled expression.

"Does that mean anything to you, Uncle Alessandro?" Tony asked.

"It's interesting." The priest ran his index finger along the spine of the foot-long feather. "I have no idea why someone would send this to me."

"Does it maybe symbolize anything?" Alicia asked. "Maybe from a historical context?"

"Well, that is certainly possible." Father Montelaro pursed his lips. "In ancient Egyptian culture, the symbol that represents truth, justice, morality, and balance is the Feather of Maat. Maat was the goddess who personified these concepts. You may have seen images or heard stories of a feather being used in the weighing of the heart ceremony in the afterlife. The Ancient Egyptians believed it was crucial in determining whether a soul was allowed to enter the realm of the dead or not. The ceremony involved weighing the heart of the deceased against Maat's feather to assess the purity and righteousness of their life lived on earth." He shrugged. "Or it could just be a feather."

The idea that the feather was used in part of a death ritual sent a chill through Alicia. Was the feather a threat of some kind?

The waiter arrived with a younger man at his side. He asked the teenager in Arabic, "What did the man look like that gave you the feather?"

Alicia's ear bud translated the Arabic seamlessly.

The teenager hesitated and replied in a hushed tone in Arabic, "Sir, but the man who gave me the feather paid one-hundred pounds for me to remain silent."

Knowing that one-hundred Egyptian pounds was only about two dollars, Alicia pulled a ten-euro note from her fanny pack and handed it to the waiter. "For him to speak the truth."

The waiter passed the money to the teenager and snapped his fingers. "Out with it. Let's hear the truth. What did he look like?" He demanded.

The teenager stared wide-eyed at the money for a second, pocketed it, and said with a pained expression, "Well, he came out of the bathroom and saw me—"

"Our bathroom?" The waiter pointed at the ground. "This restaurant's bathroom?"

The teenager nodded. "I thought he was a customer, but I'm not sure. He pointed to table thirteen," the young man pointed at their table, "and said give the older man the feather. He was dressed in a dark brown robe. His face was hidden in a hood."

"Like in a monk's robe?" Alicia asked.

The waiter translated and the young man nodded. "I'm sorry if I did something wrong. I don't know what he looked like, otherwise I would say. His hands though..." the teenager pointed to the back of his own hands. "They seemed like younger hands. Definitely not an older man's hands. And the voice sounded foreign, but spoke good Arabic." He shrugged. "That's all I know."

The waiter looked to her and asked, "Did you need me to translate?"

Alicia shook her head. "No, that's fine. I understood. Thank you."

"Of course." The waiter motioned for the teenager and they both left.

"I didn't know you understood Arabic." Tony put his elbows on the table. "What did he say?"

"Whoever gave that feather was dressed in a dark brown monk's robe, or at least that's what it was described as. He also said it was someone who spoke Arabic with a foreign accent and he thought, by the look of the back of his hands, that it was someone who wasn't very old."

Tony frowned.

"Interesting," the priest twirled the feather and shrugged. "I'll be honest, I don't know what to make of it. The truth? Morality? Justice? Balance? Or it's just a feather from an unusual source. I don't know." He glanced at the clock on the wall. "But it is almost noon already, we should go and visit the catacombs during the day. Understand what we're dealing with."

Tony looked over at Alicia. "What are you thinking? Do you think it's our *Obscura* friends?"

"I have no idea." Her mind was racing with all variety of

paranoid conjectures, none of which had anything to do with a feather. Alicia shook her head. "To be honest, I don't know what to make of the feather. It seems ominous. Maybe it was just a crackpot. But to give it to your uncle, specifically... my instincts tell me it's not good. I just don't know what to make of it. We need to keep our eyes open."

"Why are you two so paranoid?" Father Montelaro asked, his brows furrowed and looking back and forth between Alicia and his nephew.

Alicia gave Tony a look that she intended to mean, "Explaining this is on you..."

Tony got up from the table and said, "Uncle Alessandro, let's head to the catacombs. On the way there, I'll explain everything we know."

CHAPTER
SEVENTEEN

"Turn left on El-Nasereya." the navigation system blurted through the SUV's speakers as Alicia took in their surroundings.

"You're telling me that Moretti and Rossi, those two were part of some dark group of antiquities smugglers?" the priest's voice held an uncharacteristic edge to it. "And they'd arranged for my passport to be stolen?"

"I'm afraid so, Uncle Alessandro. I won't even go into some of the other things, but trust us. These were not good people."

Alicia looked at the priest through her visor's rear-facing mirror and saw the look of frustration.

"I'm embarrassed to have been so duped." He shook his head. "I should have seen it."

Tony pulled into a nearby parking lot and said, "We're here."

Alicia and the others stepped out of the SUV and approached the unassuming location. Had she not known that this was the place of a major archaeological dig, she'd never have guessed, largely because everything was underground.

Alicia, Tony, and Father Montelaro stood at the entrance of the Catacombs of Kom El Shoqafa, a historical site shrouded in mystery and darkness. The air was thick with the scent of age and dampness, and the stone walls seemed to whisper tales of ancient secrets. As they approached, a few signs posted by the Ministry of Antiquities warned visitors of off-limits areas due to flooding and ongoing restoration efforts.

"Flooding?" Alicia frowned. "I wouldn't have guessed that flooding would be an issue in this area."

"We're not far from the ocean, so such things are very possible," the priest noted, taking the news in stride.

Tony squinted at the signs. "Looks like some parts aren't going to be so easy to take a look at," he remarked.

Father Montelaro nodded knowingly. "We must respect the boundaries set by the ministry, at least stick to the permitted areas for now, certainly while playing the part of tourists."

They paid their ticket fees and joined the group of eager tourists gathered at the entrance of the Catacombs of Kom El Shoqafa, their excitement palpable in the air, the tour guide stepped forward, ready to lead them into the depths of history.

"Welcome, esteemed travelers, to one of the most fascinating sites in Alexandria," the guide began, his voice echoing against the ancient stone walls. "The Catacombs of Kom El Shoqafa, or the Mound of Shards, as it translates, are a testament to the rich cultural tapestry of Egypt. It is thus called because when first discovered, this area aboveground was covered with shards of terra cotta, which archaeologists believe were fragments of jars and plates made of clay. Objects that were left by those in the second century who were visiting the tombs. Some speculate that these remnants were offerings to the dead, leaving behind the platters, jars, and other objects that contained the offerings, and some speculate the visitors would bring food and wine for their own use and leave behind the plates and dishes."

With a dramatic sweep of his hand, the guide gestured towards the yawning entrance of the catacombs, inviting his audience to follow him into the darkness. "Legend has it that these catacombs were accidentally discovered by a donkey in 1900," he explained, his words tinged with excitement. "The animal stumbled into a concealed shaft, revealing a vast network of underground tunnels and chambers that had remained hidden for centuries."

As they ventured deeper into the catacombs, the guide's voice reverberated through the ancient corridors, recounting tales of the past.

Alicia noticed that there were darkened passages the

group was bypassing and noted to Tony in a whisper. "Flashlights. Definitely are going to need flashlights."

He nodded as they followed the group.

"One of the most remarkable discoveries within these catacombs is the Hall of Caracalla," he announced, leading the group into a vast chamber adorned with intricate carvings and statues.

"It was here, in this very hall, that archaeologists uncovered a stunning array of Greco-Roman artifacts, including sculptures, pottery, and sarcophagi," the guide continued, his words echoing off the walls. "This chamber is named after the Roman Emperor Caracalla, whose likeness can be seen in the exquisite frescoes adorning the ceiling."

The catacombs were surprisingly cool, although the air felt heavy with the scent of ancient earth.

There were lights along the way, illuminating the main paths that were meant for the tourists to see.

"Imagine that this was all carved by hand," Father Montelaro noted as they walked through the carved passage in the bedrock. "The amount of work and effort it took, without the benefit of tools, and only a torch to light their way. It's an astounding feat."

Their guide led them through a labyrinth of tunnels, each passageway adorned with mesmerizing designs etched into the rock. Symbols of forgotten gods and mythical creatures danced before their eyes, their meaning lost to Alicia, but Tony's uncle seemed enraptured by what he saw.

"These carvings are representations of ancient deities

and guardians," the guide explained, his voice barely audible over the echoing whispers of the catacombs. "They were thought to protect the souls of the departed on their journey to the afterlife. Throughout the catacombs you will see an unusual mix of the Egyptian, Greek, and Roman influence of the day."

With each step, the air grew cooler and the atmosphere more somber, as if the weight of centuries pressed down upon them. The group passed through a series of chambers adorned with intricate carvings and cryptic inscriptions, each telling a story of life and death in ancient Alexandria.

"As we descend further into the catacombs," the guide continued, his voice growing more solemn, "we must be mindful of the dangers that lurk below. One of the greatest challenges faced by the custodians of this site is the threat of flooding, particularly in the lower level."

As they continued their journey, Alicia couldn't shake the feeling of being watched. The eyes of the carved figures seemed to follow her every move, their expressions frozen in eternal vigilance.

As they explored further, the guide pointed to a side passage that was cordoned off from the main hall.

Alicia spotted several people, likely archaeologists, some of which were taking notes while others were on their hands and knees brushing the dust away from something.

"I'd like to highlight the tireless work of and ongoing research efforts by the Ministry of Antiquities. Just last month, a team of archaeologists made a groundbreaking discovery," he revealed, his eyes alight with enthusiasm. "They uncovered a previously unknown chamber buried beneath centuries of rubble, and it is only beginning to shed new light on the ancient mysteries concealed within these walls."

With each step, it dawned on Alicia just how big this place was. As they delved deeper into the heart of the catacombs, her imagination ignited by the stories of the past, she couldn't help but know that there was no way they'd be able to go through this entire place in a sensible frame of time. She needed to get home. Her leave from the Outfit did have a timeline of sorts.

Nonetheless, she marveled at the wonders around her, feeling a sense of awe at the timeless secrets this place could possibly be hiding.

Could the old man be right and a lost Gospel was actually somewhere in here?

As Alicia emerged from the depths of the Catacombs of Kom El Shoqafa, she noticed the sun was getting lower in the sky, casting ever-longer shadows across the ancient stones.

The group began walking back to the car, and Tony asked, "So, what's the plan for tonight?" his voice tinged with excitement.

They all piled into the SUV and Alicia said, "We need to

be prepared for anything. First things first, we need lights for the unlit areas. I also want to find a place where I can get a GoPro," she added, catching Tony's curious glance.

"Why a GoPro?" Tony inquired, raising an eyebrow. "If we need pictures or need to record something, we have our phones."

Alicia hesitated for a moment before answering. "Just in case," she said cryptically, a hint of mischief dancing in her eyes.

Tony shrugged. "Okay. We'll also need shovels, brushes, and a pry bar in case we encounter any obstacles," he suggested, ticking off items on an imaginary checklist.

Father Montelaro nodded in agreement. "And don't forget a water pump," he added. "In the off chance we come across a flooded room, it might come in handy."

As they discussed their plans, Alicia couldn't shake a rising sense of anxiety. "You guys realize just how big this place is, right?"

Tony turned in his seat and looked back at his uncle. "That brings up a good point," he remarked. "It could take weeks, if not months, to explore it all. And let's face it, Uncle Alessandro, you're not as young as you think you are."

Father Montelaro chuckled, brushing off Tony's concern. "Most of the catacombs have long been explored," he reassured. "Our focus will be on the newest area. We just need to get a look at it, and maybe that's just a few evenings' worth of investigation. No more."

Alicia and Tony looked at each other and shrugged.

What choice did they have?

All Alicia knew was that she needed to put some kind of boundaries on this exploration, because unlike the priest, this search for a lost holy relic, which almost certainly was in vain, was not something she had unlimited time for.

She had another life to get back to.

Tony put the vehicle into gear and they were off.

Setting aside her doubts she mentally prepared herself for what needed to be done. They had a plan in place and their determination steeled, Alicia was ready to give it her all.

They'd return to the Catacombs of Kom El Shoqafa under the cover of darkness, ready to uncover the secrets hidden within its ancient depths.

CHAPTER
EIGHTEEN

Alicia shrugged her shoulders as she adjusted her backpack filled with digging tools and other seemingly random items. Bagel shifted around in his sling as she stood in front of the entrance to the Catacombs of Kom El Shoqafa, the darkness of the night surrounding her. The only sound was the faint whisper of the wind, sending shivers down her spine as the tiny team of would-be explorers prepared to descend into the depths once more.

Father Montelaro stepped forward, holding out the paperwork from the Ministry of Antiquities, and showed it to the guards stationed at the entrance. The guards examined the documents briefly before nodding and stepping aside, allowing the trio to pass.

As they made their way down several narrow staircases,

they finally reached the newly discovered section of the catacombs.

Stepping over the rope barrier, Alicia and the rest of the team turned on their flashlights, casting beams of light through the darkness.

Father Montelaro spoke softly as he said, "We must proceed carefully," his voice echoing off the ancient stone walls. "The floor may be unsteady, there might even be a shaft that isn't cordoned off for safety's sake. Keep your eyes open and your mind focused."

Alicia nodded, and despite her fervent belief that they'd find nothing, her heart pounded with anticipation. She'd had strange dreams the night before about being buried alive, and those memories came to the fore as they walked into a large, mostly unexplored chamber.

Bagel squirmed and climbed out of his sling, landing soundlessly on his feet.

"Bagel, don't go wandering around," Alicia warned. "This place is a maze and I'll never be able to find you if you get lost."

The cat raised his nose, sniffing the air as if looking for something.

Father Montelaro pointed to the frescoes adorning the walls, depicting scenes of daily life from the third century AD. "These frescoes may hold clues to the specific things that we're looking for," he said, his eyes scanning the intricate designs. "While Rome still held sway, Christianity was a hidden sect. We remained in hiding, using clandestine symbols and for all we know, secret handshakes to identify each other. Look for symbols, signs of early Christianity."

"Such as?" Alicia asked.

The priest's eyes widened as he retrieved a pair of gloves from his belt, put them on and stepped closer the wall. He aimed his flashlight at what looked like a random pattern. "Look here. You see this?"

Both Alicia and Tony nodded. "It looks like an X with a P laid over it."

"It's called the chi-rho symbol." Father Montelaro explained. "It's a monogram consisting of the first two letters of the Greek word for Christ. In Greek, the letter 'X' (chi) and the letter 'P' (rho) are used to represent the sound 'ch' and 'r,' respectively.

"Remember, it wasn't until the Edict of Milan in 313 AD that Emperor Constantine granted religious tolerance to Christians. Before then, the chi-rho symbol was a secret sign for those of the faith to identify each other." The priest patted the wall with reverence. "This was almost certainly painted in the 200s, well before the practice of our faith was even legal."

Alicia took in the pastoral scene and felt a warm sensation in her chest. It had been nearly two thousand years since anyone other than a small handful of people had seen this artwork, and she felt the immensity of that fact deep in her soul.

Even though she wasn't sure what she believed anymore,

she felt the presence of something in this chamber that she hadn't experienced elsewhere.

A strange ominous feeling. Not a corporeal presence really, but it felt like she was on the precipice of something.

It was almost as if she were beginning to believe they might find what this overly optimistic priest was searching for.

Tony's uncle panned his gaze across the wall and said, "You might also look for a fish symbol. It's a symbol usually of two intersecting arcs resembling the profile of a fish."

"I've seen those before." Alicia nodded. "I just never really understood what the association was with Christianity. It's probably silly, but is it about eating fish on Friday or something?"

The priest chuckled and said, "It's not as silly as you might think. Fish was considered a symbol of abundance and blessing in the Bible, particularly in the stories of Jesus miraculously multiplying loaves and fishes to feed a multitude, such as in Matthew 14:13-21, Mark 6:30-44, and likely other passages that slip my mind at the moment. The fish symbol is often associated with Jesus Christ himself, and was an early secret symbol for those who were in the know."

"Okay." Tony motioned across the large chamber. "Let's each take a wall and see if there's anything we can find."

Alicia aimed her flashlight at the far wall and was about to walk over when she heard Bagel yowl from somewhere in the darkness. She panned the beam of her flashlight over to where she thought she'd heard him. "Come over here, I can't see you."

Bagel yowled once more, bounded out of the darkness, his black fur blending in almost perfectly, and immediately turned and raced back to wherever he'd been.

Alicia followed the cat, aiming her flashlight in his direction until she paused mid-step.

Bagel was frantically pawing at the wall; clods of dirt being tossed back in her direction.

"Tony, I need one of those tiny hand shovels. Bagel found something!"

Within seconds the group converged on what looked like a crack in the wall.

"Here, use this hand trowel," Tony said as he handed her the tiny shovel.

"I got this, Bagel." Alicia scraped at the dry clay and said, "This is some hard stuff."

"It looks like a hasty patch that likely dates back to when this place was built," The priest said, his voice full of excitement. "There's only one reason that they'd do—"

"Holy crap!" Alicia exclaimed as her trowel broke through the clay and she fell forward against the wall. "Sorry, Father. I didn't mean to say that, but there's another room behind this wall!" Her heart raced as she frantically scraped more of the clay from the crack in the wall.

"Can you see what's back there?" Tony asked.

Alicia shook her head, sat back and removed her backpack.

She pulled out the GoPro she'd bought and called Bagel. "Let's get this on you, my guy."

With a tiny body harness that she found in a pet store, she jury-rigged a setup where the portable video camera could attach and Bagel stood quietly as she strapped him into the harness.

Alicia brought out her phone, which she'd already paired with the GoPro and gave Bagel a kiss on his head. "Okay, just like we did in China. Let's go exploring."

Alicia brought up the remote viewing app and saw the world at Bagel's shoulder level. She turned on the 0 lux night vision, which was really an infrared light coming off the front of the camera, letting her see whatever the cat was aiming at.

Bagel walked into the crack as the three of them gathered around her phone and watched as a new chamber appeared.

"Nobody has seen this in nearly two millennia," The priest said with a reverent tone. He pointed at the phone. "Look at the Egyptian hieroglyphs. There's a sarcophagus on the far end, do you see it?"

"Bagel." Alicia leaned down and projected her voice into the other chamber. "Can you go to the far end of the room? Just go back and forth so we can see what's in the room."

Alicia turned back to her phone and smiled as Bagel did exactly as he'd been asked.

"Mr. Bagel is one smart feline," Tony remarked.

The priest's eyes were wide as he stared at the video feed. "It looks like a pretty typical burial chamber. Do you see the canopic jars? That's a sure sign that whoever is buried there came from the Serapeum."

"Why do you say that?" Alicia asked.

"The use of canopic jars, which traditionally held the deceased's organs, that practice ended around 30 BC or so. By the time this place was dug from the ground, Egyptian mummification was still a thing, but the use of canopic jars had mostly been replaced. Egyptian burial practices underwent changes with the influence of Roman and Greek customs. Instead of canopic jars, some mummies were buried with small amulets or figurines representing the four sons of Horus, who were the traditional protectors of the organs in Egyptian mythology." The priest pointed in the direction of the chamber and said, "I'll bet you inside that sarcophagus you'll find just such protections."

"It doesn't seem like the place we'd find a holy relic," Tony said as Alicia thought exactly the same thing.

The priest nodded. "I concede that point, but we'll definitely have to alert the Ministry when we're done. The idea that we may have an undisturbed chamber that's thousands of years old is monumental."

Alicia bent down and called through the crack. "Come on out, Bagel. We're done with that room, you did great."

As the cat emerged, he let out a high-pitched sneeze.

Alicia rubbed the side of the cat's head and said, "You did great."

She stood, the air in the unexplored chamber was thick with anticipation as Alicia, turned her flashlight to another section of the wall, looking for anything that might stand out. The others did as well, and even Bagel, ever the intrepid explorer with his GoPro strapped securely to his side, sniffed the air eagerly and walked away into the darkness. "Bagel, please don't go leave this chamber."

As she scanned the expansive wall, Alicia wished they'd bought some floodlights. It would made this search a lot easier.

She looked over her shoulder and the other two were also panning their flashlights from the roofline to the floor.

About thirty minutes had elapsed, and just as Alicia was finishing with her section of the wall, she heard another yowl from the one area cloaked in darkness.

Alicia's heart began racing as she turned to the darkened section of the room, evidently Bagel had taken it upon himself to begin exploring the fourth wall, and as all three of them converged on the cat, the priested exclaimed, "Praise Mary, he's found another crack!"

Alicia rushed over and saw Father Montelaro's eyes wide with excitement as he examined the painted image on the wall, while Bagel scratched away at the clay at the priest's feet.

"Look at this image!" The priest spoke, his voice shaking with excitement."

Alicia added her light to the others and took in the image that had so excited the clergyman.

It depicted a boy fishing, with a chi-rho symbol prominently displayed on his forearm. In the distance, there was a walled city and hill that seemed to glow with light.

With a shaking gloved hand, the priest pointed at the image of the city. "Jerusalem, it has to be." Father Montelaro breathed; his voice filled with awe. "And perhaps the hill of Golgotha, where Jesus was crucified. Can you imagine? This image could have been painted from direct witness testimonial of that event."

Alicia began sweating in the cool air.

The man's excitement was contagious and with renewed determination, Alicia crouched down with her hand trowel and began to dig at the mortar, her heart racing with anticipation. Tony and Father Montelaro both crouched low and shone their lights onto the hardened clay. This crack was smaller than the other. If there was a chamber behind this wall, would Bagel even be able to squeeze through?

Finally, after what felt like an eternity, Alicia's trowel plunged through the crack in the wall, revealing yet another chamber beyond, and all three of them gasped.

Somehow, the priest had made them all believers in this unlikely quest.

Tony took over as he scraped with the trowel, widening the crack as much as he could while Alicia adjusted the harness on Bagel and said, "Are you ready to explore one more chamber?"

The cat purred in response. And with bated breath, she sent Bagel in to explore, watching anxiously as the images from his GoPro appeared on Alicia's phone.

"Look!" The priest pointed excitedly at the video feed and smacked his nephew on the shoulder. "Wooden boxes! Dozens of them, seemingly sealed and untouched for centuries. It's almost like someone packed up something hastily and brought it here to hide."

Alicia's heart soared with excitement as she realized they might have stumbled upon something truly extraordinary.

Suddenly, the chamber vibrated, and before Alicia could even react, a loud, heavy thud echoed through the chamber, followed by the sound of cracking stone. Dust billowed out from the crack, filling the air and obscuring their vision.

Alicia's heart plummeted with fear as she frantically screamed, "Bagel!" her voice barely audible over the chaos.

She choked.

The dust clogged her lungs as she struggled to breathe.

Lifting her shirt, she breathed through it, filtering the dust, her vision obscured by the grit in the air and her tears.

Her mind raced with thoughts of the worst.

Tony appeared out of the darkness, his face covered in dirt. He grabbed her by the arm and began pulling her from the chamber.

Then, suddenly, a yowl pierced through the dark haze, and Alicia ripped her arm from his grip, feeling a surge of relief.

She'd lost her flashlight in the chaos and couldn't see anything.

"Bagel! I'm here!"

Something bumped against her leg in the darkness, and

she reached down, feeling a surge of relief as she scooped Bagel into her arms, putting him under her shirt so he could breathe.

Tony physically lifted her up in the air and carried her through the darkness.

The next thing she remembered was waking up outside the chamber as a paramedic put an oxygen mask over her face.

Bagel yowled at her as he sat next to her, patting her leg in a pattern. *"Breathe."*

"I'm working on it, buddy. I'm working on it."

She turned and saw another paramedic administering oxygen to the priest. He looked over at her and shot her a thumbs-up.

"Tony?"

"I'm here." His face came into view and he looked terrible, but somehow must not have breathed in too much of the crap, since he seemed to be filthy, but otherwise breathing okay.

"Thanks," she managed to say as the world grew dim.

CHAPTER NINETEEN

Alicia pulled in a deep breath and only felt a twinge of pain. She'd probably be coughing up ancient dust for the next week or so. Luckily, neither she nor Tony's uncle had to go to the hospital, despite Tony nearly pitching a fit when they'd both insisted they were fine.

Some time with bottled oxygen to get the blood flowing, along with some rest was all either of them had needed.

Tony was a bit chagrined that they'd both insisted on coming back to the catacombs first thing in the morning.

Alicia stood in the harsh light of day, peering down into the collapsed section of the catacombs twenty feet below. It was a bit shocking how suddenly the ground had given way. Rubble was strewn everywhere, and the remains of crushed boxes were visible amidst the debris.

Tony stood beside her, surveying the scene with a furrowed brow. "Look at those boxes," he remarked, pointing to the crushed remnants. "Even though they're crushed, they look like they were empty. Empty shells from 2000 years ago."

The priest, his shoulders slumped with weariness, sighed forlornly. "It's likely that whatever was stored in those boxes—grain, perhaps, or some other perishable—was eaten by rats long ago."

He looked tired, defeated by the realization that their discovery had been for naught. Tony placed a hand on the priest's shoulder, his voice gentle but firm. "Uncle Alessandro, it's time to go back to Italy. We've done all we can here."

Reluctantly, the priest nodded in agreement. "You're right," he admitted. "In archaeology, you often come so close, only to realize that someone beat you to it hundreds, if not thousands, of years ago. It's a hazard of the trade. I'm tired." He looked over at his nephew and gave him a smile. "You're right. It's time to get home, back to my books, scrolls, and other old things like me."

Alicia felt a rising sense of satisfaction. Her mission was in fact accomplished, even though she wasn't one-hundred percent sure that the old priest wouldn't have made his way back on his own at some point, that possibility was certainly not guaranteed had they not intervened.

As if sensing what she was thinking, Tony looped his arm over her shoulder and gave her a light squeeze. "Without a doubt, a job well done, young lady." Bagel poked his head out of his sling and mewed up at Tony. "You too, Mr. Bagel. We couldn't have done this without you. Let's get going, all three—sorry, all four of us have to get back to the real world."

Just as she was about to turn away, Alicia noticed something unusual amidst the devastation below. A white feather, pristine against the backdrop of destruction, lay on the floor of the chamber.

Two men clad in fatigues, their insignia unrecognizable to any nation, worked in silence as they wheeled a cart containing several large crates into a sprawling, dimly lit warehouse. Each crate bore a long series of seemingly random numbers and letters.

One by one, some of the crates were meticulously placed on shelves, obscuring their contents from view. Each crate was stamped with a unique alphanumeric number, offering the only clue to their mysteries. Among the remaining crates on the cart, one stood out, boldly labeled with the word "Alexandria."

The only other common feature shared by the thousands of boxes scattered throughout the warehouse was a single graphic image of a feather stenciled onto their sides.

As the workers moved about their task with practiced

efficiency, an aura of secrecy hung heavy in the air. The atmosphere crackled with anticipation, as if the crates held secrets too dangerous to be unveiled.

With a final push, the cart was wheeled into its designated spot, vanishing into the depths of the warehouse.

EPILOGUE

A wave of emotion washed over Alicia as she walked into Gerard's for the first time since leaving on her mission to help find Tony's uncle.

Everything was just like she'd remembered it. Familiar faces were at the tables as they ate, drank, and argued over normal everyday type of stuff.

"Hey, look who's back!" Denny yelled across the bar as he motioned for her.

Alicia's throat tightened as she walked toward the back of the bar, trying hard to keep control of her emotions.

Get yourself together, girl!

She cleared her throat as she met Denny at the bar.

He smiled and gave her a quick fist bump as he lifted up a section of the bar's counter and motioned for Alicia to follow.

Alicia followed him past the beaded curtain and into the back room.

"I was just going to get something to eat—"

"I'll take care of you once we settle things a bit, but that needs to be in the back."

Alicia winced, knowing that she almost certainly owed Denny some substantial amount of money for all the help he'd given her while she was overseas.

They walked into the small windowless room, lit by a weak fluorescent bulb overhead, and faced a tiled mural of a beach scene.

He turned to the mural and said, "Time and place."

Alicia heard a click somewhere in the room.

"Wasn't the password something different before?"

Denny grinned as he put his hand on the tiles of the mural. "It changes on a regular basis. You can't be too careful."

He pressed on a combination of tiles, and with a beep, the outline of a door appeared. He pushed the door open, and the two of them stepped through the hidden entrance, which sealed itself seconds after Alicia walked into the darkened room beyond.

Lights flickered on to reveal a large supply room filled with rows of shelving holding a variety of electronic equipment and her father got up from a chair, giving her a beaming smile. "Congratulations, you've finished your first solo mission." He opened his arms for a hug and said, "I'm proud of you."

Any emotional facade she'd maintained crumbled and her unbidden tears fell as she stepped into her father's embrace and sobbed as he squeezed her tight. "I didn't know you were in town."

"I just got in." He put his hands on her shoulders, held her at arm's length and asked, "Do you know what you're going to do?"

Denny handed Alicia a box of tissues and walked toward the far end of his hidden sanctuary.

She wiped her face and asked, "What do you mean?"

Her father motioned to one of the chairs next to a table that had a closed briefcase on it. "Well, I know you were having some doubts about the Outfit. You're probably going to have to make some decisions about that. And believe me, I completely understand your concerns regardless of what you decide. I've been offered to go full in by Mason before, and I've opted not to do that, I prefer my freedom and I don't like being beholden to anyone."

Alicia nodded. Mason was the head of the Outfit, or at least for her purposes, as high a person in the organization as she knew of. Working for the Outfit had a level of security, just like any other government job, it was somewhat reliable.

"Dad, to be honest, I like the idea of being flexible and having freedom, kind of like you describe, but I just don't know. I mean if I wanted to go it alone, I don't even know what it means yet. I don't understand the economics of it all."

Her father nodded. "That's a fair concern."

She hitched her thumb in Denny's direction. "Denny helped me *so* much while I was out there, for all I know I owe him tens of thousands of dollars."

"*Millions!*" Denny's voice broadcast through the room, and she heard him snickering.

"See?" Alicia shrugged with a half-smile. "Millions. Other than the money Tony gave me up front to start this strange little adventure, it's not like I have a huge savings. And where would I get customers? I just don't—"

"Alicia, hold up a second." Her father motioned for silence. "To be honest, I wasn't sure whether or not you would be cut out for this kind of work. Sometimes, things can get ugly. Tony told me what you did at Don Vianello's place. The thing you had Tony do with the phone regarding that assassin's sister. Would you be able to do that in real life? If need be, would you be able to hurt someone?"

Alicia winced and shook her head. "I don't think so. I mean, if they deserved it and I knew that, then maybe, but torture someone who was innocent? No, I couldn't do that. I don't care what kind of money is involved. I'm sorry, Dad. I just can't."

"Good." He smiled. "Neither could I. You're a smart girl, and from the way Tony described what you did, you seem to do well under pressure. I'll make you this offer: I often get things referred to me that I just don't have time to even think about. I need someone I can roll tasks to and can work independently. I think you could do that." He turned in his chair and opened the briefcase.

Alicia's eyes widened as she saw stacks of hundred-dollar bills.

"This is your seed money to start your independent business. It's yours regardless of what you decide, even if you don't want to go independent. You and your sisters don't know this, but each of you girls has a briefcase like this as an inheritance when you turn thirty. I think if you want to start your own thing, you can get this a bit early. It'll give you time to figure out the economics of it all, and work your own deal with Denny and possibly some other people I might introduce you to. What do you think?"

Her skin tingled with excitement and for a moment, she sat there stunned, not sure how to respond. "Um, what about the Outfit."

Her father waved dismissively at her comment. "Don't go full-time with the Outfit. Do what I do, contract with them instead. Mason won't like it, but I'll help make him see it in a positive light. That way, you can live in both worlds." He nudged the briefcase closer to her. "So, what do you think?"

"Well, if I go independent, I can't always just take things that you don't want to do, how—"

"Your reputation will build, as mine has. Believe me. Soon enough, people will be looking for Alicia Yoder's services, and they'll have to wait in line."

Alicia couldn't help but smile at that visual and her mind raced for a few seconds before a calm washed over her. She knew what she wanted to do. She had no doubts. "Okay. I can't believe I'm saying this, but I think this is what I want to do. I want to go independent. I'm sure of it. And thank you so much for everything you've done and are doing. I don't say it enough, but I love you, Dad."

Her father smiled, and for the briefest of moments, she caught a flash of emotion on his face. Even her father, the man whose iron grip usually held steady on everything around him, allowed his emotional barrier to slip just for a second.

She stood, leaned over and gave her father a kiss on the top of his head, like he always did to her. "I'll call Mason tomorrow and tell him I want a change to my contract."

"Good. Then it's settled." Her father stood and called out, "Denny, get your butt over here, I'm taking you and Alicia out for a nice celebration dinner."

"Okay, be there in a second."

"Dad, quick question."

"Sure."

Alicia tilted her head and looked at her father. "Do you have something in mind for me to do next?"

"Probably." He unsuccessfully suppressed a look of amusement. "Let's talk about it over dinner. By the way, how's your Russian?"

AUTHOR'S NOTE

Well, that's the end of *Vatican Files*, and I sincerely hope you enjoyed it.

If this is the first book of mine you've read, I owe you a bit of an introduction. For the rest of you who have seen this before, skip to the new stuff.

I'm a lifelong science researcher who has been in the high-tech industry longer than I'd like to admit. There's nothing particularly unusual about my beginnings, but I suppose it should be noted I grew up with English as my third language, although nowadays, it is by far my strongest. As an Army brat, I traveled a lot and did what many people do: I went to school, got a job, got married, and had kids.

I grew up reading science magazines, which led me into reading science fiction, mostly the classics by Asimov, Niven,

AUTHOR'S NOTE

Pournelle, etc. And then I found epic fantasy, which introduced me to a whole new world, in fact many new worlds, it was Eddings, Tolkien, and the like who set me on the path of appreciating that genre. As I grew older, and stuffier, I grew to appreciate thrillers from Cussler, Crichton, Grisham, and others.

When I had young kids, I began to make up stories for them, which kept them entertained. After all, who wouldn't be entertained when you're hearing about dwarves, elves, dragons, and whatnot? These were the bedtime stories of their youth. And to help me keep things straight, I ended up writing these stories down, so I wouldn't have it all jumbled in my head.

Well, the kids grew up, and after writing all that stuff down to keep them entertained, it turns out I caught the bug—the writing bug. I got an itch to start writing... but not the traditional things I'd written for the kids.

Over the years I'd made friends with some rather well-known authors, and when I talked to them about maybe getting more serious about this writing thing, several of them gave me the same advice: "Write what you know."

Write what I know? I began to think about Michael Crichton. He was a non-practicing MD, who started off with a medical thriller. John Grisham was an attorney for a decade before writing a series of legal thrillers. Maybe there was something to that advice.

I began to ponder, "What do I know?" And then it hit me.

I know science. It's what I do for a living and what I

AUTHOR'S NOTE

enjoy. In fact, one of my hobbies is reading formal papers spanning many scientific disciplines. My interests range from particle physics, computers, the military sciences (you know, the science behind what makes stuff go boom), and medicine. I'm admittedly a bit of a nerd in that way. I've also traveled extensively during my life, and am an informal student of foreign languages and cultures.

With the advice of some New York Times-bestselling authors, I started my foray into writing novels.

My first book, Primordial Threat, became a USA Today bestseller, and since then I've hit that list a handful of times. With 20-20 hindsight, I'm pleased that I took the plunge and started writing.

That's enough of an intro, and I'm not a fan of talking about myself, so let's get back to where I was before I rudely interrupted myself.

This story was born out of my childhood fascination with anything "secret."

When I learned that the Vatican literally had something called the Secret Archives, I couldn't help but make it a goal of mine to first visit the Vatican, but ultimately to bring a story forth that involved some of the mysteries and what-ifs that are possible in such places.

I wanted a launching point for Alicia to have to make a decision about her future, and the only fair way to do it was to give her some experience both in the "public" sector and

AUTHOR'S NOTE

"private" sector of her line of work. Arguably, the Outfit isn't exactly very public, but I think you get my meaning.

I also didn't want to make Alicia a copy-paste female version of her father, so I hope that came across, because ultimately her approach to things and her background are very different—yet she has the undeniable spark of refusing to quit that she shares with her father.

There are a lot of tales to be told, and the only reason this tale, and in fact this entire series has been told was because I heard your comments and listened.

One thing about this series is that it shares a common structure as the Levi Yoder series in that it's a serialized set of stories with a focus on its namesake, Alicia Yoder. Even though each story is set in our world, our time, and with many of the same cast of characters, each of the planned stories are independent of each other. Meaning that each book is a self-contained story that starts and ends with each book, but readers of the series will be able to appreciate a growth in the main character as well as those she surrounds herself with.

I would be remiss if I didn't mention the second "main" character, our golden-eyed cat named Bagel. I can't even begin to tell you how much positive feedback I've gotten on his presence in the story. The intent is that he will play a recurring role, and I hope to do both him and Alicia justice along the way.

I should note that some of you might have come into the

AUTHOR'S NOTE

Alicia Yoder series without having read her father's stories that started everything off.

Alicia actually first appears in his books, and I will include a sneak peek into Perimeter, book one of the Levi Yoder series so that I can at least introduce some of you to that series. I'll freely admit that she does not appear until book two, after all she is only twelve at that moment, but I think those of you who enjoy the Alicia stories will almost certainly enjoy her father's stories as well, with the added bonus that it gives you more of her backstory that is lightly glossed over in this series.

Thanks for reading *Vatican Files*, and there's lots more where that came from.

--Mike

I should note that if you're interested in getting updates about my latest work, I have a link below so you can join my mailing list.

M.A. Rothman: https://mailinglist.michaelarothman.com/new-reader

PREVIEW OF PERIMETER

"Mr. Yoder, I'm sorry to have to tell you this." Dr. Cohen looked concerned, hesitant, but he spoke quickly, as if to get it over with. "You have stage-4 pancreatic cancer."

That was certainly not how Levi had expected his nine a.m. follow-up visit to go. A chill spread through his chest and sent a shiver down the middle of his back.

The gray-haired doctor sat across the table from Levi and nudged a box of tissues in his direction.

As if tissues could help anything.

"How can I possibly have cancer?" Levi's fingers dug tightly into the arms of the padded red leather chair as he leaned forward. "I'm only thirty, and I've lived a clean life. I don't drink alcohol or do drugs. Are you sure?" He realized it sounded like denial.

Dr. Cohen stood, walked around his large mahogany

desk, and put a wrinkled hand on Levi's shoulder. "Son, I'm genuinely sorry." He sighed, his breath smelling of peppermint tea. "Unfortunately, the early stages of pancreatic cancer have almost no symptoms. I sent the biopsy samples to two different labs, and they both came back with the same results. The radiology scans we took last week also confirmed the level of metastasis. The cancer has spread into your lymphatic system."

Levi took a deep breath and let it out slowly. The tautness of his muscles dissipated as a feeling of resignation came over him.

"Stage 4? What does that mean? How do we treat this? What's the next step?"

Pulling a chair closer, the doctor sat across from Levi, their knees practically touching. "Stage 4 simply means the cancer has spread to other organs. In your case, we've detected the cancer in your pancreas as well as your lymph nodes. As to treatment, Sloane-Kettering and a few other research hospitals conducted clinical trials in 2005 that dealt with this type of cancer. Nowadays there are experimental radiation treatments that we could try, coupled with multiple rounds of chemotherapy, but at this stage of your disease, I'm afraid the odds aren't good." He leaned forward and with a solemn expression said, "My best estimate would be that without treatment, you might only have four to six months to get your things in order. And even with treatment, I'll be frank: only one percent have survived five years. Nonetheless, I've already made some calls and we've got world-class treatments that can hopefully improve those odds. I'll do everything in my power to help you get through this."

Levi's mind raced as he absorbed the doctor's words.

He'd always been known to those in his line of work as a fixer. He took care of sensitive issues when the mob bosses needed someone with a deft hand and not just pure muscle. He also fixed issues that the cops couldn't or wouldn't fix.

For this, he had no fixes.

However, he knew there were a few things he needed to take care of right away.

He stood and shook the doctor's hand. "Dr. Cohen, I know it must be hard to deliver this kind of news. Thank you for being honest with me. I'll be back in a couple weeks, after I've set my affairs in order, and we'll talk."

"But Mr. Yoder, you really should start the treatments right away. I called Sloane-Kettering and I've gotten you into one of their treatment programs—"

Levi waved dismissively and turned toward the exit. "I appreciate it, but I'll be back."

As Levi opened the door and left the doctor's private office, all he could think of was Mary.

When Levi walked into the bedroom, Mary, already in her nightclothes, shot him a brilliant smile while she placed a record on the turntable. "I just found this in an old record shop. You have to hear it."

The sound of Nat King Cole, one of Mary's favorites, came over the speakers.

"Love me as though there were no tomorrow..."

The haunting lyrics of the ballad brought a lump into his throat.

Mary danced toward him with a dreamy smile on her face, enraptured by the music. Just as her gaze met his, she froze mid-step. Her smile faltered, and lines of worry formed on her forehead.

Levi had never been able to hide his feelings from her.

He stepped closer, cupped his wife's face in his hands, and stared into her beautiful dark-brown eyes. Her face was framed by a thick mass of jet-black hair and she looked as beautiful as the day he'd met her.

As he explained what the doctor had told him, his mind flashed back to when he'd first laid eyes on her. It was only five years ago when she'd arrived in America as Maryam Nassar, a twenty-two-year-old refugee from Iran. She spoke passable English and had responded to one of Levi's ads for a personal secretary. The moment he first saw her, it was like he'd been struck by lightning. His skin had tingled, and he'd barely managed to catch his breath.

They were married nine months later.

His chest tightened as a storm of emotions flashed across her face: disbelief, hurt, anger. Her dark eyes glistened with tears and her chin quivered as she exclaimed in her strong Persian accent, "B-but you prom—"

She pulled in a deep, shuddering breath, and Levi wrapped her in his arms.

"Honey, I know..."

He pressed her to his chest and rubbed her back as she sobbed. Mary was the only person in her family who'd chosen exile after the Iranian revolution. None of her family had any deep religious convictions, yet the moment she left Iran and married a non-Muslim, she'd sealed her fate. She couldn't go back. Mary had nobody else in this world, and that's what made telling her about his prognosis so difficult.

She also wasn't the type of person to let her emotions out freely—yet now she trembled in Levi's arms.

His throat thickened with regret. He could only imagine the fears she had going through her head. "I'll make sure that you never have to worry about anything for the rest of your life," he said. "This will always be your home, no matter what happens. Do you understand me?"

"I don't need *things*. I don't need Levi Yoder, the businessman. I *need* my *husband*." Mary fiercely grabbed both of Levi's wrists and stared at him with bloodshot eyes. "I love you."

He'd only heard her say that a handful of times. Each time had been a euphoric experience. Yet this time, it pained him to hear it.

He'd helped hundreds of people in the past. But this time, when it mattered most, when the person who needed help was the one person he cared more for than anyone in the world ... he couldn't help. He couldn't fix this.

"I'll stay with you as long as I possibly can—that much I promise you." He wiped the tears from Mary's cheeks with his thumbs. "I love you more than you'll ever know."

She grabbed Levi tightly around his chest and they held each other in silence, knowing that no words would fix what they were going through.

Yousef Nassar's skin prickled with anxiety as he watched the laborers empty the ancient burial chamber of an early-Egyptian priest. It had been only two days since Yousef had discovered the long-forgotten chamber, and already it was nearly empty.

Thieves! These men were all thieves, and knowing that he was in some way enabling this ... the guilt gnawed at Yousef's stomach.

Trying to ignore the men who were stealing irreplaceable artifacts, he turned back to the wall with the faded hieroglyphs and continued transcribing them into his notebook. With his mind focused on the task, the world and its goings-on vanished.

"Dr. Nassar?"

Yousef flinched as he heard his name spoken in English, but with a heavy Russian accent. He turned to see one of

Vladimir's men. Despite the heat in the underground chamber, the man was dressed from head to toe in a black suit. His chiseled face and stone-gray eyes showed no emotion.

"Yes?"

The large man stepped closer, and a small, precious, amber bead cracked under his foot. He pointed across the tomb toward the six-foot statue of Anubis with its arm extended. "Vladimir had instructions in case such a statue was found. Has the ankh been packed properly?"

Yousef's pulse quickened, and he struggled to keep his face neutral. "We didn't see anything near or on the statue."

The man's jaw muscles clenched and relaxed. "You're certain of this?"

"I am." Yousef hitched his thumb toward the wall. "When you talk to Vladimir, let him know that some of what is written here needs to be preserved—"

"I'll inform Vladimir of what's been found."

The broad-shouldered man turned, and the workers scattered out of his way as he walked stiffly toward the tomb's entrance.

Yousef cleared his throat, and the sound echoed off the stone walls of the chamber.

Despite the oppressive heat, he felt a chill race through him as he began unraveling the meaning of a few of the images. The scenes depicted in the pictographic messages told of a time when southern and northern Egypt had yet to be unified.

"Yousef," a woman's voice whispered. "Have you gotten further in the translation?"

He glanced over his shoulder at Sara. In Farsi, he asked, "Did you...?"

She nodded.

Breathing a sigh of relief, he gave his wife a brief kiss and smiled. "I really think this might be one of the earliest tombs we've ever encountered. This is definitely from the early First Dynasty."

Sara peered at the notebook in his lap. "What do you have so far?"

He flipped to a prior page and scanned his notes. "Like you suspected, this is definitely a tomb of an early priest, but I don't see the markings of Atum, the sun god. It's something else. The messages are talking of a great war with the south. Here, listen to this."

"The land is aflame with disease and pestilence.

"A piece of the sun came down and it was a man—"

Yousef put his finger on the next symbol and frowned as he wracked his mind on how to best translate it into something meaningful.

"Glowing like many stars in the night, his breath was like a crocodile."

"What does that even mean?" Sara asked.

He shook his head. "Your guess is as good as mine. It doesn't make sense. We'll need to research that when we get back to the university. In fact, the next several passages seem nonsensical."

Yousef shifted his gaze to the remaining symbols he'd yet to transcribe. He tensed as he recognized one of the hieroglyphs. "My God, what could *that* mean?"

Sara pointed at two of the symbols on the faded wall. "The catfish and chisel ... doesn't that depict Narmer?"

Yousef nodded as he tried to glean meaning from the other nearby symbols. "It does, but it almost seems like the message is saying that this man who was a piece of the sun gave something to Narmer."

As he leaned in closer to the wall, the sound of something metallic clattered behind him. He whirled to see a grenade rolling over the sand-strewn floor, like a cluster of dark grapes.

Yousef's yell was trapped in his throat as the grenade exploded.

"I guess today's a banking day for the Yoder family. Your wife was in a few hours ago."

Never having been one for small talk, Levi simply nodded and showed the man his key.

The well-dressed, gray-haired bank manager glanced at Levi's safe deposit box key and returned his nod. "Follow me, Mr. Yoder."

The manager turned, stiffly walked into the bank's vault, and panned his gaze across the metal wall. He moved toward the right-most section of the vault, and paused in front of the safe deposit box that held the number found on Levi's key.

Pulling a second key from his vest pocket, the manager inserted it into one of the keyholes on the front of Levi's box.

He held out his hand. "The key please, Mr. Yoder."

Levi handed the bank manager his key, and the manager inserted it into the remaining keyhole. As the manager turned both keys at once, Levi heard the snick of a lock disengaging. His box slid out half an inch from the wall.

The manager returned Levi's key to him. "Mr. Yoder, allow me to lead you to a room where you may go through your belongings in private."

Levi pulled on the handle of his safe deposit box. It slid smoothly out of its alcove.

Moments later, Levi found himself in a private room smelling faintly of wood polish and leather. The bank manager closed the door behind him as he left, leaving Levi alone.

Levi withdrew a thick envelope from his suit coat pocket and placed it in the metal container. Within the envelope were several legal documents regarding the house and his assets. Upon his death, everything would be placed in a trust, and Mary would never need to worry about anything from here on in. Their home had been paid for, and monthly expenses would automatically be debited from the trust.

Levi felt some small comfort that he'd done all that he could to arrange for Mary's needs.

Placing his hands on the safe deposit box, Levi bowed his head and sighed. The lump under his armpit, which he now knew was a tumor, had grown bigger over the last few months. It was the first of many that had spread through his body, but this one in particular was hot and throbbed angrily, keeping pace with his heartbeat.

He wasn't going to have much more time with Mary, and that was what he regretted the most.

His throat tightened for a brief moment, and he allowed himself to feel the sadness that he normally didn't dare show in public. He'd overcome so many things in life, yet this was going to be the end of him.

Levi wiped his eyes with the back of his hands and took a deep, shuddering breath. He gave one last glance at the contents of the box, and just as he was about to close it, he spied a package he didn't remember seeing before.

He pulled it out. It was a bit larger than his hand and about the same thickness, but heavy for its size. It was addressed to Maryam Nassar—that was Mary's maiden name—yet the address on the package was their current place of residence. Heavily laden with postage markings, it had come from far away, yet it was still sealed.

"What in the world?"

Levi retrieved his folding knife from his pocket. With a press of a button, the blade sprang open. The box had been wrapped with many layers of adhesive tape, and it took some effort to hack through the seal.

When at last he lifted the cover, a hand-scrawled note lay inside the box, on top of something wrapped in cloth. It was written in the feathery script common to many Middle Eastern languages, which he couldn't read.

He set the note aside and flipped open the cloth wrapping.

His eyes widened.

Nestled in the bed of gray cloth was a gold object unlike anything Levi had ever seen. It was nearly the size of his fully extended hand, and looked very much like a cross, but instead of a vertical line running through the horizontal, the upper portion was an upside-down tear shape. Almost as if it was meant to hang from the overly large loop.

It seemed like a very strange thing for Mary to have received. After all, she was an atheist.

Levi furrowed his brow. "Why would anyone have sent you such a thing," he said aloud, "and why didn't you open it?"

He sat back and stared at the golden object. Somewhere in the back of his mind, he recalled seeing such a thing when he was in the city. It was in an Egyptian museum exhibit. What was it called? An ankh?

It was probably a trick of the light, but for a moment, the golden ankh shimmered as if it were alive.

Levi lifted the ankh out of its box, and almost dropped it. It had an unexpected greasy feel to it that made it hard to hold on to. He tightened his grip. It became oddly warm to the touch.

"What the hell's this thing made of?"

The world seemed to slow as Levi's neck and face flushed with heat. His heart began thudding loudly. A burning sensation crawled up his arm, and he felt a searing pain in his hand. It was as if the thing was attempting to burn through his palm.

It suddenly dawned on Levi: *drop the stupid the thing.*

His hand unclenched, and the heavy object dropped onto the wooden table with a loud thud.

Levi's chest was tight, and he struggled to pull in a deep breath. He winced at the throbbing pain climbing up his arm and spreading across his chest and the rest of his body. There was no blistering yet on the palm of his hand, but he knew that it would soon follow. The flesh there was red and angry with whatever it was that the ankh had slathered on it.

Levi began to sweat as he wiped his hand with a handkerchief, wondering aloud, "Mary, why did someone send this to you?"

He looked back at the object where he'd dropped it on the table. To his shock, it looked different now. No longer did it have a shimmering golden hue, but instead, it held a look of dull silver.

As the heat from the palm of his hand pulsed in time with his heartbeat, Levi wondered if the gold coloration had been some type of poison.

He snorted ruefully and shook his head. *What difference does it even make at this point?*

Bring it, he challenged the dull, lifeless object.

Using his handkerchief, Levi carefully placed the ankh back into its box and slid the cover back onto the container.

Driving home from the bank was torturous. His eyes felt sticky and began to burn, and his mouth was parched. He desperately needed a glass of water. His body ached; a high fever was taking hold.

Either he was getting a terrible case of the flu, or this was some unadvertised symptom of the cancer nobody had told him about. Could that ankh really have been coated with poison? Whatever it was, it seemed dead-set on making him as miserable as possible. By the time he'd driven into his neighborhood, Levi was sweating profusely and his eyes were drooping.

The flashing lights of a police car parked in front of his house brought him out of his stupor.

Levi pulled into the driveway and climbed painfully out

of the car. An officer standing at his front door turned in his direction.

The policeman glanced at a photo in his hand and then at Levi. "Lazarus Yoder?"

"Yes, officer. That's me." Levi's heart thudded heavily in his chest as he wiped the sweat from his brow. Lazarus was his given name, but ever since he'd come to New York, he'd used Levi instead. "What's wrong?"

"Mr. Yoder, can we talk in private? I'm afraid there's been an incident."

Levi glanced toward the garage; it was empty. Levi couldn't fathom where Mary might have gone. She was a diabetic, and always came home at this time of the day to take her insulin shot. The muscles around Levi's chest tightened like iron bands, and he felt short of breath. The world began to spin.

The grim-faced officer placed a hand on Levi's shoulder. "Mr. Yoder, you're not looking well. I think you'll want to sit down for this."

Levi glanced at the photo in the officer's hand, and the blood in his veins turned to ice. The photo was blood-stained and torn, but he recognized it. It was his wedding photo.

The same one Mary carried in her purse.

It had been a week since Mary died in the car accident, and only a day since her funeral. Levi only remembered pieces of the ceremony; he'd passed out sometime in the middle, evidently due to dehydration from the flu he'd been struggling with.

Now he lay in his bed at home, a nurse hanging a bag of clear fluid on the IV pole.

"I've pushed an anti-emetic through the IV's access port, so the nausea should get under control soon," she said. She set a large plastic bottle of water on Levi's nightstand. "Please try drinking as much as you can. If you can't tolerate taking in fluids to maintain your hydration, Dr. Cohen says you'll have to be admitted."

Levi shook his head. "Alicia, you seem like a nice enough lady, and I know you mean well ..."

His head fell back onto his pillow, his energy completely drained. His muscles ached as if he'd been working out nonstop for a week, and his joints seemed particularly affected. He felt like an arthritic old man. And that was nothing compared to the burning he felt in the tumors where his cancer had spread.

It reminded him that the flu was the least of his issues.

Alicia, the dowdy middle-aged nurse from Dr. Cohen's office, studied him with a sympathetic expression. "I *do* mean well, and I'll be back in the morning to check on how you're doing."

"Okay." It was the only response Levi could muster. He closed his eyes, trying to ignore the pain wracking his body.

He must have fallen asleep, because when he awoke, the sun had broken through the gap in the beige-colored bedroom curtains and blazed its early-morning welcome onto Levi's face.

His fever was gone.

The bed was wet from nighttime sweats, his eyes weren't burning anymore, and the aches had subsided. Yet he still felt ... odd.

The sounds of the morning seemed somehow louder than ever before, as if he'd previously had cotton balls in his ears. Birds called to each other in the front yard, and somewhere in the distance a school bus's air brakes engaged. The old-fashioned wind-up clock on the nightstand ticked loudly with each movement of the second hand.

Suddenly, the sounds vanished, and for a moment it seemed like the world had paused ... and then everything started right up again. The clock continued ticking, the birds chirped, and the bus disengaged its brakes.

As Levi yawned and stretched his arms over his head, he felt a tug on his arm, and the IV pole fell on top of him. He lurched into a sitting position and ripped the IV out of his arm. He flinched as the tape that held the clear tube in place tore from his skin. The odd slithering sensation of the plastic tube withdrawing from his vein sent a shiver of revulsion through him.

His skin tingled as he swung his legs out of bed. Blood had begun oozing down his arm, so he grabbed some gauze from the nightstand and pressed it against the site where the IV had been.

The bottle of water on the nightstand was empty.

"What the hell's wrong with me?" Levi shook his head to clear the cobwebs. He hadn't slept more than two hours at a time since Mary's death, and suddenly twelve hours had vanished in one go.

He stared suspiciously at the empty IV bag, now lying on the ground, and wondered what else the nurse had put in there.

He stood, feeling remarkably steady for a person who'd felt like death warmed over just the night before. Levi touched the burning lump under his armpit and winced.

Can't I ever catch a break?

For some godforsaken reason, his tumors now all felt like red-hot pokers.

Levi turned back to the nightstand, and the world seemed to pause yet again. This time, as the clock's second hand was frozen, Levi counted aloud. "One ... two ... three ... four ... five."

The hand began ticking again.

"I'm losing my mind."

Throbbing pain issued from more than a dozen points in his body. He grimaced and took a few deep breaths.

He knew what he needed to do.

Moments later, Levi was dressed and headed out the front door.

Dr. Cohen had some explaining to do.

As Levi raced along the Northern State Parkway toward Dr. Cohen's office, the frustration within him grew.

"After all I've been through, he should have leveled with me."

Something had happened to Levi last night, but he couldn't quite make out what it was. Dr. Cohen must have had Alicia put something more than anti-nausea drugs in that IV.

Everything around him seemed more intense. Colors were more vivid than ever before, and the sounds—birds flying overhead, the noise of the cars on the highway—were clearer, more distinct. His skin tingled annoyingly as the wind blew across the hair on his arm. It was as if he could feel each individual hair stirring.

Is this what it feels like to be high?

A car raced past him on the left, and he heard the whoosh of its six metal cylinders plunging in and out of its engine in near-perfect harmony.

Levi scratched at the burning spot near his armpit and frowned. It had been the place where he'd found the first tumor. But the lump now felt ... different. Smaller? And it was even hotter to the touch than ever, like a burning ember buried under his skin.

"Damn you, Doc. What's going on?"

As Levi walked into Dr. Cohen's office, the blonde receptionist looked up from the novel she'd been sneaking a peek at and smiled brightly. "Good morning, Mr. Yoder. I don't think you have an appointment today."

"Is Dr. Cohen in?"

"He's working on his charts, but—"

Levi strode past her and barged into the doctor's private office.

Dr. Cohen was busy scribbling in one of the many patient folders stacked on his desk. When Levi walked in, he looked up from his stack of work, and his eyes widened.

"Mr. Yoder. Alicia told me you were stuck in bed." The pen fell from his hand and rolled off the desk. "I was going to come over this afternoon to check on things. Are you okay?"

The heated tingling in Levi's body fueled his anger. "What the heck did you have her put in that IV? Everything feels strange, almost like I'm high or something."

The old man stood and leaned heavily against his desk. "What are you talking about? You were given a saline drip for your dehydration and a drug for your nausea."

At the old man's confused and earnest expression, Levi began feeling foolish for suspecting something nefarious. "I'm sorry, maybe it's just ... I don't know." He rubbed at the burning sensation coming from the tumor on the side of his neck. "First things first. Why does it feel like I'm on fire?"

"I don't understand." Dr. Cohen walked around his desk and closed his office door. He put his hand on the side of Levi's face, and the furrow between his eyebrows deepened. Turning Levi's face to the side, he probed at the lump on his neck. "That's not right ..."

The old man lifted Levi's left arm and probed with his fingertips along several spots, up to and including the armpit, which was throbbing painfully with heat.

"What's not right?" Levi said. "Don't tell me—let me guess. I'm dying."

The elderly doctor took a step back and donned a pair of rubber examination gloves. "Take off your shirt." The doctor's humorless expression brooked no argument.

Levi stripped to the waist. As the doctor prodded under his arms and the sides of his chest, Levi asked, "What do you see? What's wrong?"

"You haven't taken any radiation treatments or any chemical infusions since your diagnosis?"

"No. I didn't exactly see the point."

"I don't understand," the doctor muttered. "Levi, it seems as if the tumors infiltrating your lymphatic system have all shrunk since the last time I saw you. The few I'm detecting are very hard and warm to the touch, and the others ... well, some I'm unable to find at all. I want to biopsy some of these to see what's going on."

Levi sighed. "Go ahead. Do what you think you have to."

Pacing back and forth in the wood-paneled waiting room of the Sloane-Kettering Institute, Levi couldn't figure out what could be taking so long.

His visit to Dr. Cohen several days ago had yielded nothing but full-body scans and needles. And at the doctor's insistence, Levi had spent this morning being prodded by still more doctors at Sloane-Kettering. It was now late afternoon, and he was still in the waiting room, already having read every magazine available.

From somewhere in the distance came the faint sound of raised voices—one of which sounded like the voice of Dr. Cohen. Curious, Levi left the waiting area and followed the sound through the hallways. He stopped outside a set of closed doors labeled "Radiology and Histology." Two voices argued on the other side. They were muffled by the doors, but Dr. Cohen's nasal tone was unmistakable.

"Frank, all I can tell you is this. Three days ago, that patient entered my office complaining about a burning sensation. I palpated some of his lymph nodes and confirmed the presence of abnormal growths, which I biopsied and brought here."

"Dr. Cohen, I'm telling you there's no way those biopsies you brought me and the ones I took this morning are from the same person. I don't mean to be rude—after all, you *were* my histology professor in med school. But are you sure you didn't mix something up? I couldn't feel any swelling or anything out of the ordinary in my exam. I felt bad putting that man through another biopsy, yet I did it anyway based solely on what you said."

Levi removed the bandage from his neck and touched the spot where the Sloan-Kettering cancer specialist had biopsied him. He couldn't find a hint of swelling where the biopsy had been taken.

As the doctors continued to argue, he leaned against the yellow cinder-block wall. The room wavered unsteadily. Levi shoved his hand into his shirt, accidentally popping off a button as he felt along the crook of his underarm. He couldn't feel the hard burning nodule there, either. It had been there only a couple of days before.

How is that possible?

The second doctor was speaking again. "Based on the biopsy and the PET scan results, all I can tell you is this: that man in the waiting room doesn't have a thing wrong with him."

Madison frowned as she suited up for her role as the mission's standby diver.

"Maddie, calm down," Jim whispered as he shrugged into his own diving gear. "It'll be okay."

It had been only fifteen minutes since they'd transferred

onto a nameless ship off the coast of Turkey, but from the moment she'd set foot on the deck of the diving vessel, Madison hadn't liked anything about their mission.

There were five others on board. All of them seemed to be Americans, but it was pretty obvious that the ship was well shy of a standard Navy dive crew.

She clipped on her weight belt and leaned closer to Jim, who was adjusting his dive vest. "This is crap," she whispered. "They're expecting us to do a mixed-gas dive at four hundred feet and they don't even have a full crew. That's just a slap in the face."

With a slight shake of his head he tossed her a lopsided grin. "It'll be fine. This looks like a pretty typical commercial dive setup."

Did it? Madison was used to the standard twelve-man crew that the Navy employed, but she trusted Jim. He'd been an explosives specialist, diving everywhere in the world for over fifteen years. He'd seen it all.

She took a deep breath and released it slowly, trying to rid herself of her pre-dive jitters.

Jim snorted. "Sometimes the spooks take shortcuts."

Spooks?

All of the travel under the cloak of darkness, skirting the spotlights in the Bosphorus Strait, the lack of specifics regarding their mission ... it all suddenly made sense.

Madison turned her gaze suspiciously to the others on the ship. Most of them were dressed like merchant marines, which meant they looked like a ragtag bunch of civilians. But they clearly knew their way around a boat, expertly scrambling from one station to another. They were taking care of business. Two of them were handling the platform while another operated the controls of the winch it was attached to. Another crewman operated the dive console.

But one man stood out from the rest of the crew. He was in his forties, blond hair, in khakis and a dark polo. He was no sailor. Madison wasn't sure about the rest, but if there was a spook on board, it was him. This guy screamed CIA.

The spook stepped forward and addressed them all with an authoritative tone. "Divers, we've got an old airplane wreck lying directly below us at about 380 feet. It's been down there a long time, and it has a pretty narrow cross-section. It looks like there was a landslide and part of the entrance is covered by the debris. If it weren't for that, we'd have used an ROV to survey the interior."

"What are we looking for?" Jim asked.

The spook pressed his lips together and hesitated. "I'm sorry, but the exact nature of the aircraft's payload is classified."

"Classified?" Madison scoffed, feeling a rising sense of indignation. "You're asking us to do a technical dive onto a wreck we know nothing about and you're not even telling us what we're looking for? How the hell—"

"Enough!" the agent barked. "I'll be asking you to be my eyes down there and tell me what you see." He picked up a box-like device that resembled a metal detector and pressed a button on its handle. When a green LED on the box turned on, he handed the device to Jim. "Take that down with you."

Jim turned the box over in his hands. It looked like a sealed metal box with no markings, a telescoping handle with an already depressed button, and the now-glowing LED.

"What is it?" Jim asked.

"If it starts flashing, I'll want to know right away. It probably means you're near one of the items we're looking for."

Jim hooked the device onto his dive belt.

The agent addressed the full crew once more. "All right, let's move. We've only got five hours until dawn breaks."

Jim donned his dive helmet. One crewmember began reeling out the umbilical that would be Jim's lifeline and sole means of communicating up from the depths, while another man, at the console, yelled, "Comms check. Chief Uhlig, can you hear me?"

Jim's voice echoed through the dive console's speaker. *"Roger Topside, hear you loud and clear."* He gave a thumbs-up and stepped onto the metal stage. The stage swung over the side of the boat as the men called out instructions to each other.

Just as the winch operator began lowering the stage into the water, Madison made eye contact with Jim, and he shot her a thumbs-up.

She returned the gesture and recited the same prayer she did for every dive. "Guide us. Keep us safe. Let us live to dive another day."

Madison worried as she sat in her gear. As the standby diver, she'd only be getting wet if there was an issue.

Ten minutes passed.

Finally, Jim spoke. *"I'm at 375 feet. Panning the spotlight all around me and I'm not seeing anything yet. Just water in every direction."*

The man at the dive operator's console leaned in to a microphone. "Diver, the current has pushed you 75 feet away from the cliff's edge. If you turn to 255 degrees and move in that direction, you should see the ledge and the target."

"I need more slack on the umbilical."

"Roger that."

One of the crewmembers reeled out more of the thick cable containing air and communication lines.

Focusing on staying calm, Madison listened to the waves lapping against the side of the boat. The speaker crackled with the sound of Jim's breathing.

He must be swimming.

"Topside, I've spotted the wreck. It looks like the front half of an airframe got sheared off and fell to the ocean floor. The back half is barely visible with all the debris covering it."

The agent walked over to the console and pressed the microphone button. "Diver, I'll need you to clear a passage into it. The structure should be fairly wide open once you get in."

The sound of Jim's grunting echoed across the deck.

The console operator announced, "His heart rate has increased to 140 beats per minute."

"Topside, I've cleared a wide enough opening. This must have been a recent landslide—"

"Why do you say that?" the agent asked with a worried tone.

"The debris was only loosely stuck together. It just sort of pulled away as I picked at it. Topside, I need more slack. I'm standing at the edge of the drop-off."

The spool unreeling more of the umbilical made a loud clacking sound.

Madison licked the salt crystals off her lips. She closed her eyes and imagined herself down there with Jim.

Jim spoke again. *"Okay, this is obviously the remnants of an old bomber. I see the crumpled remains of the bomb-bay door lying on the floor ten-feet ahead.*

"There's lots of growth in the interior. Sponges and hints of coral. I see some rails attached to the floor, and we've got two large metal racks on either side of the doorway."

"What do you see on the racks?" the agent asked, his voice tense.

"Nothing. They're empty."

Madison opened her eyes and studied the agent. He seemed to deflate just a bit, his shoulders sagging.

"Topside, the box you gave me. Is there anything you want me to do with it?"

"Yes. What light is showing on it?"

"You mean the LED? It's still glowing green, if that's what you're asking."

"Wave it along the racks and the bottom of the cabin. See if the light changes at all."

"Roger that."

The agent paced back and forth with his head down. The frown on his face made him look as if he'd swallowed a lemon.

"No change in the LED," Jim said. "But it looks like the lockdowns on the racks were sheared off, and not that long ago. The metal looks like it was pinched off by bolt cutters or something. There's no encrustations or remnants of paint, and it has no patina. Definitely way after this thing crashed."

"Damn!" The agent turned away from the console and dug into his front pocket.

"Sir," said the sailor manning the console. "Is there anything else you want from the diver?"

"Just bring him back up." The agent retrieved a satellite phone from his pocket and walked toward the front of the boat.

The console operator flipped open the dive chart. "Diver, you've given us the data we were looking for. Start your scheduled ascent. First stop at 260 fsw for one and a half minutes."

"Copy that. Leaving the wreck and starting my ascent."

As Jim began the slow ascent with the scheduled decompression stops, Madison studied the agent, who stood twenty feet away with the sat phone pressed against his ear. He was still pacing and talking animatedly to whomever was on the other end of the line. When a light breeze blew in her direction, she caught fragments of his conversation.

"... B-47 ..."

"... stolen cargo."

"... Russia ... Turkey."

"... no detected radiation."

Madison's stomach did a somersault at the word *radiation*.

When the agent put the phone away and walked back toward the others, Madison waved him closer.

The blond man approached, his eyebrows furrowed in frustration. "What?" He didn't even look at her; it was as if his thoughts were a million miles away.

"Are you seriously telling me that you asked us here to dive on a missing nuke?"

The agent stiffened, and his gaze focused laser-like on hers, his expression turning to stone. "I don't know what you're talking about."

With a sudden surge of fury, Madison shoved the man, pointed at the ocean, and yelled, "You asked for Navy divers to go down onto a crash site that could easily have exposed us to radiation—and you didn't tell us!" Her heartbeat thundered in her head as she pulled in a deep breath and stared daggers at the agent.

He returned her gaze unblinkingly and said nothing.

"This is a Broken Arrow incident, isn't it? Does the Navy

know?" *Broken Arrow* was the military term for an incident involving a nuclear weapon.

Glancing at the other men on the deck the spook shook his head ever so slightly. "I'm sorry, but this isn't something I can talk to you about."

Madison took a step back. She felt the rage drain from her, replaced by a cold chill that crept up the middle of her back.

Could the US have actually lost a nuke?

Worse yet, did we lose a nuke and someone else reclaimed it ahead of us?

"Diver," said the console operator, "you're now at 180 feet. Your heart rate is just a bit above normal. I'll be switching you from heliox to air at 170 feet and then to a fifty-fifty mix at 90 feet."

"*Roger that, Topside. Pausing at 180 feet.*"

Jim was fine, and he'd be back up on the boat in another forty minutes or so. No harm done ... this time.

Madison returned her attention to the agent. "I'm sorry I shoved you," she said. Her temper was one day going to get her in some serious trouble.

The agent's expression softened. He cracked a smile and rubbed his chest. "Hey, I understand. And I'm sorry, it's just..." He left the sentence unfinished and chuckled. "Join the agency someday, and ... aww hell, even then I'll probably never be able to say anything. You know how it is."

Madison nodded. She'd been read in on more than a handful of highly classified matters before, and he was right.

The list of people she could talk to about any of those things might as well have been zero.

She took a seat next to the dive platform and shivered.

A nuclear bomb is missing.

Levi had prepared himself for death; what he hadn't prepared for was having the rest of his life ahead of him.

Without Mary.

He'd received a copy of the final accident report, and its details haunted him. Mary had taken an off-ramp too quickly, her car had flipped, and she'd died at the scene.

It made no sense.

She'd always been a hesitant driver—in fact, Levi had been the one who'd pushed her into getting a driver's license in the first place. He'd never seen her speed. Mary had been frustratingly predictable, always driving five miles per hour under the speed limit.

Guilt weighed heavily on him as he considered an alternate explanation for the accident. She'd repeatedly told him that she wouldn't want to live without him. Did she commit suicide to ensure she wouldn't have to?

Perhaps the reason didn't matter. Either way, here he was—alone, with constant reminders of her everywhere he looked. His home, the city, even the clothes he wore reminded him of Mary. Her absence left him with a gaping wound that was too much for him to bear.

He found himself going on ever-lengthening walks. The smell of the spring air calmed his nerves. As he wandered farther from home, into residential areas he'd never seen before, the sense of unfamiliarity struck a chord deep within him.

He needed a change.

A dramatic one.

As he set foot onto the tarmac in Okinawa, Levi found himself surrounded by many unfamiliar sights and sounds. The roaring of aircraft engines thundered over the airfield as military transports took off to parts unknown; from somewhere in the distance came the chop-chop sound of a helicopter landing; and closer in, a hundred boots marched on the hot black asphalt in perfect lockstep. The drill sergeant's voice rang loudly for all to hear.

"Sound off, one two! Sound off, three four! Cadence count, one two three four, one two ... three four!"

Someone placed their hand on Levi's shoulder and spoke loudly over the surrounding din. "Mr. Yoder, welcome to Kadena Air Base. I wasn't given any instructions on what else you might need; it's not often we get civilian visitors. I can arrange for a bunk in the officer's hall and—"

"No." Levi shook his head at the officer who'd come to meet him. "I'll be fine, Captain Lewis."

Levi had gotten here by calling in a few favors from people who owed him—although the New York senator who'd arranged the flight had tried to convince him to go somewhere more "civilized" than a backwater island. The senator had warned him, "Levi, the locals harbor resentment for us having a base there. They actually think that our being there is corrupting the island's culture. That and a few bad eggs with discipline issues have led to some serious tensions. Hell, it doesn't help that some of their elders have some awful memories of our occupation in World War II."

The senator's characterization of the island had only hardened Levi's resolve. The people of the island were scarred; that was exactly how Levi felt. The idea that Mary might have taken her own life because she refused to live without him was too much for Levi to accept, yet it was the only thing that made any sense—and he'd carry the scars of that survivor's guilt forever.

"Just point me to Okinawa City," he said to the captain. "I'll find what I'm looking for."

The captain pointed southeast. "It's about five miles in that direction. I'll get one of the men to drive you in."

"No need." Levi waved the captain away as he began walking toward the gated entrance to Kadena. He yelled over his shoulder, "Thank you for your help!"

Levi knew that the captain probably thought he was nuts. A lone man, walking into a foreign country with nothing more than a backpack of clothing hoisted over his shoulder.

Wiping a bead of sweat from his brow, the morning sun beating down on him, Levi felt a sense of satisfaction in finding a completely new environment. Ages ago, when he first heard the term "walkabout," he'd been intrigued by the idea that a person might just travel as a rite of passage. To break from one's past life, do something different—see other places, experience other cultures.

To not look back.

It was time for Levi to start over.

During his twelve years in New York City, Levi had experienced all manner of problems as he built his own connections—but he had proven himself repeatedly as someone who could take care of almost any bad situation. Sometimes, he'd found himself squaring off with people who were more than willing to use violence to stop him from getting what he needed, and many times he'd had to fight for his success.

The feeling he'd had after those fights was ... extraordinary. Other than when he was with Mary, the sense of exhilaration he'd felt as he overcame physical obstacles was probably the most alive he'd ever felt. Being a fixer was a mental game. If you were prepared, you almost never had to pull your hands out of your pockets. But when he was forced into a confrontation, he never pulled a punch.

Sure, there was plenty of pain, and once even a broken arm. But Levi had never backed away from a challenge. There were entire shelves in his library devoted to the prowess of the Japanese fighting spirit. He needed to experience that sort of life-giving energy once again. Immerse himself in it.

Hence Okinawa.

His first challenge was learning the language. He spent the first three weeks trying to find a karateka who would take in an American as a live-in student. But even though he was more than willing to pay for lodging and lessons, he was repeatedly rejected. The senator's warning about the resentment of the islanders was proving to be well-founded.

So Levi decided to take a transport from Kadena to Tokyo. It was there that he was introduced to Mr. Saito, a local friend of the Yokota Air Base commander.

As Saito drove carefully through the busy streets of Tokyo, Levi explained what he was looking for.

Saito, a fifty-something Japanese man, frowned. "I know of such a place. It teaches something called Kyokushin, which is roughly translated to 'the ultimate truth.' But I worry for you."

"As long as you believe they would take me on and they are masters in their style, why worry?"

Saito slowed the car as he turned into a narrow street. "The dojo has a reputation for being severe with its students. I fear you may be injured if you aren't careful. It is very—"

"Perfect." Levi nodded grimly. "That's exactly what I'm looking for."

The car slowed to a stop in front of a building with a placard featuring images of girls in ballet tutus executing pirouettes, and the two men got out. Levi was about to ask about the sign when Saito motioned for him to follow, and scurried around the back of the building.

Moments later, Levi was in the presence of a stone-faced Japanese man wearing a karate gi. While Saito spoke to the man in Japanese, presumably explaining Levi's odd request, Levi looked around the dojo. Two dozen students sat in a wide circle while two others sparred brutally in the center. Punches were blocked, kicks were batted away, and students were tossed heavily to the dojo's floor.

Feeling a tap on his arm, Levi turned back to Saito. "Yes?"

Saito motioned to the man he'd been talking to and gave him a slight bow. "This is Sensei Yasuda, one of the dojo's senior instructors. He finds your request extremely unusual, but he believes your story might be compelling to his master. He is willing to take you on, but you must take your lessons seriously or you'll be immediately ejected from the school."

Levi nodded.

"And there is another thing. As a *gaijin*, you'll be required to pay twice what others would pay."

"*Gaijin?*" Levi asked.

Saito paused, with a pensive expression. "It means outside person. It is what non-Japanese are called."

PREVIEW OF PERIMETER

Levi turned to the instructor and bowed. "Sensei, *doi suru*."

Levi thought he'd said "I agree," but Saito immediately corrected his pronunciation and chuckled. "You have good pronunciation for a *gaijin*."

With a loud harrumph, the instructor, looking unimpressed, turned and yelled, "Tomiko!"

A woman jumped up from the sparring circle and raced to the instructor.

He spoke in Japanese to her while nodding toward Levi.

Saito bowed to Levi and said, "It was a pleasure meeting you, Yoder-san. Best of luck." He turned and walked out the door.

The short woman pointed at Levi's feet and barked in broken English, "Remove shoes now!"

As Levi began to unlace his shoes, the woman grabbed a white karate gi from a table and threw it at him. She pointed to a folding screen that separated a section of the dojo. "Dress there!" she yelled.

After yanking his shoes off, Levi grabbed the gi and jogged behind the screen. His heart hammered as the excitement of something new warred with the uncertainty he felt within.

At first, he was one of the many students watching the others grapple and fight, with the instructor occasionally yelling instructions, and Tomiko translating for him.

But then it was Levi's turn.

The moment he stood and walked into the ring, he knew he was going to get his ass handed to him. But for each hit he took, and for each time he was slammed to the floor, he learned just a bit more.

Levi remembered someone telling him that it was easier to learn through making mistakes than to be shown how something is done. If that was true, he learned a lot on that first day. He was tossed, kicked, punched, and otherwise taught lessons of humility from nearly half the class.

Tomiko was the last—and would soon prove to be the worst.

Licking the sweat from his lips, Levi stared at the pale-skinned woman. She had an ageless quality about her, and he couldn't tell whether she was twenty or maybe even twice that. She couldn't have been more than five feet tall, and he was twice her weight. Despite his lack of training, Levi felt a bit of confidence. He had done better than he'd expected against the others. On occasion, he'd managed to land a few blows, and as he was larger than most of the other students, he could absorb a lot of punishment without receiving any real injuries.

Tomiko stared defiantly at Levi and growled, "Attack."

She circled him, not making any sudden movements. It

registered with him that she moved almost like a dancer. No ... a cat. A cat that was probably toying with him.

Rolling his shoulders, Levi took on the ready stance he'd seen employed by the others, and leaped forward with the intent of landing a kick. But Tomiko sidestepped him, dropped to the ground, and swept his legs out from under him.

Levi landed heavily on his back, his breath whooshing from his lungs. He scrambled back to his feet, tiny sparks of light dancing in his vision as he struggled to catch his breath.

He moved much more cautiously around the ring now, searching for an opening.

With near-blinding speed, Tomiko leaped forward with what would surely have been a devastating kick to his groin.

But for a split second, it was as if the world slowed, and Levi ducked to the side and rolled out of the way—just barely.

Tomiko's eyes widened slightly.

Was that a look of surprise?

The tiny woman came at him again, and Levi managed to block her swift front kick—but before he could even appreciate his minor victory, she followed up with a spinning back fist that came out of nowhere.

The next thing Levi knew, he was on the bamboo mat spitting blood from a split lip and what felt like loosened teeth.

That was the end of the match.

After the sparring, Levi suffered through group exercises

on the use of proper form. At the beginning of each form, he'd try to emulate what the others did—and inevitably, one of the instructors would race to him and shout a string of Japanese that needed no translation. They'd roughly correct Levi's form until they felt he was doing it properly.

Then came strength conditioning exercises that at times were beyond what Levi was capable of. As he was larger than the others, it took much more strength for him to maintain the stances that he was asked to perform. The muscles in his legs felt like they were on fire. But he gritted his teeth and pushed through the pain, even when the instructors walked by, pushing and pulling at the students, trying to knock them off balance.

By the time the sun had set, and Levi realized that he'd managed to survive his first day at the dojo, a great sense of relief flooded through him.

He'd survived.

The students ate their communal meal together. It consisted of rice, some kind of grilled fish or possibly eel, and a large bowl of pickled vegetables. As Levi ate, the others talked in Japanese. Tomiko wasn't among those who remained at the dojo, so Levi had no one to translate. He focused on his meal and listened to the foreign sounds of Japanese being spoken all around him.

When he and the other students had finished clearing away the meal, Levi walked slowly to the back of the dojo, trying not to make it obvious he was in a lot of pain. Following the lead of the others, he stripped out of his uniform, splashed water on his face and body from the faucet, and grabbed a change of clothes that had been provided for him. In a back room, some of the other students rolled out their tatami mats to sleep, and with a barely suppressed groan, Levi lay on the wooden mat he'd been assigned.

As he stared up at the ceiling, the throbbing aches he felt reminded him that he'd pushed himself far beyond anything he was used to.

He wasn't sure if the pain was an affirmation of life or a punishment for having lived when Mary didn't.

His first day at the infamous dojo had been a lesson in pain. So when Levi woke early the next morning, he fully expected to feel his entire body bruised, battered, and non-functional.

Yet as he sat up and stretched, he felt only the slightest bit of stiffness. Even lying on a wooden mat for the first time hadn't stopped him from getting a good night's sleep. He licked his lips, and barely felt the cut that he'd received from Tomiko.

He hopped up onto his feet, rolled up his mat, and set it in its place. He walked out of the sleeping quarters, weaving past a half dozen of the other students, who were still asleep. As he entered the main area of the dojo, he saw Tomiko stretching with some of the senior instructors, along with another man he hadn't seen before.

Levi bowed and began stretching like the others. Sensei Yasuda looked up, stone-faced, and said something to him in Japanese.

Tomiko translated. "Sensei Yasuda wants know why you not resting with the others."

Levi stretched his legs and reached for his toes. "I feel rested, and didn't want to risk missing any lessons."

Tomiko translated for Yasuda. The instructor's face registered no change in expression, but he gave a slight nod.

The new man said something in Japanese while giving Levi an amused smile.

Again Tomiko translated. "Master Oyama hopes that you continue to show excellent attitude. He says that only intense focus will purge that which haunts you, and he will ensure that you're pushed harder from now on."

Levi was unsure how to respond to that. He bowed his head to the master, and silently wondered what he'd gotten himself into.

— end of preview —

ADDENDUM

Even though *Vatican Files* is very much a mainstream thriller, I couldn't help but include nods toward science in one form or another. Given that, I feel somewhat compelled to either explain some of the science or maybe give a bit more detail than the story otherwise demanded.

Obviously, my goal in this addendum isn't to give you a crash course on college-level science, but instead give you enough information or keywords so that you have the data necessary to do more research, if you're interested.

Alicia's Contact Lens:

The idea of a contact lens that can deliver real-time information to the human eye has been around in movies for years, and a staple of many a thriller. But until recently, it's

ADDENDUM

been a thing of science fiction, in that the technology hadn't been developed to properly merge the matrix of the contact lens itself with something that could deliver visual cues to its wearer.

But during CES 2022 (Consumer Electronics Show) just such a technology was presented by InWith Corporation. Its claim was to be the first company to develop the world's first soft electronic contact lens. The lenses work in conjunction with a smartphone or another device, presumably paired via BlueTooth, and it allows the lens to present real-time information.

The details are scant, but the real triumph in technology is the marrying of a smart-device with the contact lens, such that visual elements can be displayed onto what amounts to be the world's smallest TV screen—the contact lens itself.

And borrowing from concepts that already exist such as AR (Active Reality) – which is a form of Virtual Reality that takes your current sounding and overlays things that aren't already there.

An example of such a thing in today's world would be the game Pokémon Go. It's played by millions of people on their smartphones around the world and it allows users to look through their phones at their surroundings and the application overlays certain game elements to what the user sees. They might be looking at the beach in front of them, and a monster appears on the sand, as an example.

Well, with what has recently been developed, the contact lens that Alicia is using can easily be envisioned to do something a bit more practical. In the software world, we have many algorithms to enable facial recognition and ultimately it works through a means of capturing an image of what someone is looking at (a person's face) digitizing it, and then using that algorithm to turn it into a stream of numbers.

These numbers would be communicated from the contact lens to the phone it's wirelessly connected to, and with an internet connection, the phone could use that hash of numbers, which represent the face, and search for a match.

Once a match is found, information about that person can be pulled from various online sources, and the information discovered can be broadcast back to the contact lens.

In other words, the contact lens acts both as a camera of sorts and as a miniaturized TV.

So, even though what I described in the book might have seemed fanciful, it is by no means science fiction. I'd even hazard to guess that in some classified sections of the Intelligence Community, we might have exactly this type of device deployed with our agents in the field.

Automatic Translation? It's a thing?

In recent years, technological advancements have revolutionized the field of hearing aids, offering individuals with hearing impairments greater accessibility and functionality than ever before. One of the most exciting developments in this area is the integration of automatic translation capabilities, which allow users to seamlessly communicate across language barriers.

The device that Denny gave to Alicia isn't something out of science fiction, it's actually a practical reality, though not necessarily something you can buy at your local convenience store quite yet.

Traditionally, hearing aids have been designed to amplify sounds and improve the clarity of speech for individuals with hearing loss. While these devices have been invaluable in helping people navigate their daily lives, they have often presented challenges when it comes to communication in multilingual settings.

However, with the advent of advanced digital signal processing and connectivity features, modern hearing aids can now be equipped with automatic translation capabilities. These innovative devices are designed to connect to a user's smartphone via Bluetooth technology, allowing them to access a wide range of translation services and apps.

The key components of these next-generation hearing aids include:

1. Built-in microphone: The hearing aid is equipped with a high-quality microphone that captures sounds from the user's environment.
2. Bluetooth connectivity: The device seamlessly pairs with the user's smartphone, enabling real-

ADDENDUM

   time communication between the hearing aid and translation apps.
3. Digital signal processing: Advanced algorithms analyze the incoming audio signals and extract speech patterns, filtering out background noise and enhancing the clarity of speech.
4. Translation software: The hearing aid is integrated with translation software that can recognize and translate spoken language in real time.
5. Audio output: Once the spoken language is translated, the hearing aid broadcasts the translated speech directly into the user's ear, allowing them to understand and respond to conversations in their preferred language.

The benefits of these advanced hearing aids are profound, particularly for individuals who frequently encounter language barriers in their daily lives. Whether traveling abroad, participating in multicultural events, or communicating with non-native speakers, users can rely on their hearing aids to facilitate clear and accurate communication.

Even though I don't advocate a brand, ever, nor do I own any such device, I would argue there's even publicly available devices on the market that feature exactly these abilities, it's just that they aren't yet completely miniaturized. They're more in stick form, imagine something the size of a candy bar, but there's absolutely nothing barring the ability

ADDENDUM

for such a device to actually be incorporated in a hearing aid form—and I'd argue it might already be available, but not quite for the public consumer to use, yet.

Denny's Amazing Data Collection:

This would be the first time that Denny has been introduced into an Alicia Yoder novel, but he's a very present feature of Levi's world and just like in this novel, has present some rather fantastic abilities.

Some might ask, how does he get all that data? It seems very convenient, almost like a Deus ex Machina element to the story.

Well, let's talk about one small aspect of Denny's resources, and that would be something he's even referred to in this novel, and that's the Utah Data Center.

It's a real thing.

The Utah Data Center, located in Bluffdale, Utah, is a state-of-the-art facility operated by the National Security Agency (NSA) of the United States. Designed to store, analyze, and process vast amounts of data collected from various sources, the center plays a crucial role in supporting the intelligence community's efforts to safeguard national security.

Purpose and Mission:

The primary mission of the Utah Data Center is to gather, store, and analyze signals intelligence (SIGINT) data collected from both foreign and domestic sources. This includes intercepted communications, electronic signals, and other forms of digital information. By centralizing these capabilities in one location, the center enables intelligence analysts to identify threats, track adversaries, and protect critical national interests.

Capabilities and Technologies:

The Utah Data Center boasts an array of cutting-edge technologies and capabilities designed to support its mission. This includes massive data storage systems capable of storing exabytes of information, advanced data processing algorithms, and sophisticated analytical tools. The center also houses powerful supercomputers and data visualization systems that enable analysts to extract actionable intelligence from vast amounts of raw data.

Information Gathered:

The Utah Data Center collects a wide range of information from various sources, including:

1. Communications Intercepts: The center intercepts and analyzes communications data, including phone calls, emails, text messages, and internet traffic, to identify threats and track the activities of adversaries.
2. Signals Intelligence: The center collects electronic signals from foreign adversaries, including radar

emissions, satellite transmissions, and radio communications, to gather intelligence on their capabilities and intentions.
3. Cybersecurity Data: The center monitors and analyzes network traffic and cybersecurity threats to protect critical infrastructure and defend against cyber attacks.
4. Metadata: The center collects metadata, such as phone call records and internet browsing history, to identify patterns and trends and support intelligence analysis.

Role in the Intelligence Community:

The Utah Data Center plays a central role in the intelligence community's efforts to collect, analyze, and disseminate intelligence to support national security priorities. By consolidating SIGINT capabilities in one location, the center enhances the intelligence community's ability to detect and counter threats posed by foreign adversaries, terrorist organizations, and other hostile actors. Additionally, the center collaborates closely with other intelligence agencies, law enforcement agencies, and international partners to share information and coordinate efforts to address emerging threats.

In conclusion, the UDC is a real thing, and it's a critical asset in the intelligence community providing essential capabilities for gathering, storing, and analyzing intelligence data.

ADDENDUM

Officially it uses advanced technologies and data analytics to help intelligence analysts identify and mitigate threats to national security, safeguarding the interests of the United States and its allies.

Unofficially, it's one of the many real resources that Denny pulls from to help as he can.

Arguably, we could all use a Denny in our lives.

About the Author

I am an Army brat, a polyglot, and the first person in my family born in the United States. This heavily influenced my youth by instilling in me a love of reading and a burning curiosity about the world and all of the things within it. As an adult, my love of travel and adventure has driven me to explore many unimaginable locations, and these places sometimes creep into the stories I write.

I hope you've found this story entertaining.

- Mike Rothman

You can find my blog at: www.michaelarothman.com

I am also on Facebook at:
www.facebook.com/MichaelARothman
And on Twitter: @MichaelARothman

Made in the USA
Middletown, DE
09 August 2025